T0158135

Praise for Lynn Cahoon and Her Irresistible Cozy Mysteries

THREE TAINTED TEAS
"A kitchen witch reluctantly takes over as planner for a cursed wedding... This witchy tale is a hoot."
—*Kirkus Reviews*

ONE POISON PIE
"*One Poison Pie* deliciously blends charm and magic with a dash of mystery and a sprinkle of romance. Mia Malone is a zesty protagonist who relies on her wits to solve the crime, and the enchanting cast of characters that populate Magic Springs are a delight."
—**Daryl Wood Gerber**, Agatha winner and nationally best-selling author of the Cookbook Nook Mysteries and Fairy Garden Mysteries

"A witchy cooking cozy for fans of the supernatural and good eating."
—*Kirkus Reviews*

A FIELD GUIDE TO HOMICIDE
"The best entry in this character-driven series mixes a well-plotted mystery with a romance that rings true to life."
—*Kirkus Reviews*

"Informative as well as entertaining, *A Field Guide to Homicide* is the perfect book for cozy mystery lovers who entertain thoughts of writing novels themselves...this is, without a doubt, one of the best Cat Latimer novels to date."
—*Criminal Element*

"Cat is a great heroine with a lot of spirit that readers will enjoy solving the mystery (with)."
—*Parkersburg News & Sentinel*

SCONED TO DEATH
"The most intriguing aspect of this story is the writers' retreat itself. Although the writers themselves are not suspect, they add freshness and

new relationships to the series. Fans of Lucy Arlington's "Novel Idea" mysteries may want to enter the writing world from another angle."
—*Library Journal*

OF MURDER AND MEN
"A Colorado widow discovers that everything she knew about her husband's death is wrong... Interesting plot and quirky characters."
—*Kirkus Reviews*

A STORY TO KILL
"Well-crafted...Cat and crew prove to be engaging characters and Cahoon does a stellar job of keeping them—and the reader—guessing."
—*Mystery Scene*

"Lynn Cahoon has hit the golden trifecta—Murder, intrigue, and a really hot handyman. Better get your flashlight handy, *A Story to Kill* will keep you reading all night."
—**Laura Bradford**, author of the Amish Mysteries

TOURIST TRAP MYSTERIES
"Lynn Cahoon's popular Tourist Trap series is set all around the charming coastal town of South Cove, California, but the heroine Jill Gardner owns a delightful bookstore/coffee shop so a lot of the scenes take place there. This is one of my go-to cozy mystery series, bookish or not, and I'm always eager to get my hands on the next book!"
—*Hope By the Book*

"Murder, dirty politics, pirate lore, and a hot police detective: *Guidebook to Murder* has it all! A cozy lover's dream come true."
—**Susan McBride**, author of The Debutante Dropout Mysteries

"This was a good read and I love the author's style, which was warm and friendly... I can't wait to read the next book in this wonderfully appealing series."
—*Dru's Book Musings*

"I am happy to admit that some of my expectations were met while other aspects of the story exceeded my own imagination... This mystery novel was light, fun, and kept me thoroughly engaged. I only wish it was longer."

Books by Lynn Cahoon

The Tourist Trap Mystery Series
Guidebook to Murder * Mission to Murder * If the Shoe Kills * Dressed to Kill * Killer Run *
Murder on Wheels * Tea Cups and Carnage * Hospitality and Homicide * Killer Party * Memories and Murder * Murder in Waiting * Picture Perfect Frame * Wedding Bell Blues *Songs of Wine and Murder
Novellas
Rockets' Dead Glare * A Deadly Brew * Santa Puppy * Corned Beef and Casualties *
Mother's Day Mayhem * A Very Mummy Holiday

The Kitchen Witch Mystery Series
One Poison Pie * Two Wicked Desserts * Three Tainted Teas * Four Charming Spells
Novellas
Chili Cauldron Curse * Murder 101 * Have a Holly, Haunted Holiday

The Cat Latimer Mystery Series
A Story to Kill * Fatality by Firelight * Of Murder and Men * Slay in Character *
Sconed to Death * A Field Guide to Murder

The Farm-to-Fork Mystery Series
Who Moved My Goat Cheese? * Killer Green Tomatoes * One Potato, Two Potato, Dead *
Deep Fried Revenge * Killer Comfort Food * A Fatal Family Feast
Novellas
Have a Deadly New Year * Penned In * A Pumpkin Spice Killing

The Survivors Club Mystery Series
Tuesday Night Survivors' Club * Secrets in the Stacks * Death in the Romance Aisle

Songs of Wine and Murder

A Tourist Trap Mystery

Lynn Cahoon

Lyrical Underground
Kensington Publishing Corp.
www.kensingtonbooks.com

LYRICAL UNDERGROUND books are published by

Kensington Publishing Corp.
119 West 40th Street
New York, NY 10018

All Kensington titles, imprints, and distributed lines are available at special quantity discounts for bulk purchases for sales promotion, premiums, fund-raising, educational, or institutional use.

Special book excerpts or customized printings can also be created to fit specific needs. For details, write or phone the office of the Kensington Sales Manager: Kensington Publishing Corp., 119 West 40th Street, New York, NY 10018. Attn. Sales Department. Phone: 1-800-221-2647.

Lyrical Underground and Lyrical Underground eBooks logo Reg. U.S. Pat. & TM Off.

First Electronic Edition: June 2023
ISBN: 978-1-5161-1111-4 (ebook)

First Print Edition: June 2023
ISBN: 978-1-5161-1112-1 (print)

Printed in the United States of America

DEDICATION

To the radio DJs who man the small stations and bring joy in the night.

Chapter 1

Early summer was a busy time for South Cove's businesses, so it didn't surprise me that the attendance for the first Tuesday of the month's business-to-business meeting was light. What did surprise me was that Darla Taylor, the owner and manager of South Cove Winery and our promotions chair for the business council, looked like she was going to be totally AWOL. Since we had the Moonstone Beach festival coming up this weekend, which was her baby and she'd begged the council to support it, I'd assumed that she wanted most of the agenda time to make sure everyone was on the same page.

I'd already gone through the few agenda items I'd brought, including a recommendation from the council to support Josh Thomas's request for the city council to increase trash pickup on Main Street from once a week to twice, if there was a business supported festival that week. Of course, our recommendation held as much weight as a food scale for a deprivation diet program, but from the look on his face, Josh thought he had won the lottery.

Deek Kerr held up the shop phone and pointed to me as I tried to stretch out the time. I was the liaison between the business council and city hall, so the meeting was typically held at my combination coffee shop and bookstore, Coffee, Books, and More.

I nodded and addressed the group. "I need to take this call, and I'm sure Darla will be here in just a few minutes to finish up the meeting. While we're waiting, Deek will bring out a cookie platter of all the amazing treats our own Sadie Michaels makes at Pies on the Fly. If you haven't tasted her lemon bars, you're missing out."

Deek nodded and set the phone down while he set up a cookie platter. He moved fast, and by the time I reached the back to take the phone call, he was already on his way to the table with the cookies. I heard him call out the types of cookies as he set the platter down on the table. A lot of the traffic I got in the store was to chat with the surfer dude turned barista turned author. His blond dreadlocks were tinted purple this month, and the color matched his almost-violet eyes. At least the female attendees would be distracted for a few minutes.

I picked up the line. "This is Jill Gardner. How can I help you?"

"Jill, it's me. Darla. I'm about five minutes out. I was on the phone with Matt, and I lost track of time. He's in Boise tonight. Then they're heading back." Darla rattled off the tour stops of the band her boyfriend had just returned to touring with. The band had broken up a few years ago, and this was a revival tour. They'd lost their contract, mostly due to their lead singer being admitted to rehab one too many times for the record label. Now, Matt Randall and the lead singer, Axel Poser, were sober and trying to recreate the magic they'd had before. A smaller label had picked them up and set up this northwest tour to hopefully spur some creativity and get some new songs out of the group. Or at least that had been the story Darla told me when Matt left on the tour last month.

"Darla, I'm dying here. There's nothing else to talk about except the festival. What do you want me to do to get them to stay? I've already fed them twice now." I watched as several of the members looked at their watches and started packing up their notebooks.

"Tell them I'm on my way, and anyone who leaves will be put on any committee I need help with. Including the trash-collection committee." She honked her horn and yelled out a cussword. "I'm turning onto Main Street from the highway. Three minutes, I promise."

I knew it took more than three minutes to drive from the coastal highway where my house was located to the shop. At least it did if you did the speed limit. I glanced at the clock. "Greg has his staff meeting now, so hopefully there's no one on speed-trap duty. If there is, you're going to get a ticket."

"Won't be the first one. Just keep them there. I need everyone to support the kite festival on Saturday. With that and the battle of the bands, I think we can really blow up the festival this year."

With that, she disconnected our call, and I hurried over to the podium again. Pat Williams, the co-owner of Vintage Duds, had just stood up and was putting on her jacket.

"Hi, everyone, I'm back. That was Darla. She's just outside parking. She needs to talk to everyone about the plans for the kite festival Saturday morning and the battle of the bands that starts up right afterward and finishes on Sunday morning. I know she has a lot of bands already signed up; however, she needs some help with the kite festival."

Two other people stood and grabbed their papers.

"And she said anyone who isn't here when she arrives, well, she still has plenty of slots left on the trash-collection committee. Josh, you're in charge of that committee, right?"

Josh Thomas stood and looked at Pat and the other two who were gathering their things. "I'll be glad to put your names on my call list. I'll just need your cell phone number, landline number, home address, email address, and a second number of someone who can always get a hold of you. I've got a pamphlet of information, and I've developed a comprehensive test on the material. It should only take you about six hours to complete the training. Thanks for volunteering, this is awesome."

Pat sighed and sat back down, as did the other two people.

Josh frowned and looked at me. "Does this mean they're not on my committee?"

Before I could answer, the front door swung open, and Darla Taylor ran inside. She was about five foot nothing tall, and since she'd been working out with Matt for the last year, she didn't even look winded. I smiled and waved her up to the front of the table. "I'll leave that answer to Darla. I'm so glad you could make it. The Moonstone Beach Band Blowout is going to be amazing! Right, guys?"

I stepped away from the podium and let Darla take over. She talked about the kite festival and how they still needed assistants for the kids. "It's from seven to nine in the morning, so it shouldn't interfere with opening your shops."

Pat raised her hand to volunteer, as did a few others.

Darla scribbled names down and then went on. "The band competition will run from noon to ten that night, when the local police have asked us to shut down that section. I'll be running an after-party at the winery for everyone. Then on Sunday, the top three bands will face off at noon, and we'll have a winner by three that afternoon. You can close down your shops any time after four on Sunday, but I think our traffic is going to be strong up until about six, based on other festivals."

"What about the beach crowd? Are we feeding them there, or will they come into town for food and water?" asked one of the art dealers.

Darla nodded to me. "Jill's going to have a food truck with treats and drinks. And Diamond Lille's is doing a limited-menu truck both days. I think you both are opening for the kite festival and closing at ten on Saturday?"

"Nine on Saturday and five on Sunday," I corrected her. I was going to be hiring temps to keep both the food truck and the storefront open. I didn't even want to have Lille's schedule to figure out. But the money would be great, and we'd had a slow spring.

Darla finished up the meeting and made her assignments. Then she called it to a close, and everyone bolted except Darla and my best friend, Amy Newman-Cross. Amy was the mayor's assistant as well as South Cove's city planner, so she'd been assigned to attend the business meetings to take notes for the council. Except for the couple of months before an election. Then Mayor Baylor and, more often than not, his wife, Tina Baylor, attended and made some sort of nonpolitical, political speech that screamed, "Vote me back into office!" It was an annual tradition. Amy and I had a running bet on the number of town enhancements the couple would take full credit for even if they weren't in on the planning or implementation. As the mayor always said, "A united South Cove is a winning South Cove." Which meant, "Keep me in office, please."

Darla sank into a chair after filling a glass with water from the hydration station we kept available all day. "I'm so sorry I was late. I just lost track of time. Matt loves being out on the road again, but Axel Poser, the lead for the band, is a little high-strung. I'm worried that Matt's going to have issues."

"You mean like telling the guy off?" Amy asked as she took the last cookie off the plate.

Darla flushed and shook her head. "Sorry. I shouldn't be projecting my fears onto him. I'm just worried."

"Well, long-distance relationships can be hard," I said to give her some support. I hadn't had one, but during my time as a family lawyer, I'd had a lot of divorces that were brought to court because the couple never saw each other. "Or at least that's what I've been told."

"Don't stress about Matt. What you need is a girls' night. Esmeralda was talking about this amazing bar in Bakerstown. It just opened. We should head there tomorrow night. It's ladies' night, and we get in without a cover. Unless anyone has plans." Amy grinned at the two of us.

"The only plan I have is the upcoming festival." Darla paged through her notes. "And I think, with these last volunteers, I'm good until the next shoe falls and I have to start all over."

"You're stressing too much. Your festivals are always fun and profitable. Which is the bottom line. Did the mayor pony up city money to pay for the bandstand?"

Darla laughed and nodded. "Tina has a nephew whose band is playing at six on Saturday night. They got a good slot for exposure, and we got a nice check from the city growth fund for the festival. It's going to pay for the bandstand, the lights, and a small honorarium for the bands who attend. And Lille kicked in the grand-prize money to go along with the contract offer from a record label. Of course, Matt's band thinks they have it in the bag."

"Why would they want a contract offer? Don't they already have one?" Now I was confused.

Darla shrugged. "According to Matt, the contract they have is for four songs. And if all of them bomb, it's over. The contract for the competition is for an album. And it has a lot more money attached to it."

Amy glanced at her watch. "I need to go. Esmeralda can only cover the phones until eleven. Then she goes to lunch. So are we on for tomorrow night? I'll drive."

"I'm in. I'll check with Judith and see if she wants to go. She usually has plans on the nights she doesn't work. I swear she's got more activities than anyone else I've ever known." Judith was our latest hire, or I should say, my latest hire. Aunt Jackie still hadn't forgiven me for hiring Judith without running the decision by her. Mostly I think Judith got on her nerves because the two women were so much alike. Amy and I turned to stare at Darla.

She held her hands up in surrender. "Fine, I'll have my manager handle the winery, and I'll come too. It's been a while since we all went out together."

"Can I invite Esmeralda?" Amy asked as she put her tote over her shoulder. "I know Evie's probably working, right?"

"Yes, Evie's working. I'll ask Judith, and you invite Esmeralda. I haven't had time to catch up with her for a while." Esmeralda lived across the street, but her fortune-telling shop in her house seemed to be booming. There was always someone parked in her driveway. At least when I was home. I wondered if she was going to have to quit her job as dispatcher at the police department soon to expand her hours. "This is going to be fun."

"Oh, you have no idea," Amy said as she walked out the door.

Darla looked at me as she tucked her notes back into her tote. "Do you feel like we just got set up for something?"

Amy was my friend, but I wouldn't put a twist in the upcoming plans past her. "I just hope it's not male strippers again. Remember when we drove into the city for a 'cultural' event, and it was that group from Australia?"

Darla grinned as she headed out the front door. "It was a fun night."

After I got the dining room reset, I poured myself a cup of coffee and went to the bookstore section to relax and read an advance reader copy

I'd started that morning. Before I got too far into the book, Deek sat down across from me.

The shop was empty. He leaned against the back of the chair. "Why don't you just go home? I've got this. And there shouldn't be a random bus dropping off tourists today. I think the first one is scheduled for Thursday."

"I can hang around." I held up the book. "I really like this. It falls into the fantasy genre, right?"

"Actually, that's middle-aged women's paranormal fiction." He took the book from me. "This author kind of invented the genre, self-published the first three books, and now she's published by one of the traditional publishers. It's a good win-win author story." He gave the book back.

"I love that you have the author side of the gossip tree around publishing. Have we set up any author visits I need to know about?" I set the book aside.

"I thought I sent you the calendar. We have one next week on Friday night, one the following Saturday afternoon for a kids' book, and then we have three more scheduled in May. Since I have to block out the festival weeks, people are really scrambling to get a slot."

I had seen something in my email, but I hadn't read it. "I'll look at it this afternoon. Am I going to get blindsided by Jackie about the book costs?"

He shrugged. "Maybe, but we had good sell-through last month with the author events. The kids' books seem to sell out within a week, especially if it's signed by the author. I've been keeping all of them. If you want me to order less, I can."

"Let's just watch what sells, and if you can give me a weekly update on what we don't sell and how long it takes to sell off the signed stock, that would help. Maybe we should set up a signed bookshelf? That way if a buyer is looking for a gift, they have an option. Even if the receiver has read the book, if they loved it, they'd probably cherish a signed copy."

Deek blinked and scribbled something down on his paper.

"What, do you think I'm wrong?" I was beginning to worry I'd said something stupid. Deek was our marketing guru. He had all the tricks.

He grinned and stood as the doorbell went off, announcing a new customer. "No, I can't believe I didn't think of it. I've put signed copies up by the register the week after the talk, but a dedicated shelf? That's a great idea."

I picked the book up and went back to reading. "I have them, sometimes."

My stomach grumbled right as my shift was ending. My body was trained. It knew when to expect food. I texted Greg King, my fiancé, to see if he wanted to meet me at Diamond Lille's, the only full-service diner in town.

His response came fast. *How about tomorrow instead?*

I texted back a short *okay*, then went to grab my tote and say goodbye to Deek. He was restocking the dessert case.

"Do you need anything before I leave?"

He shook his head. "Tuesdays are usually slow. I'm going to pull out the pages I printed off this morning and do some editing. Judith's not scheduled to work until tomorrow, so I'll be here until Evie shows up this evening."

"I already took Toby off the schedule this week," I said, thinking about the festival hours. "Aunt Jackie's working the store Saturday night and Sunday. I'll be going back and forth from the food truck to the shop."

He nodded. "I saw the schedule in the back. Do you think it's a good idea to put Jackie and Judith on the same shift in the same place?"

I understood his concerns. My aunt could be opinionated, and she'd been less than happy when I hired Judith a few months ago. But the woman was a natural bookseller. And she upsold more treats than anyone on staff, even when she only worked part-time hours. "It had to happen sometime. If there's a blowup, I'll never put them on the same shift again. But for this weekend, we need to try."

He nodded as he cut into a fresh cherry cheesecake to put in the case. "If you need to switch me out, I'll be ready."

"I'll keep that in mind." I left the shop and paused a minute, taking in the quiet Main Street. Josh Thomas was out sweeping the sidewalk in front of his antique shop. I saw a couple of women go into the Glass Slipper, a stained-glass shop across the street, probably for a class. But mostly, the town's streets were void of people. The only life, the flowers blooming in the pots that lined the street. It felt like I'd stepped in between two moments of time. I loved instants like that. The problem was, they never lasted.

Chapter 2

I woke to the smell of bacon the next morning. As I reached from the bed to the floor, I didn't find Emma. She'd abandoned me. Greg must be making breakfast. He'd talked about starting a breakfast routine a few months ago, but then there was a murder investigation, and I'd thought he'd forgotten. I stretched and got ready for my day. Breakfast must have floated back up to the top of his to-do list.

Greg set a plate on the table as soon as I came down the stairs. "I was about to send Emma up to get you, but I heard you stomping around."

I ignored him and went to the coffeepot. After a couple of sips, I took my cup to my place at the table and set it down. "Good morning. One, I don't stomp. And two, I can't believe you actually cooked."

"You knew I was thinking about adding breakfast to our routine. I just had to finish up a few things at work so I didn't have to run into the office to do paperwork as soon as I woke up. Esmeralda is really helping with my organization. Each morning, she puts a calendar on my desk with that day's appointments, reports that are due and when, and a list of things that need to be addressed. Like hiring more staff for your rock concert weekend." He sat down, opening a black planner. "So I add everything in here, use this book to work my day, then give any notes or things I didn't get done to Esmeralda to find room on another day."

"Planning. It's a relatively new concept. I'm sure Henry Ford invented it with the Model T." I dug into my omelet and found the bacon I'd been smelling. My man was an amazing cook. "This is good."

"Thank you. I have a gift for you." He brought a pink gift bag out from under the table.

"This is so sweet." I was floored. Greg wasn't much of an impromptu gift giver. He'd take me out for dinner or tell me to plan a vacation on a whim. But the gifting gene was not in his DNA. I opened the bag and found a leather-bound book that matched his planner. Except mine was bright pink. With a sequined star in the middle. If it had a feathered pen, it would be the perfect gift for a sixteen-year-old girl. I looked up into his smiling face. "This is really something. So sparkly."

"I know. Esmeralda told me to get you the navy blue one, but I wanted you to have something pretty." He took the gift bag away and handed me a pen. Then he turned the page to this week's planning pages. "Okay, let's synchronize our schedules. What are you doing this week?"

"Working morning shift all week except Friday through Sunday, when I'm working the festival, so I'll be on call all the time." I drew a line through Friday to Sunday and wrote in big block letters: MOONSTONE BEACH BAND BLOWOUT. I pointed to his calendar. "You should add the festival to your schedule as well. That way we don't forget about it. Of course the fact we won't be able to get out of our driveway on those days might clue us into what's happening that day."

"You're not being very open about this couple thing." He pointed to Wednesday. "Doesn't our couples' financial class start this week?"

I stood and got the calendar off the fridge. "Nope, that's next week, thank goodness. I have plans tonight. Oh, you should add that to your calendar so you can either plan on making your own dinner or hitting Lille's. The girls and I are going to Bakerstown to a new bar Amy wants us to try out. It's ladies' night."

"I thought ladies' nights were held on Thursday." He wrote "Jill gone" in his book. Then he turned the page and added "Couples Class" to the next Wednesday. I did the same.

"How many weeks is this class?" I saw notes on our kitchen calendar for all of May's Wednesdays.

"Eight weeks. We might as well mark all of them off. It starts at seven. Maybe we should plan on going to Lille's for dinner before class. Make it like a date." He tapped his pen while I took another bite of breakfast. "What do you think? Five? Class starts at seven."

"Sounds perfect." I didn't want to say it sounded like a date, because it sounded more like a class or a chore. Which reminded me that I needed to get back to school in the fall and wrap up my MBA. I'd stopped going for a while when things just got too busy, but I was determined to finish. "I'm also going to get a fall calendar from the college when I'm in Bakerstown. I'm going back to school this fall."

"Another reason you needed your organizer." He looked extremely pleased with himself as he glanced at his watch. "I wanted to add menu planning for the week, but we'll have to do that later. Maybe we should sit down every Sunday night and plan out our week."

"That would be great," I said, trying to be supportive.

He closed his planner and stood up, taking his coffee cup to the sink. "I told Esmeralda you'd love this. For some reason, she didn't think you'd be all that interested. Isn't that hilarious?"

I nodded and went back to eating. Greg kissed me on the head and whistled his way out of the house. I looked at Emma, who was watching me with a doggie grin. "Stop it. I couldn't tell him I hate these things. Anyway, maybe I can use it as a running shopping list or something like that."

She turned and stared at the door, her way of saying either she needed to go out or that this pretending to like an organizer was going to end badly for all involved.

I let her out.

That night, I agreed to drive. Esmeralda, Amy, and Darla all met at my house, and we headed to Bakerstown. Judith had other plans. I turned down the music as we buzzed down the Pacific Coast Highway. "Thanks for making time for this. The weekend's going to be crazy, so having some R and R time first was a great idea."

"My great idea." Amy grinned and turned the music back up. It was going to be a Bon Jovi kind of night.

I drove through town as Amy navigated. When we got to the other side of town, where there wasn't as much development, I turned to her. "Amy? A little help here?"

She pointed to the next strip mall up the road on the right. "Turn in there. The bar's at the other end of this building."

"I didn't realize this was even here." I slowed the Jeep down and turned where Amy pointed. "Last time I was here, this was a soybean field."

Darla laughed from the back seat. "Jill, you need to get out more. This mall's been here for over a year. My hairdresser moved her salon here when it opened."

"So you know where we're going?" I glanced at her in the rearview.

"Sure." Darla pointed to the sign that had just come into view. "Lumberjack City."

"So it's ladies' night at a bar that serves guys who wear plaid and like long walks in the woods? Amy, what are you getting us into?" I pulled the Jeep into a parking spot and eyed the front of the bar. It looked like it should be in a small mountain town rather than a beach area.

"It's not just for lumberjacks." Amy unfastened her seat belt and opened her door, jumping out to the asphalt. "Come on, have I ever led you astray before?"

"Oh, let me count the ways. How many examples do you want me to give you?" I turned off the engine and climbed out of the Jeep. "I'm not in the mood for male strippers, either. I've got over a year before the wedding."

Darla climbed out of the Jeep and slapped Esmerelda's outstretched hand. "I'll remember that for when I plan your party."

"Heaven help us," I said as the four of us headed inside. The bar was decorated like we were in a lumberjack camp. A long, old-fashioned bar lined one sidewall, and women in plaid shirts and Daisy Dukes were carrying trays of large mugs filled with draft beer to people sitting at wood tables in red-leather upholstered chairs. They certainly kept to a brand. I tried to sit at the first table, but Amy pulled me away from it.

"We're back here." Amy pointed to a wall that blocked off the back corner of the interior. "I made a reservation. We're on lane fourteen."

"Don't tell me we're bowling?" Darla groaned. "Matt makes me go every time he's in town now. My arms are about to fall off, but it's a great ab workout."

"Nope." Amy laughed and moved down the hall.

I heard a whack and turned my head but didn't see anything. As we got closer to the back, the sound got louder. And more frequent. I hurried to catch up with Amy. "What's going on?"

As we came around the wall, she pointed to the left. A dark-haired woman was standing on a white line, facing a target inside what looked like a cage. She adjusted her feet, then reached up an arm and threw an axe at the target. A cheer came from the small table where several other women were sitting, watching, a mug of beer in front of each of them.

"Did she just throw an axe? We're throwing axes?" I stared as the woman curtseyed to her friends, then went to retrieve her axe.

As she walked back, she grinned as recognition hit her. She hurried past her friends to hug Darla. "What are you doing here? Practicing so you can keep Matt in line?"

"I could ask you the same. Are you sure this is good for your shoulder?" Darla laughed as she hugged the woman back. "Girls' night out. Jules, this is Jill and Amy from South Cove. Guys, this is Jules. She's the drummer in Matt's band."

"Don't let Axel hear you call it that. He's freaking out because everyone likes Matt more than him. Of course, everyone would like Charles Manson more than Axel, but I don't think old Charlie's much of a singer. And

Lynn Cahoon

there's that whole serial killer vibe. And my physical therapist released me last week. She said I was good to go and when I brought up my axe habit, she just laughed." She turned to me and held out her hand. "Jules Cannon. Darla's worried about my shoulder surgery, but I'm good to go. Besides, I need to work out the kinks before this weekend. Nice to meet you. The band is excited to play at the Moonstone Beach event. Are you part of the planning for that?"

"Not really. Darla's our marketing maven for South Cove. I run the local bookstore and coffee shop. We'll have a food truck by the bandstand, so I'll try to catch your set." I turned and introduced Amy and Esmeralda. "These guys work for city hall as well as other side hustles."

"Looks like you all are the power center of South Cove right here. Women are the ones that get things done, right?" Jules stepped over and set her axe down. Then she grabbed her beer with her other hand. From the look of it, Darla was probably right in thinking Jules was overstressing her shoulder, but that was her problem, not mine. "I'd love to replace Axel and get us a female lead, but everyone's worried about being rock enough. Like Heart and Fleetwood Mac weren't rock? They're just worried a woman would take over."

I kind of thought Axel might be worried for his position, but I didn't point that out. According to Darla, he was a bit of a jerk, so losing him might not be a bad idea. Jules's friends were calling her back to the table, so we said our goodbyes and went to find our own spot.

I caught Darla watching Jules a little while later. "What's up? Do you two not get along?"

Darla glanced over, the trance broken. "Oh, Jules? She's amazing. I really like her, but according to Matt, Axel hates her. He's looking for a new drummer."

"Because she's a bit outspoken?" I guessed, and Darla nodded.

"That and her shoulder. Axel Poser runs his band like a small Caribbean dictatorship. If you don't like something, there's the door. He doesn't care what Jules or any other member of the band wants. He cares what he thinks the band needs. All I know is I'm kind of hoping they don't win the contest or get the record deal. I'd hate to see Matt having to be around the guy for another year while they finish the record. He's trouble." Darla drank from her mug, then stood and walked over to the throwing line. "Might as well get this over with. Amy's not going to let any of us leave before we try."

The evening turned out to be fun. I wasn't the best at even hitting the target at first, but by the last game, I'd gotten the hang of it. We were just getting ready to leave when another group came in. Amy saw the group and their leader first. "There's trouble."

I turned to watch.

A young man was dressed to look how he thought a rock star should look—tight jeans, an untucked purple silk shirt, with silver chains going down his chest. His blond hair was long and flying all over every time he moved. The guy needed to learn how to use conditioner if he was going to keep his hair that length. His gaze flitted across the room until he found Jules. "Hey, Cannon. Training for a new profession? This seems right up your alley."

"Bite me, Hansel. Why don't you go somewhere else where you can get your favorite drink with the little umbrella on top? I hear you have a collection in your bedroom in your mother's basement."

"The name is Hans, not Hansel. You can at least treat me with some respect," Hans growled and stepped forward, his hands clenched. A bouncer from the bar stepped in between them. He looked up to the man's face. "What do you want? I'm talking with my friend here. Go stand in the corner and just watch like you always do."

The bouncer didn't take the bait. "Is this man bothering you, miss?"

"Why yes, he is. Thank you for asking." Jules smiled sweetly at the tall muscle-bound man.

"She's lying. I didn't do anything to her. You can't make me leave the bar." Now Hans was livid.

I leaned over to Darla, as we all had stopped moving when the show started. "Who is he?"

"That, my friend, is Tina's nephew, Hansel Baldwin. He's the lead guitar player for his band. Kind of a loser. This isn't the first bar fight he's picked. Usually he gets out of the consequences with Tina's help. He's entitled."

"I think tonight he's being kicked out," Esmeralda commented. "Entitled or not."

"I'm sure someone from Bakerstown's mayor's office will be here tomorrow morning smoothing over the issues. His father spreads a lot of money around to keep Hansel's name clean." Darla gripped the axe handle tighter. "The guy is a true piece of work. But I guess we're the lucky ones this weekend. He'll be in South Cove for the band event. I just hope no one tries to kill him before the battle is over. I'd hate for Greg to have the extra work of trying to solve the murder of a man that's hated by everyone who's met him. He'd have too many suspects."

I watched as the bouncer escorted Hans and his group out of the bar. Jules grinned at him as he passed by. She said, "Good luck at the battle. You're going to need it."

I assumed he deserved the jab, but there was something about kicking a wounded dog when it was down. It tended to bite harder and faster when it saw its opportunity. I thought Jules had just made an enemy. My arms chilled as I wondered what and when his return strike would be. Because it was coming. Anyone who had watched the exchange knew this wouldn't be the end of it.

As I drove home that night, Hans's face kept ruining my focus on the scenery around me. He wouldn't give up that easily. Maybe I should mention the fight to Greg so he could watch out for Jules. Or maybe—which would be what he'd say—I should mind my own business.

I wanted to mind my own business, but things just kept happening around me. It really wasn't my fault.

Chapter 3

Greg showed up at the shop the next morning after my commuter customers had left. I'd gotten up early to go in and get things ready for the weekend event, but he'd still been up and out of the house before I turned off my alarm. He worked harder than me. I had a lot going on, but he made me look like a college frat boy on summer break.

He sat at the coffee bar. "Hey, beautiful. How was your night?"

"Interesting. I didn't know there was an axe bar in Bakerstown. I'm not a bad thrower. At least after a few rounds." I poured us both a cup of coffee and went to sit with him. "And we ran into one of Matt's band buddies. And one of the band's enemies. They didn't get along too well."

"I heard. The Bakerstown sheriff called me this morning, telling me that Hans was causing problems again." He sipped his coffee. "That kid really needs to go to Europe or somewhere that's not near my jurisdiction."

"I hear his dad tends to bail him out of problems." I let that statement sit. I didn't want to accuse Greg of helping sweep things under the rug, mostly because I didn't think he'd do it.

"That's the one reason the kid stays out of South Cove. He knows I won't bend to his father's or Tina's meddling. If he gets in trouble here, he pays the price. He learned that early, when he raced his new Camaro down Main Street with one of his high school buds and got a ticket that sent him back to driving school." Greg rolled his shoulders. "Tina didn't talk to me for a month. And Mayor Baylor was furious. I kept getting called in for stupid stuff he wanted me to fix. Especially after I told him I wasn't making the ticket disappear. But it was worth it. Up until this weekend, Hansel has avoided South Cove and me."

"Well, you deserve a cookie for that. From the show I saw last night, the guy is a bully. He was giving Jules Cannon a hard time. The bouncer didn't like it, and Hans got kicked out." I got us two of the Chocolate Chunkers, Greg's favorite. I rubbed my forearm. "I didn't think the axe was that heavy until this morning. My arm is aching."

"You're building muscle." He took a bite of the cookie. "So besides Hans being a jerk, did you have fun?"

"Yeah, but I'm not sure it's a place where I'd hang out. It's kind of a novelty place. Once or twice would probably be enough for me." I broke my cookie in half, then in half again. It seemed to last longer that way.

"Good thing we live in a tourist area where there are a lot of people who want novelty experiences," Greg deadpanned.

I held up my hands. "Okay, I get it. I'm not their target customer. How's prep for the weekend going?"

"Fine. We've got enough extra people scheduled. And I've got Esmeralda's trip covered starting on Monday."

I'd stopped listening and was thinking about my next bite of cookie when I realized what he'd said. "Wait, Esmeralda's going on a trip? Where?"

"You just hung out with her last night. She didn't tell you?" He frowned. "I figured she'd ask us to watch her cat."

"She didn't mention it at all. Is she going to New Orleans to meet up with Nic? Or somewhere with Rory on a girls' holiday?" Now I was curious. Nic was Esmeralda's boyfriend, at least I thought he was. She was pretty closemouthed about their relationship. Rory Kerr ran a fortune-telling shop in Bakerstown and was Esmeralda's best friend. Where did a fortune teller go to relax from the stress of the world? I would think New Orleans would have too many unresolved deaths and wandering souls to be a place to relax. But maybe she liked that.

"I think New Orleans, but you'll have to ask her. She's leaving Monday morning and will be back Sunday night. That's all I know." He finished his coffee. "And I wouldn't have even told you that, except I figured you two had already talked. Being friends with employees makes it hard to keep all the lines straight."

"You seem to do fine with it. I'm sure Esmeralda won't mind that you told me." I ate the last piece of my cookie. The question still stood though—why hadn't she told me? Maybe she didn't want Darla to know. I suspected that Amy already did know since they shared phone duty at city hall.

A customer came in and beelined to the coffee bar. "Thank goodness you're open. The coffeemaker at the hotel is on the fritz, and you know it tastes like crap anyway. I *need* coffee."

I stood and gave Greg a kiss on the cheek. "See you tonight?"

"That will work. I'll cook." He nodded to the woman standing at the counter. "Good morning, ma'am."

After he left, I handed her the coffee and rang up her purchase. She handed me her credit card. "You're a lucky lady. The man looks and acts like a keeper."

I charged the card and gave it back to her. "He is. Do you want your receipt?"

* * * *

When Deek came in for his shift, I leaned on the counter, watching him get ready. Finally, I pounced. "Did you know Esmeralda was going on vacation Monday?"

He stared at me like I had two heads. "Of course. I'm staying at her house next week to take care of her cat. Why? Is that an issue?"

I shook my head. Apparently, I was the last to know anything about my new friend. Esmeralda and I had just started hanging out. Maybe this reluctance to confide in me was just that she didn't think to tell me since we had just been neighbors. She didn't know the friend code yet. And I was making way too much of this. I had things to do.

I turned back to Deek. "Nope. I was just wondering if I needed to feed her cat."

He frowned as he started a new pot of coffee. "Are you sure? You look a little put out about the whole thing. You don't want to feed her cat, do you? I can tell her I'm busy."

Now I was getting pity cat-sitting duties. "No, it's fine. I was just wondering, that's all."

"You know you can ask her anything. She really respects you. I overheard her and my mom talking last year about you and what an amazing addition you are to the South Cove family." He put his hand on top of mine. "I'm sure she didn't want to make you feel left out."

Now Deek was trying to make me cry. I straightened and picked up the list my aunt had made for the weekend. We needed to get busy. "Touchy-feely time is over. Do you want to stock the new books on the shelves? Or do you want to handle walk-ins?"

When I got home late that afternoon, Greg texted me. *Don't make dinner. I'm bringing home some work and Tiny's chicken.*

I sent back several happy emojis and checked the weather. Warm but not too hot to run with my favorite partner. I pointed to her leash. "Who wants to go running with me?"

Emma barked and did a happy circle. I had my answer. I hurried upstairs to change; then we started down the road to the beach. My house was on the corner of what we called Main Street farther down into town and the Pacific Coast Highway. We had to cross the highway to get to the beach, but typically, I ran at off-peak hours, so I got lucky with traffic. Today was no different.

We arrived home hot and sweaty just as Greg pulled into the driveway. He stuck his head out of his door. "My two favorite girls."

I leaned in and kissed him. "You're early."

He pointed to the clock in his truck display. "It's almost five thirty."

"I worked a lot later than I thought at the store then. No wonder Deek kept throwing subtle and not-so-subtle hints for me to leave." I finished the water in my bottle and then rubbed Emma's back. "I've got to get her inside to a water bowl."

"I'll follow you." He turned off the engine and rolled up his window to keep random animals out of the cab. I could smell the chicken through the bag even with him behind me.

"I need to shower before I eat, but you go ahead." I unclicked Emma's leash, and she ran to the water dish. "I won't be long."

He followed me to the kitchen and set the bags on the table. "I can wait. Go get ready. I'm going to go lock up my weapon. I'll change when you get back down so Emma doesn't get any ideas on changing her dinner plans."

Clockwork, I thought as I ran upstairs and turned the shower on. Greg and I were perfect together since we thought the same way and had the same habits. Except for my need to inhale sugar. He could eat one cookie and be okay. Me? I needed at least two, and more if I was bored or if they were just sitting there as I watched television or did anything else.

By the time he was back in the kitchen, I had set up a mini chicken buffet. I'd added cheesecake to the end just in case we needed something sweet. Okay, fine, the cheesecake was for me.

As he picked up a plate and started filling it, I watched his face. "So what was the reason behind the impromptu dinner?"

"We had to eat. I've got to work tonight, so I didn't want to cook. And I know things have been busy at the shop. I called Deek for an update on the water supply in the beach truck to see if I could send my officers there or if I needed to source our water from Diamond Lille's. He said you'd just left." He set two legs and a thigh on his plate. Then he dished up mashed potatoes and coleslaw. "Put my cheesecake back in the fridge. I'll have it tonight as my reward for finishing these reports."

"You're a good man and an excellent role model." I didn't know what I could use as my cheesecake reward. Maybe finishing another book review for Deek? Or maybe I just needed to finish the book I was reading. That would be a reason to celebrate. I decided not to announce my goal and commit to the action. I didn't want to sacrifice my cheesecake later, just in case I didn't meet it.

"So, is the festival keeping you busy? Or is something else going on I don't know about? Like an author event?" He picked up utensils and nodded to the table. "Eat inside or out?"

"Inside. It's hot today." I finished loading up my plate and went over to meet him. "Soda or tea?"

"Water." He stood and took a bottle out of the fridge. "What about you?"

"Soda." I told him about the discussion that Deek and I had over Jackie and Judith working together. "Do you think it's a problem?"

"I guess you'll find out. Neither woman is a shrinking violet that won't ask for what she needs. I think you schedule the way you need to and let the chips fall where they may." Greg picked up his fork.

"So translated, yes, I'm making a mistake." I dug into the mashed potatoes. "I really don't care. One of these days, they're going to have to work together. It might as well be this weekend."

That evening, while Greg wrote performance evaluations for his crew, I worked on not one but two book reviews. I sent both of them to Deek, then shut down the laptop. Greg had commandeered my "home office" when he moved in. I still stored things in there, but mostly I did my work on the couch with my laptop. That way I could watch television at the same time. It was a win-win. Unless I was reading; then the TV stayed off.

When Greg came out of the office, he ignored me and went straight to the kitchen. Then he came out and handed me my cheesecake.

I took it with a smile, laying my book on the table. "Thanks. I feel very accomplished tonight."

He groaned. "I wish I felt that way. I have three great guys but only one raise approved by the city council. They all deserve and need the raise. Toby's close to his down payment goal, which means I can see a remodel of the shed coming for us. Tim needs more money since his wife's expecting their first child, and she can't work as much anymore. And Trey, he's still on the base pay I hired him at a few months ago."

I started to laugh.

"What? It isn't funny." He stabbed his cheesecake. "I'm going to lose one or more of these guys if the council doesn't loosen the purse strings."

"I know it's not funny, but seriously, you have to stop hiring people whose name begins with *T*." I took a bite of my cheesecake. "Wasn't there anyone who was named Bruno or Alphonso?"

"No. And I don't hire by name." He groaned and closed his eyes. "I promise no more Thomases or Todds or even Teds."

"Maybe you could give the raise to the first guy who files papers to change his name?"

"Not funny, Jill." He leaned his head back on the couch, where I could see his lips curving into a smile.

"Changing the subject, I guess Deek's watching Esmeralda's house and cat next week, so we're off the hook."

"You sound sad." Greg finished his cheesecake and set the plate on the coffee table. He shook a finger at Emma, who whined and lay down. "Did you want to watch the cat?"

"Why does everyone assume I want to watch her cat?" I reached down and rubbed Emma's head. "We have a dog, you know. I couldn't very well bring the cat over here. Unless we kept her in a crate, and that's not good."

"We'd find a way. But I'm glad you're not babysitting. As soon as this stupid festival is over, I'm going to sleep for a week." He reached over with his fork to take a bite of my cheesecake.

"Hey, eat your own." I dodged his attempt and started laughing. We might be crazy busy, but we had time to enjoy each other's company. "I shouldn't tell you this since you're being greedy, but I'm going to miss seeing you this weekend."

"Summer festivals are always crazy." He watched as Emma sniffed the table then leaned in with her tongue, aiming for his plate. He blocked her move. "You can't have any, it has chocolate in it."

"She thinks chocolate must be amazing since we don't let her have it, yet I'm eating it all the time." I finished off my own and picked up Greg's empty plate as well. I paused before heading to the kitchen. "Do you want to watch a movie or a show?"

"Do we still have some of that cooking show you like?" Greg leaned his head on the back of the couch, his eyes closed.

I figured he'd be asleep before the first challenge on the show was over, but it was nice having him at least attempt to watch one of my favorites. "We've got two recorded. I'll cue it up as soon as I set these in the sink."

When I got back, his eyes were still open, and he was talking to Emma. I loved that Greg loved my dog as much as I did. Of course, he'd given me the golden retriever when she was just a puppy, saying my new house needed a protector. She was so tiny that I didn't think she'd be much of a protector, until she started gaining five pounds a week. Now that she was full grown, I didn't worry about being alone in the house. Not with her around.

Greg's phone rang an hour later. He groaned and picked it up. "This had better be important."

I put the show on pause, but I was pretty sure I'd be watching the ending alone.

As he listened, he pulled himself from reclining up to a sitting position, looking more like he was ready to pounce, not stand up. "I'll be there in ten."

I sighed as I sank back into the couch. "Do you think you'll be home soon?"

He shook his head as he stood. "Sorry, Jill, someone's been killed."

Fear stabbed me as I looked at him.

He must have known what I was thinking. "It's not one of ours. I mean, not a townie. It's a guy from one of the bands. Matt's band. That was Matt on the phone. He found the lead singer dead backstage."

"Overdose? Darla said the band was a little wild with drugs and stuff. It was making her nervous. But I thought he was off the stuff?" I pulled a pillow toward me, holding it against myself like a shield from all the bad in the world.

Greg stood and got ready to leave. "No, this wasn't self-inflicted. Unless he could wrap a guitar string around his own neck and choke to death."

Chapter 4

On Friday morning, the practice sessions for the bands had been delayed until after Greg's office cleared the area. Tina Baylor stood in front of my food truck and waved me outside. I knew she wouldn't go away if I ignored her, so I asked Deek to cover my place taking orders for a few minutes. He glanced over at the mayor's wife and just nodded. Sometimes, not saying anything said a lot.

"Tina, what can I help you with? I've got a line, so this needs to be quick." I dried my hands on a towel I'd thrown over my shoulder.

"Jill, you need to get Greg to open the practice area. The bands need to get on the stage so they will know what it feels like before the competition." She waved her hands around, including the one that held a phone that was in use. I didn't know if it was the mayor on the other end, listening in on our conversation, or if Tina had just forgotten she was talking to someone when I walked up. I'd believe either.

"Tina, I'm not sure if you know, but someone was killed here last night. I think it's only respectful to be aware of the issue." I tried to appeal to her community service side. It didn't work.

"Of course I know that. You're not the only one sleeping with a South Cove man in power." Tina blew out a frustrated breath.

Ouch, that was pointed. "You'll have to take up opening the bandstand with Greg. I'm just a book-and-coffee seller."

"Whatever." Tina stormed off toward the bandstand. "Thanks for your help, not."

"I guess she didn't like what you said." A customer shook her head, watching our mayor's wife stomp off, throwing a hissy fit.

"Not my problem." I hurried back into the trailer. I had coffee to serve.

A few hours later, Amy came up to the truck. She stepped inside and leaned against the wall, watching us make coffee. "You made Tina mad."

"I don't control Greg or his investigation. She should know that." I glanced outside. For the first time since our truck had opened that morning, there wasn't a line. "Deek, I'm taking a short break with Amy. Can you hold down the fort?"

"Of course, boss." He saluted, then went to make more coffee.

When I got off the truck, Amy pointed to the left, and I followed her to a bench overlooking the ocean.

"You don't understand. Tina's furious with you. I'm afraid she's going to push the mayor into doing something. Like taking away the facilitation of the business-to-business meeting from you."

I shrugged. "Honestly, if she does, fine. I can't be worrying about what she's going to do when I just spoke the truth."

"Honey, I haven't told Tina the absolute truth since I started working with Mayor Baylor. She doesn't care if you act on what you say, just that you say you're going to help," Amy explained.

"Well, that's just stupid. I know I'm not the best with people skills, but it seems to me, she'd catch on after a while." I hoped I hadn't messed up Greg's job with my candor.

"I'll tell her you were just upset and didn't realize what you were saying, but if she talks to you, you need to apologize," Amy offered.

"You want me to apologize for something I didn't do? I'm sorry, Amy, I'm not sure I can do that."

Amy sighed and gave me a hug. "You need to take one for the team. I swear this will blow over if you apologize. If you don't? We're all going to be miserable."

I stood, noticing the line starting to back up. "I need to get in the truck. But I'll think about it. I don't want to cause a problem." Which was the stupidest thing I've ever said. I wasn't causing a problem. I'd spoken the truth, and Tina was throwing a fit like a five-year-old. But Amy was seriously worried for me. And maybe for Greg. And if Tina went ballistic, everyone I'd ever known or talked to would be in the line of fire. "Fine, I'll apologize."

"Thank you, Jill. I'll tell her the next time I see her. You won't regret this."

As Amy walked away toward town, I realized she was wrong. I already did regret saying I'd apologize for something that wasn't my fault. But that was small-town living; you had to learn to live with everyone. Even the problem children.

When I got back to the truck, Jules, the girl from the bar, was standing outside, ordering coffee with a tall man in an old rock band T-shirt and worn jeans. His hair was salt and pepper, and he had a tight goatee. I waved at the woman and stepped closer. "Hi, I'm Jill. We met a few nights ago..."

"At the axe bar!" Jules finished my statement. "You were with Darla. I love her. She's so good for Matt."

"Darla's an amazing woman. And South Cove's most energetic supporter. She developed this entire festival just for your bands." I turned to the man standing next to Jules. "I'm Jill Gardner. This is my food truck, and I own the bookstore/coffee shop in town."

"I'm Keith Jackson. I'm the manager for Atlantis Survivors."

I must have looked a little confused, because he continued to explain. "Matt and Jules's band?"

"Oh, I guess I didn't know what it was called." The name surprised me. I wasn't sure what I was thinking it was, but not that. "I'm really happy you guys are still here. I heard about what happened last night. Are you okay?"

"We are. Of course, now we're without a lead singer. Axel Poser was the heart of the band, and he'll be missed. We have to move forward, in his memory, of course. If you know of anyone who is looking for a gig, I'd be glad to talk with them." He handed Deek a twenty and then took the coffee cups off the shelf. He handed one to the woman next to him. "Jules, we need to be going. It was nice to meet you, Ms. Garden."

"Gardner," I corrected. "Jill Gardner."

He didn't seem to hear and walked away, his arm around Jules's back and his hand firmly on her butt.

"Well, isn't he special?"

I turned to see Sadie and Pastor Bill standing behind me.

"He's Matt's band manager."

Sadie and Pastor Bill were holding hands. She shot a mean look at Keith's back. "Well, that doesn't mean he can act like he can't even remember your name. Some people are just rude."

"Now, Sadie, maybe he is hard of hearing and didn't hear Jill's full name." Pastor Bill explained away Keith's attitude.

I thought Sadie was more in line with what had just happened, but I guess it could be true.

"You're always just looking for the best in people." Sadie dropped his hand and walked up to the ordering window.

Pastor Bill smiled at me, but he looked tired and worn out. "She's been on edge lately."

"I happen to agree with her assessment of the situation." I shrugged. "Sometimes people don't think about what they say. But I know it's your job to see the other side. Turn the other cheek, so to speak."

He chuckled. "Occupational hazard, I'm afraid." He looked over at Sadie, who was talking to Deek about her coffee order. "Maybe I need to show her that I can be more than just my job at times."

As he walked away, I wondered if that was why I hadn't heard about an engagement. I still thought they were an amazing couple together, but it looked like even the perfect couple had issues to deal with.

Thinking about couples, I wondered about Keith and Jules. He apparently saw her as his property, the way his hand curved on her butt. But did she feel the same way? Or was I just putting my more mundane small-town American values and expectations on people who spent their lives in the rock-and-roll world? I saw Deek waving me into the truck, so I went in to try to get the line back under control.

I heard the music start up when the bandstand finally opened. A cheer erupted on the beach from the waiting bands and their supporters. Matt's band—Atlantis Survivors—was supposed to practice from one to two, but with the practice start time being postponed until ten, I figured they had a little time to find a lead singer in the meantime. One that knew their songs. It would be a miracle if they could pull it off.

That wasn't my concern though. Right now, I needed to make a run to the store to grab more treats and more coffee. I could drive up to Diamond Lille's before the road had been closed. Local traffic—which was me—was still being given access to the alley behind Main Street, so I took the Jeep for supplies. I might need help from Greg's officers to stop traffic to get from my house to the beach and then back to my house again. But I'd deal with that when I needed to. There had to be some benefits of being the fiancée of the local police detective, right?

I told Deek and Tilly, who was the temp my aunt had brought in for the weekend, I'd be back in less than an hour and then hurried through the crowd to get my Jeep. I was going to miss hearing several of the bands practice, but I'd be here later when they actually performed. And I was only rooting for one—Atlantis Survivors. Mainly because of Matt.

The drive was uneventful, and Judith helped me load up the Jeep while telling me about the shop's day. When I drove back, I sat at the corner for several minutes until Toby saw me two cars back from the stop sign. He stopped traffic on the highway, then waved the front cars out of my way. He popped his head into the Jeep and looked around. "Restocking?"

"Yes, and I'll be back to take the Jeep home as soon as I unload this. I don't want to try to find a spot in the parking lot."

He chuckled. "Probably a good idea. Just let me know when you're done, and I'll get you through."

"Toby?" I called out his name as he started to step away.

He turned back, shaking his head. "Don't even ask, Jill. You know I can't say."

"Please just tell me it's open and shut, and Greg will be home tonight," I called after him as he walked back to the middle of the road and waved me through. "I'll take that as a no," I mumbled as I negotiated the car through the crowds in the small parking lot. I parked to the side of the food truck and started unloading. Deek came out to help.

"You got a lot of stuff. Is the regular store going to be okay with treats?"

I nodded. "We're outselling them today, and Sadie will be dropping off a delivery late afternoon. We'll probably need to restock early tomorrow morning when there's not a lot of people here. Doing this during the day is crazy. I thought maybe people would be taking a break from the beach right now. It's pretty hot."

"The bands started later, so their people are all here, watching the show and being supportive." He hefted the last box into the truck. "Tomorrow I'm going to bring out some of our South Cove travel charm books as well as all of the music books I can find. I think we'd sell them here. I've had a lot of people ask if we carry that type of book."

"I didn't think of that, and I should have."

Deek was a wiz at marketing.

"Can you write down all of your good ideas for each festival so when you take off to be a full-time author, I have a clue what to do?" I was totally serious.

He laughed. "You survived before me and will survive after me, I'm sure. But I like the idea of having a festival folder with all the ideas in it. That way, we only have to pull it out each year, and we can remember what worked and what didn't. I'll get a format set up and send it to your aunt. She'd love the standardization."

"Yes, she will." If there was one thing my aunt and I disagreed on, it was the amount of flying by the seat of my pants management I did for the bookstore/coffee shop. At least I did before she came to work for me. Or as she would say it, when she came to save my business. Another reason I needed to get my MBA finished, so I could prove to my aunt that I had some business savvy, even though she thought I was in over my head. After all these years.

Darla came up behind me and gave me a hug. "I *need* a coffee, stat. Matt's band is playing in ten minutes, and I want to be in the front row while they practice. With the mess last night, I don't think I got to bed until after two."

"I'm sorry about Axel, but I guess they found a lead singer already?" I poured her coffee and put in three caramel pumps for flavor without all the sugar. Darla had a usual since she often came to the shop to hang out before she headed to the winery she owned with her family.

"Yeah, I guess Keith's been courting this guy from another band. With the contract in hand for Atlantis Survivors, I guess he couldn't pass it up now that Axel was out of the picture." She pointed to one of the flip-flop sugar cookies I'd just filled the case with. "I'll take one of those too."

"I met Keith today. He's interesting. Are he and Jules a couple?" I wondered what Jules thought of the butt grab. She didn't seem the type of person to let someone get so familiar in public. But they were music people, so who knew. I'd been with Greg for years, and if he'd grabbed my butt like that, I'd be upset.

"He thinks so. Jules is on the fence about it. She says they're dating, but she's still playing the field. I think she just likes having someone if she has an open date on her calendar. The girl works all the time. She's in a smaller band too, but they don't play gigs as often as this band does. She just wants to make it. One band or two, or even ten, she doesn't care." Darla took the cookie and coffee and handed me her credit card. "I should just leave it here and open a tab. I'm going to be a frequent customer this weekend."

"We'll have to get you a punch card." I handed her back her card and a receipt. "Just don't forget to eat some real food this weekend too. I'm picking up some lunch for both the truck and the shop. I had everyone write down their order, and I called it in for a late pickup, but I didn't count on the practice being delayed. I hope we're not slammed when the food gets here."

"There's only two more practice bands; then the stage is clear until six, when the competition starts." Darla looked around. "Although there may only be one band left to practice. You didn't hear it from me, but Mick O'Reilly, the new singer that took Axel's place? He was from Hans's band. I'm sure Tina's going to call foul, but there's no rule saying a person can't start with one band and end with someone else. And besides, the competition hasn't even started yet."

"That's not good. Tina's already mad at me for not talking Greg into letting the practice start before they cleaned up the murder site." I hoped I didn't see Tina at all this weekend.

"You've got to be kidding." Darla sipped her coffee. "And how were you supposed to do that?"

I shrugged. "I guess I should be better at telling Greg what to do. Not. Can you even imagine? He'd just laugh at me."

"Well, we know who runs the mayor's house now." Darla glanced at her watch. "I've got to scoot. See you soon."

As I watched Darla hurry through the crowd toward the bandstand, I got mad all over again about Tina and her demands. "I'm not sure I'm going to apologize."

"Boss, you know you need to be the bigger person here," Deek said from the coffee machines, where he was stacking cups. "Your aura is all kinds of messed up right now. Calm down and get this apology over with. Then your aura will go back to normal, and you'll be happier."

"I need to apologize to fix my aura?" I didn't believe in Deek's philosophy, but he'd never told me I could change my aura before.

"Yes. That's how people get stuck, and their auras go black. They let a slight or something where they feel they were in the right just fester. You're too good a person to let that happen to you. People's auras change all the time. Your aunt, for example. Once she married Harrold, her aura took on a brightness. Of course, she still has moments, but it's so much better."

I had to agree with him on that one. Aunt Jackie had been a lot happier since I'd gotten a new uncle. I didn't know about her aura, but the result was the same. I took the next order and then turned to Deek. "I promise, the next time I see Tina, I'll apologize."

He started the coffee and smiled. "You're already turning brighter."

Chapter 5

After picking up and delivering lunches, I had my feet up and was sitting at one of the picnic tables near the food truck to eat. Deek was manning the food truck, but our line had disappeared, and he was eating while he watched for customers. The temp had run out to her car to eat. *Tilly. Her name is Tilly,* I reminded myself. I'd invited her to sit with me, but I figured she was job seeking on her lunch. She'd asked me if I was hiring on a full-time basis and had been disappointed in my answer.

I had her number and told her I'd call her first for the next festival if she was still looking, but based on her work ethic and selling skills, I didn't think she'd be available.

Greg sat down across from me and took several of my fries. "Did you get me food?"

"Did you tell me to order you lunch?" I moved my container out of his reach. "Lille's food truck is open. Go order, and you can eat with me."

"I have food back at the station. I just need to get there. I had Tiny prepare his taco bar for the crew. Especially since I never know when anyone is going to have a few minutes to eat. We've had three drunk-and-disorderly arrests already, and it's only early afternoon. I think your friend Josh is going to complain about the type of tourists this festival brought into town." Greg stood and walked over to the window and asked Deek for two waters.

When he got back, I accepted the bottle he offered and took a long sip. "I needed that."

"You don't hydrate enough. You'll drink coffee all day, but you need some plain water in that mix as well." He scanned the area as he took two more fries. "I guess you heard that Tina's upset at my delaying practice time."

"She's also mad at me for not stopping you." I laughed when he turned and stared at me. "Don't kill the messenger. I'm on her naughty list, according to Amy. I'll apologize when I see her."

"You shouldn't have to. I'm the one who delayed the practice." He groaned. "I'll talk to Marvin on Monday and tell him to control his wife."

"I'm sure that will be super helpful," I teased. "And worse, her nephew's band lost their lead singer."

He frowned and turned back toward me after watching a group of teenagers gather around Lille's food truck. "I didn't know Hansel was in Atlantis Survivors."

"He's not. The lead singer from his band quit this morning and joined Matt's band. Darla says they have a great chance at winning this thing now that Axel's out of the picture." I ate my last bite of fish and pushed the rest of the fries toward Greg.

"I hate it when you give me information that could be motive in the murder investigation." He doused the remaining fries with a packet of malt vinegar. "Okay, maybe I don't really hate the information. I just hate that it comes from you. I worry about you getting involved."

"What are you talking about?" I went back over what I'd just said. "Wait, you don't think that Mick, the new singer, killed Axel to get into the band."

"That's one potential path for motive, but not the one I was thinking of." He finished the fries. "Do I need to stop at the house and let Emma out?"

"I was just there when I went up to get everyone's lunch. I think she's good until about six. Do you want to handle that one?"

He leaned over and kissed me. "I'll see. Text me at six, and I'll let you know if it's possible. I'm afraid the murder investigation is going to be heating up in the middle of this festival. I'm not sure I'll have the energy to do both. The mayor's going to scream about overtime this weekend, especially if Hans doesn't have a band to compete now."

I watched him walk away toward town. I probably wouldn't see him for more than a few minutes here and there until the investigation was completed. I set an alarm on my phone, and when I went back to the food truck, I asked Deek to remind me to let Emma out at six. There was no reason to worry Greg about that too.

He wrote on a sticky note and put it up on the slider where orders would be placed if we were cooking in the truck. "Your dude seems a little overwhelmed right now. His aura is all kinds of jumpy."

"I'd say a lot overwhelmed. But he loves his job. Even on weekends like this." I watched as a guy fell down in the crowd, then popped up again with his glass still in hand.

"I didn't spill a drop," he called out to his buddies.

I kind of thought it might have been a good thing if he had spilled all of it and given his body a break from the alcohol.

Deek reminded me about Emma and told me to take a break at about five thirty. "I've got this until Judith shows up."

Tilly had left thirty minutes ago with a promise to be back at nine in the morning. *Tilly the temp* was what I was calling her in my head. Hopefully, I wouldn't blurt it out when she was here.

I was working the main store from six to eight, when we were closing, unless it was crazy slow; then we'd close up, and I'd send Evie down to the food truck to work until the competition ended. I was planning on rejoining the truck and sending Judith home after that. It was a game of musical booksellers or baristas. It just depended on where the customers were, and I was beginning to think the food truck would be the hot spot for the weekend.

Before heading back to the house to let Emma out, I wandered down to the bandstand. If Tina was there, it would be better to get this over with. Atlantis Survivors was still playing when I arrived. Darla squealed when she saw me.

"Aren't they amazing? This guy is so much better than Axel." She turned toward me, and her face fell. "Oh no."

I turned around to see what she was upset about and saw Tina stomping toward us. When she arrived, I stepped between her and Darla. "Look, Tina, I'm sorry about what I said earlier."

"Like I don't know what you and your friend were up to. The practices were delayed so you could talk Mick into leaving Hans's band. Don't deny it. I know," Tina yelled at me over the music.

"Tina, again, you're giving me too much credit for things I don't have any power over. I only know Matt, and I've met Hans, Jules, and Keith once, this weekend. I don't care who plays or who wins. I serve coffee." I tried to reason with her, but Tina wasn't having any of it. Greg showed up as I was talking and stood behind me.

"Whatever you want to tell yourself. I know the truth." She pointed toward Darla. "And I know you were in on it too. But it doesn't matter. Hans found someone better than Mick to sing with the band anyway. Your stupid band is going to lose, even with the shenanigans you pulled to win."

I watched her storm away as the music died. Several people had been watching along with me since they'd overheard Tina's tirade. Now they were watching me. I rolled my shoulders and mumbled to Darla, "You're my witness. I tried to apologize, but she wasn't having any of it. She basically accused me of killing Axel to get Mick in the band."

"I don't understand why you are always in the wrong place at the wrong time." Greg put his arms around me. "I'll handle this thing with Tina. Just stay away from her as much as possible this weekend. She's convinced this is all a conspiracy against Hans."

"Even Axel's murder?" I leaned into his shoulder. "I don't think anyone would go to those lengths just to get a band out of a competition."

"Oh, they would if the band was that good." Darla walked away from the bandstand with us. "It's happened before. According to Matt, Axel was a pro at getting the competition out of his way. By hook or by crook. That's one of the reasons I didn't really want Matt involved in the band. But Keith said he'd keep Axel in line this time. I guess everyone thought since there was money and a contract on the line, maybe he'd straighten up. And maybe he had."

"But you don't think so," Greg finished the thought that stayed in Darla's head but that we both knew was there.

"No. You can't just paint a horse and pretend he's a zebra. Axel was bad news. He had been since he started playing as a teenager. Everyone in the business knew that. Now he's gone, and he's still causing problems for the band." Darla nodded to Matt, who was just coming off stage. "We're going to grab some food at Lille's. The restaurant, not the food truck. Do you two want to join us?"

Greg shook his head. "I've got more interviews to do, but Jill can go."

I smiled up at him. "I need to go let Emma out, and then I'm expected at the shop. I take it you hired more staff for the winery tonight?"

"I'm off the entire weekend. My day manager is covering me, and we've got someone we're training for management covering her during the day. I haven't gotten a call yet, but the weekend's young. I'll see you around, probably." She waved and hurried over to Matt, where she gave him a huge hug.

I walked with Greg. "Are you working here, or do you want to walk to the house with me?"

"My interview is at the station. Mr. Keith Jackson and his attorney. He said he'd meet me there as soon as the set was over. I guess his attorney has been here since they found Axel. He's representing the band members as well." He watched as Matt and Darla joined up with the rest of the band. "I hate to think that Tina could be right about anything, but it is odd that the singer just knew all of the band's songs, even though he just started playing with them today."

"According to Keith, they were looking to replace Axel as lead singer anyway. My guess is Axel would have taken on lead guitar or bass. And Keith probably had fed him the songs just in case." I fell in step with Greg, who was now working his way off the beach and onto the highway, where we could cross and walk home. "I guess Keith will tell you that when you talk to him."

"It will be interesting if he doesn't tell me that part of the story. I think he'll try to say as little as possible about the discord that Axel was causing in the band. He doesn't want to point any fingers at himself or the remaining band members. It will mess up their tour if one of their own is in one of my jail cells." Greg waved to Toby as we crossed the street with the crowd. "You looked busy at the truck. Are you doing enough business to keep two locations busy?"

"The one in town is slow, but that's okay. Tomorrow's probably going to be busier since today was just practice for the bands. Then Sunday less so, as all but three of the bands will be out of the running. Most of their followers won't stay around for the finals." I rolled my shoulders as we walked. It felt good not being in the cramped food truck. "The temp is doing really well. I told her I'd call her for the next festival."

"Too bad you can't hire her now as overflow. The summer's going to be busy. Maybe that way it won't be such a bother for us to leave on a vacation." He turned up our driveway to the house. His truck, Toby's truck, and my Jeep were all parked in the driveway, and we still had to make a sign to block the area to keep festivalgoers from parking there. The joy of living in a tourist town.

I stared at Greg and paused at the gate to the yard.

He realized I wasn't following him and turned back to look at me. "What? Is something wrong with the house? The cars?"

"No, I just can't believe I didn't think of hiring her as overflow. We could give her shifts from my time to start with; then she could be the coverage person. It should be enough hours to keep her from going to work somewhere else full-time. I'll talk to her tomorrow when she comes back." I jogged up the stairs and unlocked the door and was immediately body-slammed by my seventy-pound baby, Emma.

"Who's a good girl? And you didn't eat any sofa cushions today! I wish I could take you for a run, but our beach is too crowded right now. Maybe Sunday evening?" I looked hopefully up at Greg. Most of the times when there was a serious investigation, like murder, he liked for me to not run alone on the beach trying to attract the attention of a serial killer.

"We'll see. You know how investigations go. At least this time, no one on my suspect list or the victim wanted you to sell your house. It's a refreshing change." He followed me into the kitchen with the mail that had been delivered while we were gone.

I let Emma out and then got two glasses of water with ice. I handed him one and nodded to the pile. "Anything interesting?"

"I've got a card from Mom. Did I miss an anniversary or something?" He took the water and drank it all down.

"Not that I remember." I drank my water more slowly, but it felt so good. "You have food at the station, right? I don't need to call in an order for you too?"

"A good housewife would have had a pot roast in the crockpot so I could eat a homemade meal before I go back to work to save the world." He refilled the water glass halfway.

"Too bad neither your ex-wife nor your soon-to-be wife fall into that category. Maybe you should keep shopping." I finished my water, then went to watch Emma in the backyard.

Greg grabbed me and kissed me on the neck. "No way. I've already made my choice. Now I just have to wait a year to get married. Maybe we should consider eloping to Las Vegas. It worked for your aunt."

"We could." I rubbed his arms as they circled my waist. "Now that we've started planning to have it at the mission, I'm getting a little attached to the idea. But if you want to elope..."

He turned me around before I could finish. "Don't finish that statement. We're not in a hurry. If we get that way, we'll renegotiate the date. But I want you to have the wedding you want. It's my last wedding, so it should be special."

I smiled and kissed him. "Good. Besides, we still need to get through Pastor Bill's finance and pre-wedding counseling class. And if I time it right, I'll have my MBA before our honeymoon. Maybe that will make Aunt Jackie trust my business decisions."

He turned me around, and we both watched Emma patrol the fence line for random bunnies or turtles. We had coyotes in the area, so we didn't leave her out alone a lot without watching her. "From the conversation I had with Pastor Bill and Sadie today, I'm not sure we still want to take that class. They were snippy with each other."

"I noticed that too." I leaned my head against his shoulder. "I need to call her and see what's going on. I can help with feeling like you're coming in second to a job."

"Are you telling me something?" Greg stepped away and held me out so he could look me straight in the face. I guessed it was his interrogation mode.

"Nothing you don't already know. I think when your significant other has a job where he's on call all the time, it can be hard at first to figure out where you stand. I don't think Sherry ever got comfortable not being your main concern twenty-four seven. I have my books, my friends, my aunt, and running with Emma. If I were that perfect housewife, I'd be pretty bored with my life after a while." I glanced at the kitty-cat clock on the wall. It was a holdover from when Miss Emily, the prior owner of the house, lived here. It made me smile every time I saw it. But today, it spurred me into action. I called Emma into the house. "I've got a food order to pick up. Do you want to walk with me into town?"

"I'll accept your offer." He pulled me close and squeezed me. "Even when I'm busy with other things, you're always on my mind."

"Back atcha." I gave Emma a hug and told her to be good. "I don't think either one of us will be home before ten."

"I'll send Toby home for a break around eight and ask him to let Emma out then. If he can't, she'll just have to hold it."

I laughed and checked her food and water before leaving the kitchen. "Okay then, you're on cleanup duty if something happens. Let's go."

Emma was used to being alone for about four to five hours, so I thought she'd be fine. Except for all the people walking by her house. I figured she'd be staring out the window and barking most of that time. She'd sleep hard tonight. As would I.

I said goodbye to Greg when we reached Diamond Lille's, the only full-service restaurant in town. I served breakfast pastries and treats, and Darla's winery served pizza and a few fried items for late-night snacks, but Lille's was a full diner. And I loved it. Her chef, Tiny, was amazing and was always trying out new recipes. I tended to stay with fish and chips. Or a chef's salad if I was dieting. I was a creature of habit.

The diner was packed. Carrie walked up to greet me. "I don't have a table or a booth, but I could seat you at the counter."

"I'm picking up my first order, and I'll be back in about twenty minutes for the second one." I pointed to a bag sitting in the to-go area. "Maybe that's it?"

She walked over and checked the ticket. "Yes, it is. You town people are smart. Josh called in his order this morning too."

"We've been through this festival weekend before." I glanced around the crowded diner but didn't see anyone I knew. "Can you ask Tiny to fire my second order now? I told him I'd check in when I picked up this one."

She glanced over at the window into the kitchen, where Tiny was waving at us, a ticket in hand. "I think he knows you're here. Did you prepay, or do I need to ring this up?"

"Tiny charged it when I ordered." I took the bag that she offered me and moved over to let more people inside. "I better get out of here and go feed my people. See you in a few."

Carrie was already moving to the new people, taking a name, and telling them about the wait time. One of the men glanced at my bag and nodded. "Smart idea to order ahead."

I smiled and kept walking out the door and up the sidewalk to my store. Aunt Jackie was on the counter, and Judith was walking around, cleaning tables. There were only a few people in the store. I held up the bag, then stopped at the table where Harrold sat reading. "Here's your dinner, and Aunt Jackie's, too. Did you already close the Train Station?" I felt bad I hadn't even looked in the door when I left.

"Thank you, Jill. No, my son is working the close shift. That way I can come sit with your aunt, just in case it gets busy." He nodded to Judith, who was wiping a table across the room. "That one's a hard worker. You're lucky you got her, no matter what Jackie says."

I could just imagine what my aunt said about my new hire. But Judith was solid. She upsold like a champ, and she was well-read in a lot of subjects. A bonus for a bookstore. "Judith is a gem. Deek recommended her. And that reminds me, I need to talk to Aunt Jackie about hiring Tilly as an overflow."

Harrold frowned as he watched Aunt Jackie serve a coffee. "I think that's a great idea. I don't know if she's mentioned this, but we're going into the city to see a specialist next week. It's nothing. There's just a few things that are going on that she needs to get looked at. And don't tell her I mentioned it. But if there is something, you might need more help around here for a bit until we get it under control."

I didn't turn to look at my aunt. I couldn't. The fear I was feeling from Harrold's words would show on my face, and then he'd be in trouble for telling me. I swallowed the lump in my throat, pushed positive light into my head, and nodded. "Just keep me informed, okay?"

Chapter 6

I tried to keep my aunt's upcoming doctor appointment out of my head as I sat at a table in the office with her and Judith a few minutes later. Harrold had agreed to watch the front and let us know if a customer came in. I handed Judith her dinner. "Go ahead and eat. We need to talk about how long to leave the store open."

"Thanks." Judith opened her veggie sandwich and took a big bite. "Yum."

"I expect any traffic we get now will be light." My aunt watched Judith eat and then handed her a napkin.

"I agree. I think the bars and winery are going to be busy, but these tourists don't seem like the type to buy books to take back to their room and read." I grabbed a cookie from the ones on the counter warming up and waiting to be put in the display case.

My aunt stared at me.

"I'll put it on the list. Besides, my dinner will be with the order I got for Deek and the food truck. I've already sent Tilly home for the day, but I wanted to talk to you about bringing her in part-time, for overflow."

"That's a good idea. I approve," my aunt said as she sipped her tea.

Shocked it was that easy, I grinned and pressed on. "I'll talk to her tomorrow. She's smart and fast and reads a lot. And she figured out the till on the truck in just a few tries. I think she'll be amazing. I'll train her on my shift just in case Greg and I want to take a vacation."

"Okay. That's settled. Now when to close the store tonight? I think we should close at seven. I can deal with the next hour on my own and do the closing. Judith can watch the store while I eat; then she can go to the food truck and handle it while you and Deek eat. Evie will be there to help her out as well." She sipped her tea again. "Tomorrow night, I'm thinking the same, but you know it's never the same from one night to the other, so we can talk when you bring us dinner. Does that work for you?"

"Yes." I was stunned. My aunt wasn't the easiest to work with, but this time, we'd been totally on the same wavelength.

"Okay, I'll go out and work until Judith finishes her sandwich; then I'll go spend some time with Harrold. I hope he's eating and not waiting for me."

I followed her out to the front and saw that Harrold was indeed eating, and we'd had no customers enter the store while we had our short meeting. "Do you want me to stay around?"

Aunt Jackie shook her head. She handed me a folder.

"What's this?"

"An application for Tilly. I'd like to get her into the system as soon as possible. Paying her through the temp service is crazy expensive. Of course, we'll have to pay them a finder's fee if she stays more than ninety days, but I think she'll work out."

I thanked her and tucked the folder into my bag. "If you want to talk..."

"I'm fine with you hiring someone. We'll need someone for the summer. And when fall comes, we'll reevaluate staffing. We always do, but with Tilly on board and trained, maybe we can do more festival events this fall with the food truck."

"Sounds like a plan." I hesitated. "So I'll talk with you tomorrow?"

"Stop acting like a mother hen. I can handle the shop for an hour on my own. You know this used to be my shift."

By the time I got to Lille's to pick up the rest of my order, I'd compartmentalized the news my uncle had given me. I'd call Aunt Jackie on Monday and make her tell me what was going on. Or maybe I'd wait until Tuesday after she'd seen the doctor. My aunt was a very private person. She'd only told me she'd fallen prey to a Ponzi scheme when she realized she needed to sell her condo and find a place to stay. That time, I'd called her for a favor first.

I'd let her settle, but I'd give her time to tell me. I could tell her I was going back to school in the fall. Another reason we needed to hire Tilly. I just hoped Tilly would stay around with what we were able to offer her. It wasn't a full-time position. We'd cobbled together one for Deek and Evie, but I didn't know if we could do another. Maybe one of the other stores was looking for a part-time position. If we shouldered the benefits like health insurance, she could take a few hours from maybe the yarn shop and have full-time hours.

Worrying about Tilly and what we could offer kept my mind off what was going on with Aunt Jackie. At least for a while. I might stop in to

the Train Station tomorrow and see what else I could get out of Harrold
without Jackie finding out.

Family—sometimes it was like having a degree in spy craft to keep up
with what you needed to know.

Diamond Lille's was still busy, and the line to snag a table was even
longer than when I left. I got several dirty looks as I pushed my way to the
front. Carrie spoke without looking up. "We've got an hour wait, sorry."

"I'm here to pick up."

Carrie looked up and smiled. "Yes, something I can do. I really don't
love this hostess gig, but Lille took a dinner break. Rode off on the back
of that Harley and didn't look back. I hope she'll be here in about fifteen
minutes. I don't deal with angry glares very well."

"I'm sure they know you can't kick people out of their tables." I took
the bag she handed me.

"But I can clear them as soon as they stand up." She nodded to a couple
who'd just left. Then she called out a name. When the next couple stood,
she said, "Wait here, I'll be right back for you. Jill, I'll see you tomorrow."

"Sounds like a plan. Tell Tiny I'll call in the order around six, six thirty."
I turned and left with the bags of food.

"Hey, I'll give you a hundred dollars for whatever's in that bag." A man
pulled out his wallet as I walked by.

"Sorry, I'm feeding my staff at the Coffee on the Run truck. Stop by
later if you need dessert or a drink to get through the night." I smiled as
I headed down the road to the beach. I didn't feel like smiling right now,
but it was a "fake it until you make it" moment. Besides, Harrold could
be worried about nothing. He kept close tabs on my aunt. He wanted their
story to last many years.

And I loved him for that.

Evie was already at the food truck when I got back, and she waved as
she saw me. "Food's arrived."

Deek opened the door for me and let me inside. "I don't think it's going
to slow down. How's the shop?"

"Not as busy as here." I didn't want to say it was dead and jinx Aunt
Jackie since I'd basically left her alone for an hour, but Deek deserved an
answer. "Judith should be here soon, so she can relieve me so I can eat.
You two eat now."

Evie shook her head. "I just started working about an hour ago when
I got back from class in Bakerstown. You've been working all day. You
and Deek eat, and I'll join you when Judith gets here."

"You don't have to twist my arm." I opened one of the boxes, and it was my fish and chips. Bonus, Tiny had added a small salad to the bag with Jill written on the top of the box. I took my dinner and a bottle of water and headed back outside to the small table we'd set up behind the truck. From that vantage point, I could see the now-empty bandstand. There were a few people wandering around in front, setting up chairs and coolers for the night's events. And to the side, Jules was talking to Hansel.

Or should I say Hansel was yelling at Jules. I was too far away from the bandstand to hear what was being said, but it was clear, Hans blamed Jules for losing his singer. I was just about to call Greg when Deek sat down next to me.

He followed my gaze and sighed as he opened his container with what appeared to be a Cobb salad. "Those two just need to get over each other. They've been that way since they broke up last fall."

"They were dating?" The idea shocked me. Jules was the ultimate bad girl, at least from what I knew about her. Hans looked more like a college frat boy, polo shirt and khaki shorts. Maybe he dressed more "rock and roll" for his performances, but right now, he looked like he should be in a campus library, not a beach band competition.

"High school sweethearts. I had drinks one night with Hans over at the Bakerstown Pub. He was hammered because he'd found out she was dating that Keith guy. From what I've seen, she goes back and forth, depending on who has the better opportunity. I bet Hans thought he had this gig in the bag since his uncle's the mayor here. And with Matt's band stealing the lead singer after Axel died, Hans can't assure her that he's on the fast path." Deek focused on his salad. "I feel their auras spinning around all the way up here. Are you calling the police dude? I don't think they'd go violent, but you never know."

I dialed the number, but before Greg could answer, Jules stalked away. Hans started to follow; then it was like all the air went out of him, and he headed down the beach to the shore instead. The fight was over. Neither participant looked victorious, which was what happened most times when people were in love. Everyone felt the pain of the fight, not just the loser.

"Jill? What's going on?" Greg's voice brought me back out of my thoughts.

"Hi, Greg. Nothing right now. Deek and I saw Jules and Hans fighting over at the bandstand. I was afraid it might go violent, but they've stopped now." I leaned back in my chair. "Sorry to have bothered you."

"Not a bother. Those two shouldn't be within ten feet of each other. First the bar, now this."

I looked at Deek, and he was listening, so he couldn't say I was talking behind his back. "Deek said Hans told him they were high school sweethearts."

"So now it's Jill said Deek said Hans said." Greg laid out the trail. "Not exactly court-worthy evidence, but I'll check it out. Maybe I can get one of them to tell me that, since Keith was less than up front. He didn't tell me about Axel and Jules. And he claims to not have a relationship with her outside his managerial relationship for the band."

"Then why did he have his hand on her butt? That should be either illegal or proof."

He chuckled. "Aren't you supposed to be eating?"

"I've got my food in front of me. I was just trying to be a good citizen and stop another murder in case those two went psycho." I didn't like the way he was questioning my motives.

"Go eat. I'll handle the investigation. And don't talk to Tina again. I'm talking to her tonight about my shutting down practice and explaining that you don't have the power to change my mind. We'll see how that goes."

"You know what they say about the power women have over men," I teased.

"Goof. Tell Deek I said hi."

I put away my phone and opened the salad, dumping the dressing on top. I should have dumped half, but Tiny made fresh ranch, and it was yummy. "Greg says hi."

"You really shouldn't put me into the dude's line of sight. I still don't think he's sure about me. Not like Toby. He loves that guy. He sees me as a bit of a wild card." Deek set his fork down and took a drink from his water.

"It doesn't matter how Greg sees you. I know your worth, and I appreciate everything you've done for the store. Speaking of that, tell me about next week's author visit. Who's coming again?"

Having Deek talk about the author visits got his mind off Greg and what he might or might not think of the guy. I thought Greg liked Deek enough. I think Greg loved to tease him and make him think he was watching. But Greg knew what a blessing Deek had been to the bookstore. And since I trusted him, Greg did as well. He just didn't want Deek to know that. What can I say? Sometimes Greg can be a little cruel.

The top-rated bands played on Friday night, and then Saturday morning, the rest of the lineup would take their chance at getting into the semifinals that started at noon. Both Atlantis Survivors and Hansel's band, Destiny's Run, were scheduled to play tonight. I figured both bands would get into the next round. We had a full day with the food truck. First up, coffee and treats for the kite-flying contestants and parents. Then the bands would play from nine to noon. And the second round would start right at 1:00 p.m. The main store might get more walk-in traffic on Saturday due to the kite-flying contest, but once the main competition started at one, I predicted traffic in town would slow down.

I was sure Darla was going to get some flak from the other businesses since this festival focused less on the art section of town and more on the food and drink providers. Like the winery and the bar. I suspected Toby would be kept busy tonight with the drunk and obnoxious calls he'd be getting. Maybe enough to bring him back to the coffee shop to work full-time. Except then, he'd never make enough money to buy a house and move out of my shed. I better be careful what I hoped for.

When Evie joined us at the table, I tucked my empty containers in a bag and left the group to go back to the food truck. I didn't want to leave Judith alone for long.

I shouldn't have worried. She'd handled the small line that had formed, and when I got to the truck, she was serving the last coffee. She smiled at me as I moved inside the truck.

"It's a little bit different working the truck versus the shop. The machines are different, and I didn't see where the cups were, at least not at first." Judith pointed to a box on the floor. "Those are the books Deek asked me to bring. He has a second list for tomorrow. I see a book rack in the closet. Can I set it up outside the truck so people can look at the books while they're waiting for their order?"

"Of course. Thanks for offering." I glanced around the truck and found some things to clean while I waited for the next customer.

By the time Deek and Evie were done with dinner, the crowd still hadn't grown. At least not enough to need four people in the food truck. I looked at Deek. "Want to clock out?"

"You go. And if it stays slow, I'll send Judith home next. I can write here if it stays this way, and Evie and I can handle any rushes." Deek pointed to a bag on the shelf. "I brought my computer this morning, just in case."

The boy was dedicated, that was for sure.

I looked around at the other two, and they nodded.

"Sounds like a plan. Go home. We've got this." Evie started stacking cups. "I'm here tomorrow morning?"

"Yes. You and Deek will open. I'll open the main shop with Judith at six, then come here about eight, unless you get slammed. Aunt Jackie will join Judith at nine, and we'll see where we need to shuffle so you all aren't working ten- to twelve-hour shifts or more tomorrow."

"I can use all the hours I can get," Evie said.

"When is Tilly coming?" Deek asked.

"Nine. How do you feel about her work? Would she make a good part-timer? Aunt Jackie thinks it's a good idea to have a little depth in the shift pool, just in case."

"I liked working with her today." Deek glanced over at Evie and Judith. "She's fun and knows a lot about books. She reads high fantasy, so she has a little different background."

"Sounds good to me." Judith folded a box and put it in a closet. "I'm taking a late-summer cruise to Alaska in August that I need to get on the calendar with you. If there was another body, I wouldn't feel so guilty."

"Never feel guilty about taking the time you need." I smiled at Judith and then pointed to Evie. "I'm talking to all of you. Judith, do me a favor and email me so I can get it on the staff calendar. I'll probably forget from the time I leave here to when I get to the house."

"I can do that."

As I left the food truck, the evening bands were just starting to play. I ran into Darla, who was heading to the bandstand.

"Come sit with me," she invited.

I shook my head. "I'm heading home to be with Emma. I'm sure I'll be able to hear them from my porch. Text me when Matt plays."

"Sounds good." She hurried off to watch the bands. Darla had thrown herself into this festival. It seemed to be working, at least for Lille, me, and the places that served alcohol. I'd heard the bed-and-breakfasts and hotels were filled for the weekend too. So that was good. Now, if at least a few of them bought some art, we'd have most of the stores covered, and maybe this could be an annual event.

If we made it through this one.

Chapter 7

I couldn't tell you if Greg had come home the night before or not, except I had an orange sitting on the kitchen table with a note from him. I picked it up and read it aloud. "Eat this. Love, Greg."

Apparently, the lack of fruits and vegetables in my diet was an issue not only for Tiny from Lille's diner, but now my fiancé was on the same bandwagon. Or maybe it would make me grow like Alice. I peeled the orange as I watched Emma run around the yard. The smell made my stomach growl. I needed to get today's lunch and dinner orders in. And I guessed I needed to order something for me besides fish and chips.

I made a list of who was where and checked my email for their food orders. If they didn't get it in to me before nine, they got a turkey sandwich on wheat with fries. Most people sent their order for all three days at once, so I went through each email and wrote out today's food list. Then I checked my list for what I was missing. Judith and Tilly. I'd catch both of them this morning and remind them to email me for tomorrow's order as well.

I put the food list into my tote and made sure I had an alarm on my phone to call the orders in to Lille's. Tiny might call me to remind me, but Lille wouldn't. Have I mentioned that she and I don't get along? I guessed now I could add Tina Baylor to the list of people in South Cove who weren't Jill fans. Through no fault of my own. At least with most of them.

I checked my tote and made sure I had the folder with the employment information for Tilly. I really hoped she took me up on the job offer, especially since I'd been less than optimistic about my ability to hire her just yesterday.

But that was the way life worked, wasn't it? It changed on a dime. Sometimes for positive reasons, sometimes not. Either way, you could never get too comfortable with the status quo. Just ask Axel Poser. I bet he didn't plan on being killed just before the band took off.

If the band was really going to take off. I pushed aside thoughts about why Axel was killed and headed into town to open the coffee shop.

Typically, my walk to work was pretty solitary. Today, I was greeted by a ton of giggling kids and their tired parents on their way down to the beach. I was walking against a swarm of traffic on the sidewalk, so I stepped out onto the road to make my way into town.

Not long after, the siren from a cruiser beeped behind me. I turned around to see Toby driving up the road in one of the South Cove police cars. I walked over and leaned into the open window. "What are you doing driving this thing? I would have thought you'd be in the side-by-sides today."

"I will be as soon as I move this back up to where we blocked off Main Street. Greg wanted it parked in the fruit stand lot next to the highway last night, just as a visual reminder that someone may be watching." He nodded to the barrier in front of us. "Can you move that back so I can drive in and park?"

"Sure." I hurried over to where the barrier was and moved it toward the busy sidewalk. Several people watched, and I thought they were considering taking the road instead of the slower sidewalk, but then they looked up at the police car moving slowly through the now-open barrier and changed their minds. After Toby pulled through, I moved the barrier back, and he turned the car sideways on the road.

He shut off the engine and climbed out. "Thanks, Jill. Do you want me to walk you to the shop?"

"Do you want coffee?" I brushed dust from the barrier off my hands.

"I could use a cup." He used the remote to lock the car and fell in step with me.

"Good, since I need to tell you something." I adjusted the tote on my shoulder. "I'm hiring Tilly North to come on part-time, if she'll take the job."

"Tilly North?" He repeated the name as he looked at me, shock on his face.

"That's her name. Do you know her? She's worked with us a couple of times when we've had to hire a temp in the last few months." I realized he had stopped in the middle of the street. "Oh no. She doesn't have a record, does she?"

He shook his head and hurried to catch up. "No, sorry, the name just shocked me. If it's the same girl, we went to high school together. I guess you could say she's the one that got away."

"Oh, really? That's not going to be an issue, right? I mean, you dated Sasha for a long time before I even knew you two were dating and working together. She doesn't hate you, right?" I didn't want my new hire to cause any problems with my current staff. It wasn't worth it.

"No, she broke up with me and broke my heart. She went off to college in Idaho and left California. I stayed around and tried to make a life." He shook his head. "Tilly North. Now that's a name I didn't think I'd hear again. Much less work with her."

I unlocked the front door of the shop and turned on the lights. "Okay, are you going to be okay with her working here? I can't lose my oldest employee due to a new hire."

"Boss, I'll be fine. I'm not a kid anymore. I've dated a lot of women, some even seriously, like Sasha, since Tilly took off. I'm sure my heart is healed." He straightened a table as he walked by. "Jackie must have closed last night?"

"She did. How did you know?" I poured two large coffees into to-go containers from the auto pot that I had set to come on a few minutes before I arrived.

"She likes this table by the window. Evie sets it up closer to the doorway and out of the path to the bookstore. They set their cups up differently too." He pulled out his wallet, and I waved it back.

"No charge. Take this one to Greg if he's in the office; otherwise, just give it to someone." I started turning on the other machines and getting the coffee bar ready. "Okay, so you're sure me hiring your date to the prom isn't going to mess with your head?"

"Jill, I'll be fine." He grinned. "Tilly might have a problem, especially when all the women from the cosmetology school show up and show her what she missed out on, but that's not my issue."

"You're full of yourself. You know that, right?" I called after him as he went to leave the shop.

He spun around and shrugged. "I can't help it if I'm all that."

Laughing, I watched him hold the door for Judith, who hurried into the shop. "Good morning. How are you feeling today?"

"Great. I loved yesterday. Working here, then moving to the truck just gave me a full understanding of the entire business. Did Deek tell you we sold out of most of those books I brought over? I'm going to cull out more to add to his list to take to the truck today." She took off her jacket as she walked toward me. "Did you tell Toby about the new hire? Is he happy?"

"He knows." I didn't know how much to tell my staff about Toby and Tilly's prior relationship. And I didn't know if she'd even take the job.

Maybe she didn't remember Toby at all. No, no one would forget a guy who looked like Toby. Not even if it was just a high school crush.

I distracted myself with my commuters, who were griping about the festival and the traffic. It must be annoying to be trying to go to work and having to drive around your usual route.

"You know I'm addicted to your coffee if I walk here before driving into the office," April, one of my regulars, said. "I'm regretting saying I'd come in to work this weekend. I really need to get a calendar of community events so I can plan better."

I took out my business card for the business-to-business group. "Check out the calendar here on the website. It will tell you all the events we have planned for the next six months. And Darla prints them up and has them available at the winery."

"Thanks. I think I knew that, but with life so busy, I'd forgotten." She tapped the card on the counter. "I'm updating my calendar as soon as I hit the office. Work and home. That way I'm not a grumpy coffee drinker."

"At least you got some steps in this morning." I nodded to her fitness watch.

"Always looking at the bright side. I love South Cove!" April turned, moving past the next customer. "Coffee addicts unite."

After she'd walked out of the building, the man who'd already given me his coffee order smiled at me. "That girl needs to start drinking decaf. She's a little chatty for those of us who are still waiting for coffee."

"Sorry, Randy. I try to keep the line moving." I took his five and went to ring in the coffee.

"I'm just being grumpy. Her cheerfulness is not your issue. Keep the change, Jill, and I hope the festival doesn't run you ragged. Clara and I are going down to the beach after I get home from work to listen to the music." He held up his cup in a toast. "I'll see you there."

It wasn't a question; he just assumed I'd be there, and he was probably right. I worked too much. But I didn't want to just sit around while I waited for Greg to finish his day. I smiled at the next customer. "How can I help you?"

By the time my weekend commuters had come and gone, my aunt was in the shop. I turned the counter over to Judith and went to plan the day. I pulled out my notebook. "How was closing last night?"

"Boring. After Judith left, the streets seemed to empty out. It was like someone had set up a barrier keeping people out of town. If there had been fog, I would have been worried about monsters." She opened her planner.

"I didn't know you read that book."

She smiled at me. "It was a short story, and they made a movie out of it. Kind of hard to miss the message. Anyway, I'm thinking based on last night's traffic, I'll plan on closing at seven. That way, we can snag anyone who's walking through town after dinner and wants a treat. Harrold will be here at four, after he closes his shop. They're not getting a lot of traffic from this festival."

I looked up from my notes. "Yeah, I was worried about the type of tourist it brought in. Not the usual tour bus looking for cute Christmas presents or gifts."

"I'm sure some of the businesses are doing well. We're fine, at least, because of the food truck. If we didn't have that, it would be a different story." Jackie glanced down at her notes. "You're still planning on bringing lunches and dinners?"

"Yes. And I have Harrold on my list for dinner. He deserves something for coming and being available to help out."

My aunt sighed. "The man worries about me."

This was my opening. I might be on the verge of getting yelled at, but it was worth a shot. I tried to keep my voice casual, and I kept my gaze on the notebook in front of me. "He said you have some doctor appointments next week. Anything I should be concerned about?"

"He mentioned that?" My aunt's lips tightened. For a couple of seconds, neither one of us breathed. "He must be worried. Actually, it's only a checkup. Nothing to worry about until they tell us it is, right?"

I nodded, but this time I looked up and met her gaze. "Just a checkup, then. I figured if something was actually wrong, you'd let me know. Especially if you needed help with the shop today or tomorrow."

She met my gaze. No one could play the "dare you to blink first" game better than my aunt, but to my surprise, this time she blinked first. "I promise, if I feel dizzy or need help, I'll call you immediately. If I can keep Judith with me until after lunch, then you can have her for the rest of her shift."

"Perfect." I nodded to the box of books Judith was filling. "We still have that small handcart I used to use when we went off-site to sell books, right?"

"In the closet." She glanced over her notes. "Has Sadie dropped off treats yet?"

"No, I haven't seen her." I glanced at my watch. Typically, she was here during the commuter rush. Today, that had come and gone without a delivery. "Should I call..."

As I was talking, the door burst open, and Sadie walked in with a tray of cookies in each hand.

"There's more in the van. That shelf I have closest to the door is all you," she said as she walked by.

"I guess that's my cue to help." I pointed to Sadie as she made her way to the back office. "Can you check the invoice versus the delivery?"

My aunt stood and shuffled to the counter on her way to the back room to follow Sadie. Aunt Jackie was moving slower and she kept a hand on the counter or wall as she walked. Like she was in pain. Had she fallen or run into something? Was this why she was going to the doctor? I wouldn't know unless she told me or Harrold blabbed. I was betting on the latter. My aunt was right; Harrold did worry. He wanted years together with my aunt. As did I.

It took several trips of bringing trays into the back when, finally, Sadie announced she'd brought in the last load. My aunt marked them off on the list and then made a copy for Sadie and went back out front. As Sadie helped me put the desserts in the walk-in, I asked about the elephant in the room, her relationship with Pastor Bill. "How are you two doing?"

She tightened her lips as she placed cheesecakes on the shelf. "We're fine."

"You didn't look fine yesterday. Greg said you two were having words when he saw you too. I'm beginning to think that maybe Greg and I should skip the couples' counseling sessions."

"Oh, no. Don't let my feelings change your plans." She came out of the cooler and sat on one of the chairs by the table. "Bill's excellent at his counseling work."

"But not at his relationships?" I moved books off the chair next to her and sat as well. "Tell me what's going on."

"I'm being childish." She wiped her cheeks, but I didn't think she knew she was crying.

"No, your feelings are valid. Do you love him? Is the relationship going too fast?" I wasn't sure what question to ask when my friend was dating a person of the cloth.

"Ha!" The word came out with a huff, and surprised, Sadie covered her mouth with her hand.

"Okay, maybe not fast enough?" I knew Sadie had loved her last husband deeply. His death had shaken her, but she'd needed to be strong for her son, and she had been. Now, Nick was on his own, and it was Sadie's time to find love again. I thought Pastor Bill had been perfect when they'd started dating. But then the courtship hadn't progressed.

"He's always worried about how other people are going to view our relationship. The deacons have hinted that him being married might limit his devotion to the church." She wiped her face again. "We were planning on announcing our engagement this month. Now I'm not sure we are even going to continue dating. I need him to commit to me."

"That's not unreasonable." I was beginning to not like the people who were affecting Sadie's happiness. "And any man would be lucky to have you marry him. So it's his loss if he walks away."

"That's just it. He doesn't want to walk away. He wants us to slow down. But I'm not a spring chicken. If I'm getting married again, I want my new life to start soon. This courting ritual has gone on long enough."

I let the words settle before I asked, "Have you told him that?"

Sadie opened her mouth, then closed it again. She shook her head. "No. I assumed he knew how I felt."

"The one thing I can promise you about relationships is that as soon as you start thinking the other person can read your mind, you're in trouble. Just invite him to dinner or coffee and tell him what you want. Your wants and needs are just as important as the demands of his job. If he walks away then, at least he knew what he had to do to fix it."

Sadie stood and hugged me. "How are you so smart?"

"I've made quite a few mistakes. So maybe I'll see you Wednesday night for the couples' finance class?" I glanced at my watch. I needed to get to the food truck. "Or are you dropping stuff off at the truck?"

"The truck is already supplied. I started there this morning. Now I have one last stop at Lille's; then I'm giving Bill a call." She hugged me again. "Thank you. I'll call if I have news before Wednesday."

I wasn't sure what I'd put into motion, but Sadie deserved to be happy. Even if it meant breaking up with the guy who couldn't choose her. Or maybe especially if it meant that.

Greg was right. I was nosy and opinionated. I just hoped Pastor Bill chose the right path.

Chapter 8

The food truck was slammed when I got there at nine thirty. I saw Deek's relief when he noticed me dragging boxes toward the door. I left them outside by the steps and came inside. "You need some help?"

"Can you do coffees while Tilly does desserts? We were slow, so I sent Evie home to walk Homer." He handed a cup and change to the customer in front of him. Then he focused on the next person. "What can I get for you?"

Now I felt bad that I'd stopped at the house to let Emma out and scan through the mail. I poured a cup of coffee for the order he'd just gotten and handed it to him. Tilly looked relieved to be moving over to the dessert section, and she grabbed the two cookies a woman had pointed out, quickly putting them into a CBM sleeve.

"You should have called me."

"Like I said, we were good until a few minutes ago. Then things got crazy." He reached for the coffee and treat, then rang up the book the woman had picked up off the shelf near the window as well. "The good news is we're selling the crap out of the music books."

"I've been meaning to pick this book up since it released. Thanks for having it here. You took one thing off my to-do list." The customer handed Deek her credit card. "As for your line, the kite-flying competition just finished, so you're getting the sleepy parents and overanxious kids who are starving right now. I know, sugar isn't breakfast, but we're heading back to the rental and making food now. Mama just needs a boost."

I laughed and started the next order. By the time we'd run through most of the line, Evie was back.

"Whoa, that's longer than when I left." She came inside and washed her hands at the sink.

"That's nothing," I said. "You should have seen it when I arrived. The kite contest is over. Remind me to tell Darla to separate these two events next year."

"Where should I step in?" Evie glanced around at the assembly line we'd set up.

"Take my place, and I'll set out the books that Judith culled for the truck. She's really got an eye for what people might buy." I stepped away from the coffeemaker as I handed Deek an iced coffee. "I just finished the order he's working on."

"Sounds good." Evie waited for me to move out of the way and adjusted the coffee cups to her reach. We all had our own preferences, no matter how standardized Aunt Jackie tried to make the stocking of product.

I grabbed some water and went outside to open the boxes and stack the books. I had several go as soon as I set them out.

"Oh, I love him." A woman pulled a book on Elton John out of my hand. "Is this for sale?"

"He'll ring you up with your coffee order." I smiled and got another copy out of the box.

Deek had ordered a lot of music-themed books for the weekend. I smiled at him as I finished stocking the last of what I'd brought over from the bookstore. We'd probably have a few books left over, but I'd make a music shelf with pictures from the event and maybe even the date for next year's event, if Darla had set that yet.

Thinking of Darla made me think of Matt and the unfortunate Axel Poser. I wondered if Greg had found his killer yet. I should have stopped by the station to chat, but after spending some time with Sadie, I'd been late and knew the truck needed my help. Right now, the flow was regular but not overwhelming.

I broke down the boxes and put them in the closet. I probably wouldn't need all of these to take the books back tomorrow, but I also didn't want to try to drive my Jeep over to the recycling center. Walking the books to the food truck had been more work, but with the little dolly, it hadn't been overwhelming. I'd deal with the cardboard and cleaning the truck on Monday.

I glanced over to the bandstand. A band had just stopped playing, and another one was setting up. I squinted and saw Darla sitting on a blanket with her computer. She must be writing her column for the paper. I called out to Deek, who was at the window. "Hey, hand me a water please. I'll be right back."

He leaned down, grabbed a water, handed it to me, and kept talking with his customer without a break. The boy had skill. I walked across the beach, weaving through screaming kids that had just come out of the cold water and their tired parents, who were sitting on a blanket watching the waves.

Not quite ten thirty, and they already looked beat. Another reason I knew I was a perfect pup parent versus having a kid right now. I'd need to slow down my working hours if Greg and I had a baby. He couldn't just "decide" to slow down as the lead police detective for South Cove. Unless he could ask all the criminals to take a break from committing crimes so he could take a paternity break.

I held the water out to Darla. She looked up and grinned. "I was just thinking I needed to get up and go get some. How did you know?"

"You looked hot." I sat down next to her. "And it was an excuse to see how you're doing. Did Greg find the killer?"

"You don't know?" Darla sipped her water and replaced the cap. "He's questioning Jules right now. He scheduled it early so it wouldn't affect the competition. But I'm worried. What if she killed Axel? She hated the guy, and she was always saying he was out to get her."

"Was he?" I brushed sand off my legs.

"Out to get her? Most definitely. Matt told me all the time how Axel was trying to replace her. The problem is Jules is amazing on drums. And Keith likes her." She closed her laptop. "I'm trying to write an objective piece on the murder for the paper, but everyone hated Axel, so I'm not sure how to not make the entire music community a suspect."

"You'll find a way. You're always insightful and fair in your reporting." I made marks in the sand while I talked. "So if it wasn't Jules, who else could be on the list? In your opinion."

Darla laughed. "Besides me and Matt?"

I nodded. I liked that she realized she could be on the suspect list if Axel had turned on Matt and tried to ruin Matt's dream. She'd already told me she was worried about Axel's drug use and lifestyle affecting Matt's sobriety. "Yeah, besides you two. Because if you did kill him, I think you and Matt would be on a plane to some South American country without an extradition treaty."

She rolled her shoulders. "Actually, after the last few days, that sounds wonderful. I should think about a vacation soon. But back to your question. So Jules, Keith, Eddie, the bass player, and Hans. He probably hated Axel the most, since Hans used to be part of Atlantis Survivors before Axel kicked him out. And you can add Tina to the list, but the mayor's not going to look kindly on Greg if he puts his wife in jail for killing someone."

"Well, if the shoe fits, or something like that." I watched the stage as the next band announced itself. I stood and brushed more sand off my capris. It always seemed to get everywhere. "Looks like it's going to get a little loud here. I hope everything goes well with the festival. We're killing it on the truck."

Darla grinned. "That's good to know. I suspected this festival wouldn't be good for all the businesses, but I thought having the kite contest might help. We'll have to look at the numbers everyone turns in to see if we get to do it again. I know Josh is a firm no."

I laughed. "Isn't he always?"

When I got back to the food truck, it was time to go get our lunches. I grabbed my tote and headed back across the highway to my house to let out Emma. I wasn't missing my runs this weekend since walking back and forth into town and back to the beach was getting my steps in. Emma, on the other hand, whined at the leash hanging by the back door when I let her out. "Sorry, girl, I'm only here for a little while; then I've got to go back to work."

She turned her face and stood at the door, waiting for me to open it. Message received but not appreciated.

I picked up a book I'd brought home to read and review and sat down to read a chapter, giving her time to do whatever she needed to do. When I was finished with the chapter, she was at the back door, watching me. Reluctantly, I put the bookmark between the pages and closed it. With Greg working the murder investigation, I should have plenty of time to read tomorrow since the contest finals didn't start until noon and only went to three. I tucked the book into my tote, just in case I found a little bit of time to read during the rest of the day. What can I say, I'm an optimist.

I said goodbye to my dog and tucked the sofa pillows into the office, closing the door so she couldn't get inside. Saying Emma liked sofa pillows was like saying I enjoyed ice cream. We both were addicted.

Hurrying to Diamond Lille's, I didn't want my aunt to think I'd forgotten. I opened the door and almost groaned out loud. Lille Stanley stood at the hostess station and narrowed her eyes when she saw me walk in. You would think with all the business I bring to her diner, the woman would at least tolerate me. That wasn't true.

"Hi, Lille, I've got a takeout order."

She grunted and left the stand to go into the kitchen. She came out with a bag and shoved it into my hands. "Already paid. You can leave."

"Thank you so much." Yes, I groveled, mostly because I would hate to be banned from the place. "Can you tell Tiny to start the other order for me? I'll be back in about thirty minutes."

"Great. I'm so looking forward to seeing you again." Lille kept her face still and her eyes dead. I knew she wasn't looking forward to seeing me, but her attitude freaked me out, just a little bit.

I pushed my way through the crowd and headed down the street to my bookstore. I opened the door and saw Judith standing at the counter. I walked around her and said, "Lunch is ready. Come eat, and I'll watch the front."

"You want me to eat with Jackie? Alone?" Judith's eyes widened.

"Well, the plan is, if you're not too busy here, you'll go to the truck and work while the others eat. I can watch the shop for a bit." I knew my aunt could be intimidating, but I'd never seen Judith back away from a challenge. "I'll go drop off the food, chat with Aunt Jackie, and then be back to cover you."

Judith nodded in response. I didn't think she trusted her voice to respond.

"Have you been picking on Judith?" I asked my aunt, who was working on a computer, probably analyzing our profit margin for the weekend.

"No, what did she tell you?" My aunt looked up from the computer.

I glanced back at the door. Maybe I'd read the situation wrong. Besides, I couldn't make my aunt like all of our employees. "Nothing, I just got a feeling. Never mind. Do you want to eat lunch alone, or should I send Judith in to eat with you, and I'll cover the front?"

"No, I'll go cover the front and give her time to eat. I was just finishing up this report. We're doing well this week, even with the additional staff costs. I think if we add on a few more festivals where we take the truck out, we'll cover the costs of the new hire in no time." She closed the file and shut the computer down. "I'll send you the final evaluation on Monday, but for now, please make the offer as we discussed."

As she stood, I set the food on the table. "You're sure you're okay? This doctor visit is just a checkup?"

She paused at the door to the front. "Jill, I promise, if there is something wrong, you'll be one of the first to know. Right now, I don't know anything, which is why I'm going to the doctor. And your questions are why I didn't tell you. I don't know what, if anything, is wrong. When I do, I'll tell you. Okay?"

I turned and met her gaze. "Okay. I'll stop asking. I just worry."

"I know, and I appreciate the concern. Just give me some space please." She went out to the front, and I heard her telling Judith that she could go eat, and Jackie would watch the front.

I took Judith's meal out of the bag and set it on the table for her. When she came in, I nodded to the walk-in. "Feel free to add a drink and a dessert to your meal. Salad goes a lot better with a slice of cheesecake."

"I'm eating salad because of the cheesecake. I've been taking full advantage of my one dessert a shift." Judith turned and looked at the door. "I didn't start an argument with the two of you, did I?"

"Oh, no. We've got some family things going on that are making our conversations a little tense lately. I think my aunt just needs some alone time. Do you want me to sit with you while you eat?"

Judith laughed and went to where she'd hung her tote. "I've got all the company I need right here. I'm loving this young adult time-travel book Deek recommended in the last newsletter."

"He's got an eye for good storytelling." I'd also read the book, but Deek had done the review and brought out the characters in a way I hadn't thought of doing. The joy of having an author working on the newsletter. "Okay then, I'll leave you be. Clock back in when you're ready, and Aunt Jackie will take over. I think she'll send you to the food truck after she eats. But she'll let you know."

"Sounds good. I'll see you later, then." Judith went to the walk-in and grabbed a soda as I headed to the door to the front.

I paused at the counter to talk with my aunt. We didn't have any customers. "You make the decision when you're going to send her down to the truck and when to close."

"Now I'm thinking just after six, but I'll let you know when you bring dinner. Don't forget Harrold will be here too."

"I've already ordered his meal." I noticed she had the laptop on the counter. "Are you going to work on financials today while it's slow?"

"I think so. Then I can take a day off next week. I'll be off Monday through Wednesday, unless you need me."

"We'll manage. And you don't typically work Saturdays or Sundays, so that pays you back for stepping in for the festival."

She smiled at me. "Owners and managers don't usually get comp time for the work they do off-hours. It's nice we have a little bit of leeway with the shop. After you get Tilly trained, we should have more."

"There's a bit of a possible glitch there." I decided to tell Aunt Jackie up front.

"She's not working out in the food truck?" Aunt Jackie frowned. "From what I remember, the last time she worked in the shop, she was easy to train and a quick learner."

"She is working out. And she is those things." I paused, biting my lip. "She's also Toby's high school sweetheart."

"He has a problem?"

I shook my head. "He said it was fine, water under the bridge type of thing, since she broke up with him, but I haven't mentioned to her that he works here. She might not know since she's only worked festivals, and Toby never works during a festival."

"I didn't think of his other commitments when I hired him." My aunt sighed. "Well, if she doesn't work out, we'll hire someone else. Let the team know we're looking. Referrals have been our best source of staffing."

I thought about Tilly as I made my way back to Lille's. I'd have her sit with me to eat and make the job offer and tell her about Toby. If she didn't choke on her sandwich, that would be a good sign.

"You should have stayed out of this," a man yelled at a woman on the other side of the road, bringing me out of my practice run on what I was going to say to Tilly.

The woman struggled to get out of his grip. "How was I to know that Axel would wind up dead? I told you I could fight my own battles. Besides, as long as you didn't kill him, it's a nonstarter with the police, right?"

A driver honked his horn at a boy who'd followed his ball into the street. The couple turned and saw me watching them. It was Jules and Keith who were yelling at each other. Keith turned and walked back up to town. Jules watched him for a bit, then turned and headed the other way.

I wasn't sure what I'd just watched, but I figured Greg would find it interesting.

Like I've always said, I'm usually at the wrong place at the wrong time. At least in my cop fiancé's eyes.

Chapter 9

Dreading the conversation, I pulled Tilly aside when I arrived back at the food truck. "Can we eat together? We need to talk."

"Sure, but did I do something wrong? If so, tell me now so I don't pick at my food. I'm starving, and I don't want to worry about what you're going to say." She followed me out of the truck. Evie was going to eat inside, just in case Deek needed her until Judith showed up.

"Nope, nothing is wrong. In fact, quite the opposite. I'd like to invite you to join our crew, part-time for now. I just want you to know everything before you make a decision."

She opened her lunch box and pulled out an overstuffed French dip and fries. Opening the container with the au jus, she sighed. I wasn't sure if my words had comforted her, or the food. I could agree with both. "Great, because I love Tiny's French dip. I always order it when I come into town. So you think you have enough hours for part-time? What's that going to look like? I can't accept one day a week. I need a full forty-hour job or a couple that add up to forty. The rent here is pretty crazy."

"I know. Several of my friends here in South Cove have more than one job. Anyway, I can promise you thirty-two—which will also get you the full benefits package. Some weeks, it could be full. Other weeks, it might be just the thirty-two. And I know at least one other business in town who is looking for a part-part-time person. The owner of the yarn shop needs someone for like one full shift a week."

Her eyes brightened, and she set down her sandwich and wiped her mouth. "Full benefits? You're kidding, right?"

I shook my head. It cost the business a lot to do health care and retirement benefits, but I was dedicated to giving the staff what they needed. And if it was a slow year, we could supplement the profits with some of the inheritance money I'd received from a friend. I called it the Miss Emily fund, and I had granted money for college, day care costs, and supporting a mission being rebuilt. There were other causes I felt I should support, but I needed to research different agencies, and time was a limited resource in my life right now. "No. As long as you get over thirty a week, you keep your benefits. I can't pay you a lot compared to warehouse or factory jobs in the area. But you also can read all the ARCs—that's advance reader copies—you want."

"I'd love to work for you," Tilly said. She frowned. "I'm not sure what the downside is. Don't tell me the shop is haunted. Or owned by organized crime."

"No, neither one of those, that I know of. I mean, I own the shop, so there's no connection with the mob." I rubbed my forehead. I was stalling. "I'm sorry, I'm rambling. Okay, here it is. Toby Killian works at the shop."

She stared at me like I was speaking another language. "I'm sorry, who?"

"Toby Killian, your high school sweetheart? At least that's his story." I was beginning to feel uncomfortable. She looked confused.

She shook her head. "Sorry, I don't know a Toby Killian. Tell me more about the 401(k)."

* * * *

When I went to Lille's to pick up dinner, I ran into Amy. "What are you doing here?"

"I'm working dispatch now and tomorrow. Esmeralda finished up her shift; then she'll do the early shift tomorrow, and I'll step in until the festival is over. Last festival, they tried to just have the officers on shift do it, and it was a mess. But right now, I'm following up on a couple of side dishes they missed on the delivery for Greg's crew. They love Tiny's mashed potatoes and coleslaw."

"I'm picking up food too." I nodded to Carrie, who checked the bags available, then went into the kitchen. "And it looks like I'm a little early. Come sit with me. I have a problem."

We sat on the bench surrounded by tourists and hopefully strangers. I told her the story between Toby and Tilly.

When I got done, I looked at her. "What do you think?"

Amy shrugged. "Either Toby didn't get the name right or this Tilly didn't see their relationship as significant, like Toby did. You said he told you she broke his heart. Maybe it was one-sided. I can't tell you all the boys I dated in high school."

"Maybe." I thought there had to be more to it. But it seemed like it wouldn't be a work-related issue. "I hate to be the one to tell Toby she doesn't remember him."

Lille held up a bag and called Amy's name, as she stared right at us.

"I better go. These guys were expecting a full dinner. I hope they don't get called out before I get back. It might get ugly." She grinned. "I can see the headlines now, 'Riot in South Cove Caused by Lack of Police Coverage Due to Dinner Mix-up.'"

I smiled and called after her, "It's a little long for a headline." She ignored my editing comment.

"Coffee, Books, and More?" Lille called out, even though she knew I'd made the order.

I sighed and stood, moving through the crowd. "Thanks, Lille. Can you tell Tiny I'll be back in about thirty minutes for the second order?"

"Sure. I'm at your beck and call." She shoved the bag at me and grabbed some menus. "Frank? Your table for two is ready."

I caught Carrie's gaze, and she nodded. She would let Tiny know if Lille didn't. Thank goodness Carrie liked me. If not, I'd have to go to Bakerstown when I didn't feel like cooking. And that drive would waste a lot of time.

I delivered Harrold and Aunt Jackie's meals and noticed Lille had put in two slices of cherry pie that I hadn't ordered. She'd known that this order would be given to Harrold, and she loved him like a grandfather. I suspected that Lille had a heart; it was just hidden under all that snark.

Judith had gone to the food truck around two, so Jackie was working the main shop by herself. And besides Harrold, she was totally alone.

"Traffic slow?" I asked, looking around the cleaned and set up coffee bar.

"Dead. After we eat, I'll close up and put up the sign sending them your way. I kind of like this different type of festival. It gives us a break from having both locations crazy busy." She stepped over and sat with Harrold. "Did you offer the job to Tilly?"

I nodded as I leaned on another table. "Yes, and she accepted."

"So no issue with her and Toby?" My aunt narrowed her eyes like I'd lied or omitted something in my statement.

"Not an issue at all." I grabbed my tote and headed to the door. "I'm going to see if Greg's at the station. I haven't seen him since early yesterday."

"Busy man, your fiancé." Harrold nodded. "A man who works hard is a good provider. You're lucky."

"As is he," my aunt added.

"I didn't mean to imply..." Harrold began.

I waved and left the shop. I knew Harrold didn't mean to imply I was looking for a sugar daddy; it had just come out that way. He was of a different generation when a lot of women didn't work out of the home. I'd never known anything different. My mom had worked all her life, and when she'd died, I moved in with my aunt, who owned a coffee shop with my uncle. Women worked in my life experience. And I would continue to work and run my business long after Greg and I got married.

I went through the police station entry door and waved to Amy at the reception desk. "I should have asked if Greg was around when we talked earlier."

"Sorry, Jill, he just left for the beach. There's a fight going on between two of the bands." She nodded at my expression. "You guessed right. It's Matt's band and Hans's, who are arguing over who should go on stage next. Apparently, the schedule has Hans going next, and he wants the later spot, so he's crying preferential treatment due to Matt's relationship with Darla. Then some fists got thrown, and Greg had to go be the peacekeeper. I can't believe this is turning into high school all over."

"Sounds more like elementary school to me." I glanced at my watch. Time to pick up the next round of food. "I've got to go. Are we still on for brunch next Sunday?"

Amy nodded as she turned to pick up the phone. She covered the receiver with her hand. "I'm looking forward to it. Things back to normal. South Cove Police Department, this is Amy. How can I help you?"

I left the station and hurried to Lille's. Pushing my way through the line, I thought maybe Lille needed a second entrance for pickups. Of course, if I suggested it, it would never happen. I'd suggest it to Carrie the next time I saw her. Which was just then. She was back on the hostess stand now instead of Lille. "Hey, Carrie, here for my next pickup."

"Jill, it just came up. Hold here a second." She stood, but I held out a hand.

"Hey, before I forget, has Lille thought of having a carryout door? That way people who are just picking up could come inside without pushing through the line." I pointed behind me at the frowning mob.

"That's a great idea. I'll suggest it."

"Just don't tell her it came from me," I called after her as she went to get my order. I heard her laugh through the crowded dining room.

When I got to the food truck, I let the crew eat, and I watched the window. There weren't a lot of people coming for coffee right now. Most were either somewhere eating dinner or cooling off at their hotel. No wonder Hans didn't want the current slot.

As I stood there, I opened a magazine that one of the baristas, probably Judith, had left behind. It was a decorating magazine. I was deep into how to turn your bath into one that looked like a Tuscan villa when someone stepped up.

"An iced coffee please and two cookies," Greg ordered.

"Hey, you. I went to see you at the station, but Amy said you were playing babysitter to the bands." I started his iced coffee. "What cookies do you want?"

"Depends on if you can sit and chat for a few." He glanced over to the bandstand. "I wasn't exactly a babysitter, more like King Solomon. The fact that Hansel is Tina's nephew is getting to be more and more of a problem. Do you know he actually said he paid for the bandstand and should be deciding when he should play?"

"Uh-oh." I finished up the coffee. "How did that go over?"

Greg took the coffee and took a sip before continuing. "I informed him that the city put up that money, and as far as I knew, he wasn't a resident of South Cove. He kept pushing, so finally, I decided he should go first. As scheduled. Then he said I was in cahoots with the band and Darla and the competition was rigged. I asked him if he'd like to just leave. I could have my officers escort him off the beach. So he backed off."

"I bet that didn't make him happy."

"Spoiled little rich kid, it never does. Now how about taking a break?"

"She's all yours," Deek said as I started to tell him it would be a few minutes.

I turned to Deek, who was washing his hands. "Are you sure? It wasn't a full dinner break."

"Believe me, you pay for a lot of hours where I'm writing as I wait for customers to come in. I can repay the favor." He turned, wiping his hands on a towel. "How's things going, Mr. Police Dude?"

"Festival weekends are the worst." Greg reached out and shook Deek's hand. "Thanks for letting me have her for a while."

"No worries. The girls have finished up eating and are walking the beach for a few minutes. So the table in back is empty if you want to use it." Deek waved at a customer walking toward the truck. "Come on up and let me guess the way you take your coffee."

"If you're wrong, do I get it free?" the younger man asked.

Deek grinned at me. "If I'm wrong, you pay for the coffee, and I'll throw in a cookie."

"Fine. Guess..."

As we walked away, Greg turned and looked over his shoulder. "Does he do this often?"

"Who knows? I just let him work the way he wants to work. He likes making it a game."

"Does he lose often?"

Now I turned to watch Deek and our customer. He'd guessed right, even though the man had tried to trick him. I smiled and turned away. "Probably not. I'm thinking it's something to do with their aura, or maybe Deek's served him before. Sometimes people don't notice who's serving them coffee or dinner. They're just a means to an end."

"That's a little pessimistic of human motivations." He sat and put the coffee on the table and opened the cookie sack while I unpacked my fish and chips.

Before Greg could say anything, I mentioned that I'd had a Cobb salad for lunch, so this wasn't my fourth meal in a row that was fried fish.

He chuckled. "I wasn't even going to comment. But it's good to know you're taking care of my Jill."

I loved it when he said that, even if it seemed a little old-fashioned. Like Harrold saying Greg was a good provider. Maybe I was a little old-fashioned as well. "I had to order something different. Tiny was beginning to worry. He sent me a side salad with my order last night. So what's going on with you? How's the investigation?"

"Long, boring, and everyone hates each other, so there is a lot of finger-pointing going on. Tina still feels like you killed Axel to ruin Hans's life." He broke off a piece of chocolate chunk cookie and ate it.

"Sure, and I also caused climate change and the California drought. Heck, throw in the wildfires too, as long as you're randomly pointing fingers." I stabbed my fry into ketchup. "That woman is a menace to society. Not to mention, she's just plain mean."

"I love it when you get into girl fights. Have you chosen your weapons yet? Pillows or feather boas?" He dodged the fry I threw his way.

"Keep it up, buster. I'm getting used to being home alone all the time. I might have to make it permanent." I knew he was teasing, and so was I.

"Yeah, sorry about that. I did come home last night, but it was so late, I crashed in the guest room so I wouldn't wake you. This morning, I left a couple of hours before your alarm went off. Festival weekend is hard enough. Then throw in a dead guy, and my schedule just becomes twenty-four seven." He took my hand. "Do you still love me?"

"I guess." I smiled, and he reached over and took several fries. "Okay, maybe not. Stay out of my dinner. I know you had Tiny's fried chicken. I saw Amy at Diamond Lille's."

"Without any mashed potatoes and gravy. By the time she got back, I was running out here to handle whatever this was." He glanced down at the bandstand, where Hans had just introduced the band. "Don't you think it's weird that Hans found a lead singer that fast?"

"Like he thought he might just need one to fill in once the other band stole his lead singer?" I nodded, finishing the last of my fish. "Yeah, it's coincidental. Unless Mick had told him he was looking for a new band."

"Told Hans? You're kidding, right? He'd be more likely to keep it on the down-low. Maybe this Mick guy knew someone over in Matt's band. They seem kind of all up in everyone's business." Greg handed me the second cookie. "I've got to get back to work. I just wanted to spend some time together. Do I need to stop on my way back to let Emma out?"

"I stopped to see her when I picked up dinner. She's mad at me for not taking her running, so that's first on my agenda on Monday morning. So don't give me any rules about not running. I've totally stayed out of this investigation, so there's no target on my back." I realized I hadn't told him about Keith and Jules's fight. So I did before he left.

He wrote some stuff down in his book. "That's what you call staying out of the investigation?"

"I didn't ask them to fight out on the street where I could hear them, did I?" I finished my dinner and put the trash back into the sack; then I broke the cookie in half, handing part to Greg. "Want this?"

"Of course." He stood and took the cookie. Then he leaned down to kiss me. "Okay, unless I'm convinced there's a serial killer in town, you can run Monday morning. I'd send Esmeralda, but she's taking off Sunday night."

"Yeah, Amy told me she's working tomorrow. I guess I should have figured that since I will be as well, but I miss our Sunday brunches when we don't get to have them." I stood and walked with Greg to the front of the food truck where we were just beginning to have a line forming. "Looks like I came back just in time."

"Be careful going home." He kissed me again. "And thanks for the information. I know I get grumpy, but I appreciate the intel."

I hugged him. "You might want to chat with Darla too. She seems to have all the dirt on Matt's band at least. With Axel gone, she won't have to worry about Matt getting back into bad situations."

"You realize you just gave her motive for the murder, right?" He shook his head and chuckled. "You just can't help yourself, even when you're pointing out one of your friends as a killer."

"I didn't mean that. Darla wouldn't, couldn't hurt a fly," I said, but Greg had already turned around and was walking toward the highway. "Great, Jill, rat on all of your friends."

Chapter 10

Sunday morning, I woke to no Greg, again. It wasn't a surprise, but I'd be glad when we got back to a more normal life. I drank some coffee while I watched Emma patrol the yard. I didn't have to be at the truck until nine. The competition didn't start until noon, so there wouldn't be a lot of customers today until then. I had Deek coming in at eleven and Evie working the morning shift with me. I had told Tilly to come in about ten and work until two; she'd be our safeguard. And it would give her a full training in the food truck part of her job.

It still bothered me that she hadn't recognized Toby's name, but I guessed that was between her and Toby, not me. I waved as Toby came out of the shed, or his apartment, and headed to his truck to get to work. He waved back but didn't stop.

There could have been a couple of reasons he didn't. One, he could have been in a hurry. Or two, there had been a break in the murder investigation, and he didn't want me asking about it. I could take Greg coffee and cookies, but I didn't have the strength to walk up the hill to town. Not today. Besides, I'd have to go get everyone lunch at one, so I needed to conserve my energy. I went upstairs and gathered the laundry. I wanted tomorrow to be free for grocery shopping and maybe a quick clean of the house. Or maybe some reading. I still had the book in my tote, but I hadn't had any free time to read at the shop or the truck this weekend.

It was very disappointing.

I started a load of laundry, explained to Emma again why we couldn't run, and then made myself a protein shake for breakfast. Amy swore by them, but I thought it took a little too much time to deal with on a regular morning. However, today, I had the time.

I was reading and drinking my shake when a knock came on the door. When I opened it, Esmeralda stood there. "Hey, what's going on? I hear you're taking off for New Orleans. That will be fun."

"Oh, more of a chore than fun. Nic has asked me to host a party at the house for his sister's return home. They're all about welcoming home the wandering lamb. I'm sure I'll be asked why I'm not returning to claim my rightful place by Nic's side." She had stepped back, and now she was leaning on the porch railing. She looked cool in slim capris and a soft silk sleeveless shirt that must have had every color in the rainbow mixed together.

"Did I miss something? Has Nic popped the question?"

"Oh, how can I count the ways. I'm kidding, you haven't missed some big announcement." She grinned and waved the idea away. "He's ready for the next step. I'm the one who's still wary of stepping back into a world I turned away from. He's trying to change it, but... Oh, why am I burdening you with my problems? I just came over to tell you that Deek's going to be popping in and out of my place this week to take care of my baby."

"Yes, I heard. And you can talk to me anytime. About anything."

She stepped off the porch. "You are very easy to talk to. That's a little scary. Anyway, I'm off to work. Then I'll be flying into New Orleans and a whole peck of trouble if I'm reading the signs right. Wish me luck."

"I do, but you won't need it. You're the most capable person I've ever met," I called after her.

She turned and smiled. "Jill Gardner, that is the loveliest thing anyone has ever said about me. Thank you."

After Esmeralda left, I went back to the kitchen and finished my smoothie and the chapter I was on, and maybe not in that order. Okay, fine, the smoothie was gone long before the chapter was. I loaded another bunch of laundry, told Emma goodbye and to be good, then headed down to the beach to open the food truck.

There wasn't a police officer directing traffic to move people across the highway, but since it was still early, there wasn't much traffic either. The beach parking lot was empty except for Lille's trailer and my own. No one was at Lille's, but she probably didn't plan on opening before eleven, focusing on getting the lunch crowd. I walked around the trailer to the small table and sat for a few minutes since I was early. Life was more than just working.

The waves were still crashing on the sand and clearing off any sign of a major festival. Moonstone Beach was a beautiful place to relax. Emma and I ran here several times a week, but sometimes, after I'd finished a shift on a weekday, I'd come here alone and just sit still and listen to the messages in the waves.

Relax. Feel the earth. You're enough. It didn't matter what the waves said to me; it was always the right thing. I know it was probably my brain attaching to a word or phrase I needed, but it was romantic thinking that my needed messages were being sent from the ocean itself.

I took in a big breath of the sea air and dropped my shoulders. Amy had a yoga class that met here every Saturday morning—except for festival weekends—and they did an hour of practice on the beach. I didn't like yoga enough to join her. But this centering? I could do this daily. I decided to add the practice to my workweek. Wake up, eat something, take Emma out, and spend ten minutes just sitting and listening on the beach.

"I didn't expect to find you this early. Don't you have staff to run the coffee shop?" Jules stood by the trailer, watching me. "Don't tell me you're getting ready to do yoga? Before you do, can you sell me some coffee?"

"The pots haven't been turned on yet, so have a seat, and I'll get one started for you. Plain coffee? Or something special?"

"Unless you mean alcohol as that something special, plain's fine. I have a bottle in my bag. I can add some whisky later." Jules sat at the table as I stood.

"I'll be right back. I'm not at my regular caffeine level yet either, so I need to get some in my body before I fall asleep out here."

Going inside, I realized there was now one car in the parking lot. An older blue truck sat near the back of the lot, the truck bed filled with drum boxes. Jules had parked as close to the beach entrance as possible. She'd have to make four, maybe five trips to get her set on the bandstand. Maybe the idea of having the event on the beach hadn't been the best. At least not for the bands' drummers.

I started the coffeepot, and as I waited for it to brew, I made a plate with several of yesterday's cookies. We'd almost sold out, so I only had a few to choose from, including several sugar cookies in the shapes of ice-cream cones and guitars. When the coffee was ready, I took it and the cookies out to sit with Jules. I was too early to open and still waiting for my delivery from Pies on the Fly, Sadie's business.

Jules picked up one of the guitar cookies and laughed. "Sure, guitars get all the love. Did you hear us play last night? I think Mick's a better singer than Axel ever was, even in his prime."

"I did sneak out and listen to your set. When do you know who plays today?" I sipped my coffee and leaned back, watching the waves.

"Keith will get a text by ten if we play. So I'm here, just in case. I'm sure the parking lot will fill up with most of the bands' drummers soon. We tend to think ahead since we can't just throw a drum set over our shoulder and walk several blocks. Not like a guitar player." She bit off the neck of the guitar and ate it. "These are good."

"Local bakery. I'm waiting for her delivery before opening today." I took an ice-cream cone cookie. "I hope the police interview wasn't too stressful. That must be hard to do when you're supposed to be thinking about the contest."

"Actually, playing is the only time I don't worry about things. Not my rent, not my family, not If I'll ever meet Mr. Right. When I'm playing, I'm in the zone. It's probably why I'm still pushing so hard to be in a band that makes it. I'd love to make a living doing what I love, without going to work on a cruise line or overseas playing old rock classics. But I have the invite sitting on my dining room table, just in case." She set the cookie down and sipped her coffee. "What about you? Is the coffee shop and bookstore your jam? Is this where you thought you'd be at our age?"

I nodded. "When I was younger, I thought I'd be a lawyer, and I was for a while, but I hated it. People can be ugly to each other when feelings are hurt or if money is involved. And since I practiced family law, that was most of my cases. I came to South Cove for a break before I burned out, and realized I'd already burned out. I bought the bookstore, added a coffee shop, and since then, I've been living."

"That sounds amazing. Darla's got a good setup here. I know her parents drive her crazy, but she loves running the winery. And Matt, he enjoys working with the bands at the winery. I swear he'll quit the band if we become successful." Jules laughed at me. "You don't believe me."

"I'm just shocked you think that. Why?"

"Matt isn't made for touring all day, every day. He likes being home and being with Darla. I tried to go there. He's a cute guy and a lot of fun, but he shot me down fast. He said he was a one-woman man, and she was home in South Cove." Jules sighed a bit. "Actually, that made me want one just like him. But I never went there again. I respect boundaries."

"Matt's a good person." I wasn't sure Darla would like Jules's confession, but I appreciated her honesty. "I kind of thought you and Keith were an item."

"You sound like we're in school. Keith and I aren't an"—she made air quotes—"item. We slept together once, maybe twice, but he's not what I'm looking for. He's too self-absorbed. If I'm not going to be a famous rock star, which is my first choice, I want to have a solid relationship like Darla and Matt."

I started to say something else, but then Sadie popped her head around the truck. "There you are. I've been knocking on the trailer door, thinking you were inside. I was about to go to the house and drag you out of bed."

I stood and hurried over. "Sorry, I was just chatting. Jules, this is Sadie. Jules is in Matt's band."

"Well, isn't that nice. I'm going to be late for church, and you're my last stop, so let's get this food out of my van and into your truck." Sadie used to use her purple PT Cruiser, but now she had a panel van she'd painted purple with the Pies on the Fly logo.

"I'll see you later, Jules." I waved, but she held her hand up.

"What do I owe you?"

"I wasn't open, so there's no charge. Besides, it was my treat to talk to you." I looked at the last guitar cookie on the plate. "I hope you get into the finals. I'll be rooting for you."

As Sadie handed me a tray of cookies, she looked over at Jules, who was now walking over to her truck, her coffee in one hand and her phone in the other. "She seems sad."

"I think she's just existing right now." I glanced around the parking lot and saw several vans and trucks with equipment boxes in the back. Jules had been right. Everyone was waiting to see who was going to be in the finals. "I didn't know being a rock star was such a hard life."

Sadie glanced over at the woman, who was now sipping her coffee and staring out at the ocean. "I think anytime you're chasing a dream, it can be hard. Especially when your dream isn't coming as fast as you'd hoped."

I carried the last tray into the truck. "Can I pour you a coffee to go?"

"I could use one. I've been up early getting treats for you and Lille done. I can't believe how many you've sold this weekend. I'm going to be able to pop some money into my retirement fund that Nick had me set up a year ago. He's always asking what I'm contributing. I guess he doesn't want to take care of his spinster mom in her old age."

"You're not going to be a spinster. I guess the talk with Pastor Bill didn't go well?"

She shrugged. "We're having lunch after church. Hopefully, just the two of us. I've been trying to talk to him for a while, and he keeps inviting others to the table. If he does today, we're still having the talk, even if it puts him in an embarrassing situation."

"You wouldn't." I handed her the coffee.

She smiled as she took it. "Don't tempt me. I'm fed up, and I need to know where his heart is. If it's not with me, then fine, I'll back off and find someone else who will appreciate me."

"Sounds like you and Jules want the same thing. Someone to love." I watched out the window as trucks and vans began pulling out of the parking lot. "Looks like the announcement has been made. The top three bands have been announced, so those that aren't in the running are leaving."

Sadie sighed and picked up a cookie. "Now I am going to be late while I wait for the crowd to thin out. So what did you mean about Jules looking for someone? Maybe I can find someone she'd like."

"I'm not sure you run in the same circles." I refilled my coffee.

Sadie shook her head. "You think I'm that naive? Just because I do a lot of service work with the church doesn't mean I don't know a lot of people. I even know people in the local biker gang. Of course, I know them through Lille, so it's not like I'm hanging out in their clubhouse. Anyway, I'll keep her in mind, and if I find someone, I'll send them Matt's way. He can be a good matchmaker."

"Sounds like you have a plan. I'm not sure why I worried in the first place." I stood and greeted the first customer of the day. "What can I get you?"

Sadie bagged up the cookies the woman had ordered, then handed them to me. "I'm going to try to get out of here and back home. I'll see you Tuesday morning, and don't forget our class on Wednesday night. Although I may be in the single category by then."

"Good luck with your lunch," I said as I took the woman's credit card. "I'm rooting for you."

The woman took her coffee and signed the receipt. "That's Pastor Bill's girlfriend, isn't it? Sadie, right? I've met her before at a fundraiser for my son's Scout troop. She's really nice."

"And a talented baker. She made the cookies. She has a bakery and supplies all the local food places, like my shop and Diamond Lille's."

"I didn't know that. How fun. I hope Pastor Bill appreciates her." She took her receipt and headed to the beach.

So do I. So do I. I guessed I'd find out on Tuesday morning what the answer was to our question.

As I got the food truck set up and ready to go, I saw Jules starting to unload her truck. I heard someone call her name and saw Matt jogging across the parking lot to help. He must have walked down from the apartment he shared with Darla behind the winery. He took several boxes, and Jules unloaded the rest. I saw the way she looked at him as she followed him across the beach. She might not be actively trying, but the girl still had some feelings for Matt. It showed on her face.

"Hey, boss." Evie climbed into the truck and followed my gaze to the two band members. "Does that mean they got into the finals? Cool."

"I think it does. I could text Darla and see, if you're interested." I turned away from the window and focused on finishing prep.

"No, that's okay. They'll be announcing at ten, so we mere mortals will find out then. What would it be like to be part of a band? I used to play the piano, but John didn't like the time it took from him. Especially since my teacher was a very attractive college student who was teaching piano to get through school. We lived in a small town."

"Your ex was an idiot. Have you thought about taking it up again? You have a lot of room for a piano in that new house of yours."

She grinned as she poured herself a cup of coffee. "I do have room for it. Just no time. With school and work and trying to keep up with the landscaping and the pool, I'm swamped. And then there's Homer. He's really liking the new house. He wants to spend time in the backyard with me, so I've been doing my homework out there. I think he's still getting used to the new place."

Change was always the constant in life. Whether you were a Pomeranian or a person.

Chapter 11

By the time the music started at noon, we were swamped at the food truck. Or CBM-Mobile, which was what Deek had started calling it. I wanted CBM-West, but he'd pointed out that we weren't always west from the actual shop. Especially since South Cove was on the California coast, it was hard to be more west than the store.

Technicalities. Anyway, I need to go grab lunches. "Everyone okay with me leaving?" I glanced around at the four employees in the truck. They had a system. And I'd just been in their way. As of eleven, we'd sold out of all of the books. "Do we need anything from the shop?"

"Vanilla flavoring. I'm down to my last bottle, and it's nearly gone." Judith held up the bottle to show me.

I turned to Tilly, who was working the treats section. "Are you good for the rest of the afternoon?"

Her eyes widened, and she stared at the case with the pastries. "I don't know, actually. How can I tell?"

Deek moved over to her and waved Evie up to take his place on the till. "So, we're selling a lot of the ice-cream cone cookies. And you only have three cheesecakes left. Last night, we sold out of cheesecake right at closing time. And we had less than ten cookies when we closed. He glanced at his watch. "It's noon, so we have about four hours to go, max. We're closing at four, right, Jill?"

"Unless the crowd totally dies, but yeah, that's the plan." I watched as Deek explained his process.

"Okay then, if we sell twenty cookies an hour, we have enough for ten hours. If we sell fifty, we have enough for four hours." Deek continued the lesson.

Tilly nodded. "I get it. You kind of guesstimate based on the history. Like last night."

"Thanks, Deek, for explaining that. I'll get us another two dozen cookies and make at least one dozen the ice-cream cone ones. And a cheesecake. But I'll need the dolly to carry all that." I glanced around the truck.

"It's in the closet with the boxes." Deek pointed as he went back to the register to take another order.

I got my tote and the dolly and headed out the door. The team had this. I walked up the hill and stopped at the house. My Jeep was the only car in the driveway. We still had the "private parking" sign blocking the entrance, but it didn't look like anyone had tried to block us in. I took my book out to the yard and read while Emma did her stuff. Then I tucked it into my tote and headed back into town, trying to forget the sad puppy dog eyes I'd received when I told her I had to go back to work.

Four, maybe five more hours tops, and I could cuddle with my girl on the couch. The only problem was dogs couldn't tell time.

I walked past Lille's and continued on to my shop. I'd pick up the food on the way back. When I got there, I went straight to the back door, trying to stay out of the front since, if anyone spotted me, they'd try to get me to open. The main street was empty as if it were a Wednesday in winter. Everyone who was in town was probably either at the beach, the bar, or the winery, or at Lille's eating. I began to get a little freaked out as I realized how alone I truly was here in the shop. I hurried to gather what I needed, then packed up and, as I was leaving, ran into Hansel Baldwin in the alleyway behind the buildings.

"Oh, hello. I would have thought you'd be at the beach?" I kept walking. I had been going to cut through the buildings to the main street, but Hans had blocked that walkway.

"Why would I be at the beach? My band didn't make the cut." He fell into step with me. "Where are you going?"

"To Lille's. My team at the food truck is waiting for lunch." I sped up my pace. Hans kept up with me.

"My aunt's not very happy with you. She thinks you should have told your boyfriend to move the practices along." He glanced behind us to see if anyone was following. "Maybe if he had, Mick wouldn't have had time to defect, and I'd be playing this afternoon for that contract."

"I don't think that would have happened. It sounded like Keith had Mick on speed dial just in case Axel went off the deep end." I needed to keep him talking until we got back on Main Street. We were only three buildings away from safety. I was beginning to sweat and wondered if I'd make it. I might not be the reason he didn't get into the finals, but in his eyes, I was part of the problem.

"What do you know?" Hans's voice got high and loud. "I should be playing today, not your druggy friend Matt."

I saw him move and pull out what looked like a big knife from his pocket. Instead of running, I stopped, frozen in place. His momentum sent him ahead of me. Then I felt hands on my arms, pulling me even farther back.

"Jill, what have I told you about walking the alley? I was meeting you at the front of the store. Didn't you remember?" Greg now stood between me and Hans. And, I noticed, Toby was on my left.

"Sorry, I forgot. I must have missed the turn." I kept my gaze on Hans, wondering if he'd try to stab all of us.

But to my surprise, when Hans turned, he had an inhaler in his hand, not a knife. Maybe he wasn't the villain, but he mostly fit the part. He glared at me. "I guess I'll see you around."

I watched him walk away as some part of me fought to keep down the giggles or to call out, *Not if I see you first.* I turned to Greg. "I thought he had a knife."

"So did I. I'm still not convinced that he wasn't going to try to harm you. Spraying the medicine from that inhaler might have given him enough time to hurt you or steal from you. The kid's just a bad seed. That's all there is to that." He nodded to Toby. "You can follow him. See where he goes."

Toby jogged past us.

"Okay, how did you know I was here?" I could finally breathe without screaming.

"I stopped by the truck, but you'd just left. Emma didn't want to go out, so I knew you'd already been there. And when I tried to look into the shop, I couldn't see anyone. I figured you must have gone through the back door."

"I was planning on coming back out front, but Hans was blocking the pathway. I had to just hoof it down the alley and hoped I could outrun him or actually run into someone. And I did." I couldn't catch my breath.

"Because I went looking for you," Greg reminded me. "I wish I had enough to throw him in jail for a day or two, but I don't."

"If you did, Tina would throw a fit." I pulled on the dolly and started walking again. "I need to get back to the truck."

"I know, but I'm going to walk you back to the beach. Just in case. You don't have Emma to keep away another attacker."

"I still have to pick up lunch, but if you want to help, I'm not going to argue." I held out the handle of the dolly. "You can pull and watch this while I go into Lille's."

"Sounds delightful. But at least I'm not talking to a bunch of musicians who think Matt's band members killed Axel just so they could win the contract. It's the leading theory in the rumor mill." Greg took the dolly and pulled it behind him. "Nobody liked this Axel guy, but everyone wants to blame his death on this contest, nothing else."

I glanced over at him. "Is there something else to blame? Or someone else?"

"He had shoddy business practices. He shorted suppliers as well as band members when he could get away with it. He tried to dump his drummer because she didn't fit the image he had for the band. And Darla didn't like him. Darla is a good judge of character." Greg pointed to the line. "Go get your food, and let's get going. I've got a bunch of officers who will be going off shift at five. Hopefully, the festival will be somewhat cleared out by then."

"I'll be right back." I moved to the front of the line and again had to deal with dirty looks from the people I was moving past. I wanted to hold up a hand and say, "I'm not cutting," but maybe they thought even picking up food was cutting. Lille needed a second door, at least for festival weeks. I went through the door and found Carrie at the hostess stand. It was my lucky day.

"Jill, I'm so glad you're here. Now I can get back to my tables." She moved to the kitchen and got my bags.

"Wait, does Lille assign you hostess duties to avoid me?" I glanced around the crowded dining room. Lille was nowhere to be seen.

Carrie dropped her voice. "Don't tell her I told you. But yeah, she asked me to cover until you got here. Man, you rub that girl wrong."

"Not my fault." I took the bags. At least I didn't think it was my fault. If I didn't think it would make the situation worse, I'd have a heart-to-heart with Lille. Problem was, I didn't think she had a heart except where my new uncle was concerned. "Hey, what's Doc say about Axel's death? Anything interesting besides the guitar string garroting?"

She nodded and leaned toward me. "I guess the guy was high as a kite. Doc said he didn't know how he was walking, much less singing. But you know how those rockers are."

As I moved outside so Carrie could get back to her tables and Lille could come out of hiding, I thought about two things. One, I needed to send someone else for food the next time we did a festival. I hated that Lille was bringing Carrie into the problem. And it was probably costing Carrie some tips. I didn't want to be responsible for that. But more importantly, why was Axel doing drugs during what he'd told Matt was their ticket to an actual contract? It didn't seem logical.

I met up with Greg, and we walked down the sidewalk.

"You're quiet. What's going on?" Greg asked as he put away his phone.

I shook my head. He wouldn't tell me anyway. "Nothing."

"Jill, I know you. Something happened in Diamond Lille's. So you might as well tell me." Greg put his free hand on my shoulder. "What's got you bothered?"

"Okay, but remember you asked." I glanced over at him. "So I heard the tox screen on Axel came back showing he was doing drugs."

"I really need to explain to Doc the importance of keeping evidence quiet even from Carrie." He sighed and nodded. "But you're right, I asked. So why is that upsetting? From what I've heard, Axel was often high or drunk. Matt said the after-concert parties were crazy, and he'd stopped going to them."

"Yeah, the after-concert parties. But according to Darla, this contest was the band's chance at a full contract with a bigger label. Why would he jeopardize that? You're telling me that the night before the biggest weekend of his life, he goes off the deep end while he's checking out the bandstand for tomorrow's practice?"

Greg stopped walking in the middle of the sidewalk. Someone almost ran into him and went around into the street.

"Dude," the man grumbled. I was sure he was going to say more, but then he saw that Greg was in uniform.

"Greg?" I pulled him to the side, making sure my dolly was out of the way. "What's wrong?"

He set the dolly down and rubbed his face. "How come you can see the obvious when I've missed it?"

"So he may not have taken the drugs voluntarily?" I didn't know what drugs Axel had been on or the volume, but his motivation was off. That was the only thing I saw.

"I'm not talking about this, but thank you. I needed a clear perspective. Let's get this to your truck. I've got some interviews to review and maybe some new questions." He motioned to the officer that was directing traffic to clear our path, and we and several others went across the street to the parking lot.

When we got there, I saw a piece of trash by the tailgate of Jules's truck. It must have fallen out when she took out the drums. I reached down to pick it up, planning on putting it into the trash can by the food truck. I paused to look at it, making sure it wasn't a receipt or something she would need.

The words on the bright yellow plastic packaging said it was a guitar string. I went to throw it away, and Greg grabbed my hand. "What?"

"That's a VanHelm string package." He took the piece of trash by the corner and took a baggie out of his pocket. He closed the package inside and looked back at the truck. "Who owns that?"

"That's Jules's truck, or at least the one she drove in here today. I talked to her this morning while she waited to see who was advancing in the competition. I guess most of the drummers came early, just in case they needed to carry their drum sets over to the bandstand. Maybe if we do this next year, we should hold it at the Castle, where there's plenty of parking."

"You're sure Jules was driving the truck?"

I waved at Deek, who was watching us stand at the trash can, a confused look on his face. "Come get the desserts before the cheesecake melts. And have someone else grab the lunches."

"Yes, boss." He disappeared inside the truck for a moment, and then he and Evie were taking the dolly and the bags of food from me.

"Send everyone but Tilly to lunch. I'll be in to help her in a second." I didn't wait for an answer. I moved Greg away from the truck and my employees.

After they'd gone back inside, I tapped his pocket where he'd stashed the package. "You don't know that Jules actually had the guitar string."

"That's why I'll have it fingerprinted. Good thing we have your fingerprints already on file and I saw you pick up the piece of evidence. Although you did try to dispose of it."

"I tried to throw away a piece of trash." I glanced over at Jules's truck. I needed to tell him the rest of what I'd seen, but it wasn't going to look good. "Matt was here this morning too. He helped her unload the drums."

"Jill, if the package fell out of Jules's truck and Matt didn't touch it, it won't have his fingerprints on it. Apparently, Axel special-ordered these strings. They're expensive and hard to get. So unless he threw an empty package into Jules's truck, it's evidence." Greg pulled me into his arms. "I know you want to believe Matt couldn't do this."

"He's one of us. He has been for years." I leaned my head into Greg's chest and lowered my voice. "And if it's him, Darla's going to be heartbroken."

"I know all that. And just because he was being nice and helping Jules this morning doesn't mean he's a killer. Go back to work. Eat something that's not ninety percent sugar, and I'll see you at home tonight. I'll be there for dinner. Maybe something easy like tomato soup and grilled cheese? I need some Jill time." He held me at arm's length, then kissed me gently on the lips. "I'll see you tonight."

"Promises, promises." I smiled as he walked away. Greg's job kept him at the office a lot, and it wasn't predictable, but I knew it meant a lot to him. Our relationship meant a lot to him as well. After this weekend, he needed a break where no one asked him work questions and he could just be Greg. And as long as another dead body didn't show up between now and dinner, I might just have a chance of having dinner with my fiancé.

When I got to the truck, everyone was gone to eat except Deek. I raised my eyebrows. "I thought I told you to have Tilly stay back?"

"Sue me, I was curious. What did you pick up by that truck that made Police Dude go crazy?" Deek glanced out the window, but for now, we didn't have any customers to overhear our conversation.

"It might not be anything." I pointed to his lunch. "Go eat. I'll hold down the fort for a while. I'm sorry it took so long for me to get back."

Deek picked up his lunch and shrugged. "I just figured it took a while at Lille's. Was there something else?"

I thought about brushing it off, but another set of eyes watching wouldn't hurt. So I told him about Hans and the creepy behavior.

"He all but threatened you, and Police Dude couldn't arrest him?" Deek grabbed some fries out of his bag and pointed them at me before he devoured them. "That's messed up."

"I agree. But if you see Hans hanging around the truck, just let me know. I don't think he's done being creepy." *Or dangerous,* I thought as Deek left the truck to eat out back at the table. In screaming earshot, as he put it.

I just hoped I didn't need the backup.

Chapter 12

The winner was announced right at 4:00 p.m. Atlantis Survivors won the competition and the recording contract. Our South Cove favorite had taken the prize. I thought as I watched the people stream out of the parking lot, heading back to their cars or their hotel rooms, this had just made the mayor's wife a ticking time bomb. Tina would not be happy that her nephew's band had lost even though they didn't make the top three. And when Mama ain't happy, as the saying goes.

Darla had done the right thing by making the judging panel music experts out of the city. I hoped that would be enough for Tina to realize that there was a reason Hans lost, but probably not.

"So we're closing up?" Deek asked as he stood beside me watching the people disappear.

"Might as well." We might sell some waters for the road, but most of these people were going to dinner or home, so treats probably weren't high on their list. "We had a great weekend though."

Deek nodded. "We probably can send Tilly home. Is she starting Tuesday morning with you?"

"Yeah." I turned around and found Tilly packing the few books we hadn't sold into a box. "Tilly, come to the shop Tuesday morning with the paperwork I gave you, and we'll start training. Ten to two for a week. Then I'll put you on afternoons and evenings for a week. Will that work?"

"Perfect." She closed the box. "So am I free to go now?"

"Free as a bird. Evie, can you stay with Deek to close up? Or do you want me to stay so you can get home to Homer?"

Evie pointed out to the crowd of people. "I'll stay. My car is up at the shop. That way, I'm not in traffic for an hour or more."

"I've got my bike, so I'll leave now." Judith took her apron off. "Tilly, do you want me to wait with you?"

"My boyfriend is in the parking lot. He texted me a few minutes ago that he'd just wait for me to be done." Tilly glanced into the mirror and adjusted her blond ponytail. "I'm glad he's seen me in worse shape. I look drained."

Evie met my gaze, and we must have been thinking the same thing. Toby wasn't going to be happy to find out his ex–high school sweetheart didn't remember him *and* had a boyfriend. But she was an amazing barista, so I couldn't not hire her just because of that.

I was about to leave when Darla showed up at the food truck window. "Jill? Are you in there?"

"I'm just coming out." I put my tote over my head and turned to Deek. "Lock it up and drop the keys off at my house when you walk by."

"I'm staying at Esmeralda's tonight through Saturday. She's coming back on Sunday." He continued, "But I'll walk the keys over."

"Maybe you can help Toby move the truck to the shop tomorrow then. You guys figure out a time." I waved at Evie. "Thanks for everything this weekend, guys. You two are my rocks."

"You're kidding, right? It's my job, and I love it," Evie said as she cleaned out the coffee machines.

"Thank goodness for that," I said as I left the truck.

Darla was almost glowing with excitement when I met her. "Congratulations. To you for a successful festival and to Matt for the win."

"I know, right? I wanted to let you know that we're having a party down at the winery to celebrate. You're welcome to come. Bring Greg and anyone else you want. The band's going to play for a few sets too. Everyone's worked up and needs to let off some steam."

"Greg said he might be home for dinner tonight." I nodded to the highway. "So I think we're a no, but if you're heading into town, I'll walk with you."

"I've got to go get everything ready." Darla fell in step with me. "Can you believe they won?"

"They're good." I didn't want to bring up issues, but Darla was being chatty. "The new singer, Mick, he's good."

"Twice as good as Axel. He'd worn out his voice with cigarettes and booze. This guy is serious about being a good musician. Axel just wanted to be a rock star." Darla sighed. "I know, I shouldn't speak ill of the dead, but I'm glad he's gone. Matt went through hell getting clean, and I don't want anyone pushing drugs on him now. It's not fair, you know."

"Darla, there's no way Matt would have killed Axel, right?" The words were out of my mouth before I could stop them. Knowing that empty guitar string package had been near Matt this morning made me wonder how far Matt would go to stay clean.

"I can't believe you even asked that." Darla's eyes filled. "You know Matt. He's been a part of South Cove for years, and you want to finger him for this murder? Why? So Greg can solve another investigation?"

"Darla, don't get mad," I started, but it was too late. She wasn't just mad. She was furious.

"I thought we were friends. If you're going to suspect Matt, you should suspect me as well." Darla's face was getting redder by the minute. "No one in Atlantis Survivors would have done this. It had to be someone else."

I wasn't sure what to say, but I didn't have to say anything. Darla stormed away from me into the crowd and got on the edge of the group that the police officer was letting on the crosswalk to go into town. Even if I'd pushed my way through the crowd, I'd still be stuck, waiting for the next group to be allowed to cross the road.

I suspected my invite to tonight's party had just been rescinded.

* * * *

By the time Greg got home, I'd already chatted with my aunt about the success of the festival and ways to improve our profits next time. Aunt Jackie was always looking for ways to make the business better. I just wanted to go upstairs and soak in a long, hot bath.

Emma, on the other hand, she wanted a run.

Neither one of us was getting what we wanted. Greg came in the house to find me on the couch, eating popcorn and watching a cooking show. He checked his watch and frowned. "Am I too late for dinner?"

"No, I'm just decompressing after a fight with Darla and an impromptu business meeting with my aunt. Emma wanted to run, but when I told her no, she said popcorn would at least soothe the disappointment." I muted the television. "Are you home for the evening?"

"I am. Although Matt called to see if we were coming to the party. I guess Darla's feeling bad about your argument." Greg went into the office to lock up his gun and take off the police belt he'd worn all weekend. When there were festivals in town, he wasn't just limited to his detective and managerial duties. He did everything, including directing traffic. "Please tell me you don't want to go."

"I don't want to go," I said between popcorn bites. "At least Darla realizes the argument was stupid. I don't think I'll get as much grace from Tina. Are you sure the mayor can't fire you?"

"I work at the pleasure of the city council. So as long as you don't make Mary Sullivan mad, we should be fine." He took the popcorn bowl away from me. "Let's go heat up soup and make grilled cheese. You can tell me how your weekend went. Or not."

"I'd rather talk about us running away together and living off the land in a cabin in the Oregon woods." I followed him into the kitchen.

"You'd miss the beach." Greg took out the bread and the cheese as I rummaged through the canned soups to find the tomato.

"You're right about that. Besides, I'd hate to have to run from bears. At least the sharks stay in the water so we can run on the beach." I pulled out a pan and, after opening the cans, dumped them in and went looking for milk. We had just enough. "I'll need to run to the store tomorrow. Anything you need?"

"I'll put it on the shopping list." He took the pan away from me and started whisking the milk into the soup. "Sit down, I've got this. You seem to have been putting some thought into this escape plan. What did you say to Darla?"

"I asked if Matt could have killed Axel. I didn't mean to say it; it just came out. You would have thought I'd gutted her favorite teddy bear." I put my head in my hands. "Sometimes I just don't know when to stop talking. And she was so happy about their win."

"If she hadn't thought the same thing, it wouldn't have stung so much. I'm sure on some level, Darla's questioning Matt's innocence as well as all her friends in the band. It must be hard." Greg checked the grilled cheese. "You know, I would think after all the investigations we've been involved in here in South Cove, this process should get easier. But anytime there's a local connection, the emotions around it make the process harder. I've got a whole list of interviews to complete next week, but at this point, I'm still trying to make a coherent story. Axel's life isn't making this any easier. The guy knew a lot of people."

"Anything I can do?" I tried to look innocent, like I just wanted to help.

He laughed and stirred the soup. "Not on your life. You just go about your business tomorrow and go to the grocery store. That's how you can help."

"Is Toby working your job tomorrow?" I took out my planner. "I need some help getting the truck back to the shop."

"He's on day shift for Monday. Tim needed the day off." He opened his phone. "I'm booked through the day, and I've got Amy doing double duty as the dispatcher. Maybe Harrold could help?"

"Actually, I'll just help Deek. He's over at Esmerelda's for the week watching her cat. I hate to cut into his writing time, but it's kind of an all-hands-on-deck week. I thought maybe Toby could help him." I found my phone and texted Deek about meeting me at the beach parking lot about nine. I'd take Emma for a run first; then she could ride doggie shotgun while we moved the food truck.

"Deek's turned out to be a pretty good employee. I have to say, I was worried when you hired him." Greg flipped the grilled cheese.

"Because of his dreadlocks? I have to say, I knew he was strong in the book department due to his multiple degrees, but I thought maybe I'd lose him pretty fast. I thought he'd be flaky about staying. Always looking for the next adventure kind. But I was wrong." I got bowls out and poured the soup into them. Then I handed Greg a plate for the sandwiches.

He checked the toast on the bottom and then slipped them off the griddle and onto the plate. "Yeah, I kind of got that feel from him too. But Toby loves the guy. And he has taken a lot of weight off your shoulders. So I'm happy."

"Nice to know. Anyway, I hired the temp this weekend. She starts Tuesday." I made a second note in my planner, just in case I forgot. I had some administrative things to do before the end of the week.

"Great. So let's plan our next vacation. Are we going to drive up the coast? We haven't been to Washington State yet." He sat down. Dinner had started, and it was time to put the business part of my brain away and just be there for the couple part. A skill that I was still working on mastering. I'd noticed it with Amy and her husband, Justin. They had to learn how to not only talk about vacations and surfing trips. They had to mix in the boring household stuff. We had that figured out. Now we had to learn how to talk about the future.

"Oh, don't forget we have that couples' finance class on Wednesday," I added as we finished up our dinner.

"Jill, with the investigation, I don't know."

"Fine, but if you're not going, I'm not either." I dunked my sandwich in my soup. Oh, so good. "I've got a book I want to finish anyway."

"No, I'm not going to let you off that easy. I'll be there. I'll just put it on the planner and make it, make us, a priority." He took his bowl and the empty plate to the sink to rinse and put in the dishwasher. "Now, let's find a movie. I'm tired of negotiating."

"So I get to choose?" I finished my soup and joined him at the sink.

He squeezed my waist. "Good try, but no. We have to compromise, and if I remember right, the last movie was your choice. So it's my turn."

Luckily, Greg chose a spy movie that I'd been wanting to see anyway. I pushed away all thoughts about the coffee shop, the band competition, who killed Axel, and even anyone outside our little cozy house bundle. This was our time.

I just hoped Greg had turned off his phone before the movie started.

* * * *

The next morning, Emma and I were running on the beach. It was still set up from the weekend festival. There were chairs all over the sand and small tents and cabanas, which the rental company would come and get sometime today. Darla enforced a strict rule that all evidence of the festival had to be dismantled and erased by Tuesday morning of the next week. That included signs in our business windows about the past event.

I regularly did a review of the policy at the business-to-business meeting, and Amy had been sent to clean up and fine the businesses who failed to comply. Mayor Baylor liked the additional income from the fines since that went into his budget rather than the festival committee's. The man knew how to work a budget and regulations to his favor. No one would argue that point.

I came up on the bandstand, and Emma stopped at the stairs. "Do you want to be a superstar?"

I followed her up, and we checked out the view. The bandstand had been angled so the bands could see the ocean over the fans sitting on the beach watching. This morning, with no people around, it was breathtaking. If you ignored the mess. I felt like I was in one of my books where the world ends for all but a few people. And they had to gather together to stay alive.

Emma was sniffing at the back of the stage area, so I followed her backstage, hoping she wouldn't find a half-eaten hotdog or something worse, like a dead fish. Instead, I realized we were in the area where Axel had been found. I snapped my fingers, and Emma came to my side and sat.

Looking around, I didn't see any used syringes or empty pill bottles. Of course, Greg's crime scene techs had come and gone already, so there was plenty of fingerprint dust, and tape blocking off the area. I knew he'd already cleared the area, so the tape had just been forgotten in the rush of getting the contest going.

I saw something blue tucked between the wall and the floor. The bandstand stage was pieces put together quickly so it could be torn down and moved to the next event. The stage floor didn't attach to the walls. I ducked under the tape and went over to see what was there.

A folder came out of the small opening. It could just be construction instructions for the workers who put the bandstand together, but I didn't think so. I glanced around and saw there was a square of dust-free floor in front of the place where I'd found the folder.

Had there been a trunk or speaker set up there?

With Emma sitting outside the tape, watching me, I opened the folder. A number of letters from South Shore Productions were in the folder. All addressed to Axel. And all talking about the missing four songs that he'd promised in the contract. The last letter was what I focused on. It started with the following lines, *You are in breach of contract. Either we receive four songs by five o'clock on the last day of April, or your band will be required to repay the advance we gave you.*

I set the folder down and dialed Greg.

"Jill, I'm a little busy. I wrote what I needed on the shopping list."

"Greg, I'm at the bandstand, and I just found a folder filled with letters to Axel. They were in breach of contract for the advance they'd gotten last year. Axel hadn't given them any songs."

"You what?"

"Do you want me to bring this to you, or will you send someone down? I need to meet Deek pretty soon." I ignored his question.

"I'll be there in a couple of minutes. Don't touch anything. Or don't touch anything else, I should say. I can't believe you were the one to find it."

"I think there was a..." I realized I was talking to dead air. Since my fingerprints were already on the letters, I used my phone to quickly take pictures of all of them and then tucked them back into the folder. Emma was watching from behind the tape. I swear she looked disappointed in me. I moved back under the tape. "Let's go wait for your dad outside."

Chapter 13

My phone buzzed as we were walking out onto the stage, and my hands were shaking from sneaking the pictures. I almost dropped the phone. I glanced at the text. Deek.

Done with your run yet?

I responded that I was at the bandstand and saw him walk around the food truck. I waved him over as I went down the stairs to wait for Greg.

When he got there, he glanced around. "Man, this would be a great start to a dystopian novel. What's going on?"

"I'm sure the rental people are on their way," I answered absently, then realized that hadn't been the question Deek asked. "Sorry, we're waiting for Greg; then we can go. I kind of found something that Axel had left."

"The dead guy? How do you kind of find something? Don't tell me you're investigating. Toby says the police dude really hates that." He glanced up at the parking lot. "You need to tell him that I didn't have anything to do with this. He already doesn't like me."

"Why do you think he doesn't like you?" After last night's conversation with Greg, I knew Deek's fear wasn't true, but I wondered why he felt that way.

"He just seems to have his eye on me all the time. And if it's not him, it's your aunt. I feel like I have to live up to some expectation around both of them." He shook his head. "I know, it's my need for authority approval since I didn't have a father figure in my early developmental stages."

"You seem to have it all worked out." I nodded to the approaching figure. "I'll tell Greg it wasn't you; it was me."

Greg nodded to Deek as he came up. "Thanks for watching out for her. Okay, Jill, where did you find the smoking gun?"

"It's not a gun. Maybe you didn't hear me on the phone. I found a folder of letters about Atlantis Survivors' last contract. The one that everyone said they were working on?"

"It's a figure of speech. Where is the folder?"

"Oh. Follow me." I handed Deek Emma's lead and went up the stairs. "Emma wanted to come up and see the view, so we did, and then we found the crime tape. Then I saw a sliver of blue over there."

Greg looked to the area where I pointed. "The area is clean. Maybe something was here, and the crime scene techs didn't move it."

"That's what I tried to tell you when you hung up on me," I said.

He looked up and grinned. "Sorry. I was a little distracted by the fact that you'd found a piece of evidence that my guys had overlooked."

"What can I say? I'm good."

"You're a pain in my butt. That's what you are." He slipped on gloves, then opened the folder. "You're right. The contract that Keith, Matt, and even Jules said they were working on went dead last month. Unless, of course, Axel actually delivered the songs that they wanted."

"Darla said that Matt had submitted several songs to Axel, and they had worked through a lot of them. Why didn't he send them in?" I lifted the crime tape as Greg tucked the folder into a large evidence bag and came out of the area.

He took several pictures of the area and turned back to me. "Don't you have somewhere else to be?"

"I love you too." I headed out of the stage area and went to meet Deek. "Let's get the food truck out of here before they come for the rest of this stuff."

He handed over Emma's leash and followed me to the truck. "We moved everything inside last night. That table and chairs are in the closet, but I had to move out the empty book boxes to get them to fit."

"I'll put them in the recycling when we get the truck back to the shop." I opened the door and nodded at the trash bags. "Put those in the containers by the edge of the parking lot. They'll dump them again tonight. I'll get this truck going."

I went up into the cab part and started the engine. I had just enough room to angle out of my parking spot and out to the exit. I noticed several cars were still in the lot. Including Jules's truck. I left the truck running and went to the back. I ran into Deek, who was coming inside. "I'll be right back. I want to check something."

I went over to Jules's truck and glanced in the windows. She kept it pretty clean. A notebook was on the passenger seat, as well as a planner.

I tried the door. It was locked. Then I checked the empty back. What had they done with Jules's drum set? It hadn't been left on the stage. That had been empty. Then I leaned down and looked under the truck. Nothing I could see, except a scrap of paper under the back tire. I reached for the paper; then a hand came from the other side and grabbed it. I glanced over, and I could see Greg waving the paper at me.

I stood up and glared at him. "What is that?"

"You mean this piece of evidence?" He held it above his head. "Wouldn't you like to know. And what are you doing checking out Jules's truck?"

"I just thought it was odd it was still here when she'd brought her drum set in it. And the drums aren't on the stage," I pointed out.

"So someone else took them back to her house. Maybe her truck didn't start, and someone helped her out?" He came over and gave me a kiss. "Go deal with your food truck before this place becomes a zoo."

"Fine." I walked over and stepped onto the truck.

"Jill?" Greg called out.

I turned back around and saw him holding up an ice-cream sandwich wrapper. "That's what was under the truck?"

"Yep. No evidence this time. I was beginning to get a complex about the thoroughness of my investigation team." He nodded to Deek who now was sitting in the driver's seat with the window down. "As soon as Jill gets inside, I'll help you get this monster out of the lot."

I shut the door and went to sit in the passenger seat next to Emma, who was grinning like she was going on a cross-country trip. "Let's go."

As Greg helped us ease out of the lot, I saw Matt and Jules drive in. He pulled his van up next to Jules's truck and got out, popping the hood as he did. My sleuthing skills had been off, and Greg had been correct. From the look of things, Jules's truck needed a jump.

After he'd gotten us to the exit, I watched Greg go over and talk to Matt. The loss of the contract didn't matter now that they had another one from the contest win. But it put Axel's death in an entirely different light. Now, every member of the band that had submitted a song to be part of the four-song collection could have motive if they found out that Axel had blown up their chance to succeed.

I watched Jules in the sideview mirror as she went to start her truck. And Jules was one of the most career focused of the band.

"You're quiet," Deek said as we drove up the street to town and my shop.

I reached out and rubbed Emma's head. "Just tired from the weekend. Lots going on, and it's not over yet. Thanks for coming this morning to help. Toby's on the day shift."

"No problem. I like helping out. And anyway, the words weren't coming this morning. I think it's the different setting. I might run upstairs to my apartment when we get to the shop and write on my desktop for a few hours before I go back to Esmeralda's."

"Are the spirits bothering you?" I teased.

He laughed as he turned the truck into the alley that ran behind my shop. "More like the setup. Esmeralda does all her paperwork at her kitchen table. She doesn't even have an office. I guess the reading room is considered her workspace. I like having my desk."

I could understand that. I liked reading in specific places. I'd read anywhere if I had to, but I had my favorite spots. Like the couch at the shop or my house. The swing on the back deck. "I guess it's what you get used to. Maybe your muse just needed a break this morning."

"Well, she doesn't get a long one. I need to get this book done so I can move into edits. I'm sure I'll need to change the pacing. I'm going to make a timeline poster on my wall to make sure I didn't mess it up. It's hard, especially with time travel, to keep it all straight."

"You mean on paper on the wall, right?" I would hate to think he was drawing on the fresh paint.

"Yes, mom. I stopped coloring on the walls when I was about ten."

"Ten?" I gasped.

He parked in the spot behind the building that we kept for the truck and turned off the engine, handing the keys to me. "My mom believed in encouraging my creative side. I'm pretty sure she regretted that decision when I went for my second degree and told her I wasn't moving out of the house."

"She's a better mother than I'm going to be." I took the keys and locked the trailer. I could do a clean-out tomorrow after my shift. "Make sure you put two hours for today on your time sheet."

"It wasn't that long." Deek fell in step with me to the building.

I paused at the pathway that would take Emma and me back to Main Street and home. "I took up some of your writing time. Don't look a gift horse in the mouth. I'm pretty sure you give more hours than you account for. Especially with the author events."

To his credit, he actually blushed. "I like talking to authors. Thanks, Jill. You're amazing to work for. Remember, we have an author event on Friday night. It's a personal finance book about reaching retirement early. The guy who wrote it has a huge podcast, so I'm thinking we're going to get a great turnout. You and the police dude should come."

"If he's got a break from this case, we will. Otherwise, I might just show up with Emma. I haven't had her out in a public setting like that for a while now. She's probably missing all the attention from strangers." I rubbed my dog's head. I loved her, but sometimes she really liked other people too. It was kind of disheartening. Like finding out your boyfriend bought flowers for all the women in the bar, not just you. "Are you working Tuesday or is Toby?"

"Toby's working Tuesday. I'm working late afternoons to evenings. I think Judith has a few days off for a family trip this weekend. I hope Toby's other job doesn't get crazy and leave us short."

I shrugged. "We have Tilly. And she's almost trained, so we'll use her for Judith's slots. We should be fine, even with the author event. I'd like as many people as possible to work that night though."

"I figured, so I let your aunt know when I sent her the schedule. The other two events this month probably won't be as big, but this one I'm a little worried about. I'll have him sign bookplates if we run out of books."

"You may want to ask him to bring his stash as well. A lot of authors keep a box or two of their books, just in case. We'll buy them from him." I shrugged when I saw the grin on Deek's face. "Okay, so you've already thought of that. I don't know why you talk to me about these events. You always have everything covered."

He turned and jogged up the stairs to his apartment on the second floor. "I like to keep you in the loop."

Deek was an excellent employee. I would be sad when he decided to take his talents elsewhere, but Coffee, Books, and More was a small store. I was always replacing employees, except for the ones like Toby and my aunt, who lived in South Cove and just wanted a second income to help with bills or to just keep busy.

Emma whined, and I realized I'd stopped walking. Instead, I was staring at the back of my bookstore, thinking about the people in my life now. "Sorry, girl. I was lollygagging. Let's go home and get some lunch."

Josh was sweeping the sidewalk in front of his antique store as I attempted to walk by.

"Miss Gardner. I want to have a little time to chat about the last festival. Those hoodlums who came didn't buy antiques, and I'm sure I lost sales to normal people who would have come to the shop this weekend but didn't due to that music thing." He used the broom to emphasize his words, shooting out his arm each time he wanted to make a point.

"Josh, the entire committee voted to try this festival. If it didn't work, we won't do it again, but it wasn't my decision alone." I tried to move around him, but he blocked my attempt.

"But you are the leader of the group. If you support something, it gets passed. You have a lot of responsibility as well as power in that group. People respect you." Now that I was closer, he was using his finger to make his point. Every time he said the word *you*, he shook his finger at me.

"I understand your feelings. But not all festivals work for every business." That wasn't quite true, but this was Darla's discussion, not mine. "I'll put a slot on the next business meeting for you to talk about your results and ways you think it can be changed to increase your traffic."

"You want me to come up with a solution to my own problem?" He almost dropped the broom.

I smiled and moved around him as he took in the idea. "Exactly. If you complain, you have to bring a workable solution, or there's no complaining."

The idea had come from a childhood under my aunt's raising. If I complained that dinner was too late because she was working, the solution was for me to start cooking dinner before she got home. If I complained about anything, I learned to bring a solution to the problem with it. One that didn't burn me in the process.

As I walked down the street, I saw Keith on a motorcycle in front of city hall. He was smoking a cigarette and staring at the door to the police station. I crossed the street, since I had to anyway, and went over to congratulate him on the new contract. I also wondered if he knew the old one had been terminated. "Keith. Congrats on the win this weekend. I bet everyone's crazy happy about the new contract."

He looked at me like he didn't know who I was, then stood. "Thanks. You're Matt's friend who runs the coffee shop, right?"

"Jill Gardner. And this is Emma." I put my hand on Emma's head and realized she had a low growl going in the back of her throat. Apparently, she didn't like Keith. Or she felt that I didn't like Keith. Which was sort of the same thing. I didn't want him to try to pet her, so I said, "Emma, be nice."

He looked from her to me and then back. "It's good to have a guard dog sometimes. There are bad people in the world."

"I probably know that more than most since my fiancé is the police detective here." I might as well get all the cards on the table, just in case Emma's warning didn't adjust his bad mood. "Emma's just protective. I think after last week's festival, she's a little tired of people."

He smiled, but it didn't reach his eyes. "I know how she feels. Sorry, I'm late for an appointment."

He walked off toward the police station. Emma's growl got louder, causing me to glance around and make sure there wasn't anyone else around. But no, it was just the three of us. She didn't like Keith Jackson one bit. And I didn't blame her. I didn't like the man much myself.

We headed back toward the house, and as I went past the Train Station, my aunt waved at me from inside. I poked my head in the door. "I've got Emma with me, or I'd come in."

"There are no customers. Bring her on in. I'd like to see her." Harrold was at the back counter, working at the register.

My aunt frowned at him, then waved us inside. She met us at the replica of the town of South Cove and the trains that Harrold kept running during the day. At Christmas, he decorated his miniature town with lights and trees. It was fun to watch Santa running through the town on a train caboose rather than in his sleigh. "Jill, did you move the food truck yet? You know if it's not off the lot by five, we'll be ticketed."

"I just finished moving it. Deek helped me get it up to the shop. I was planning on cleaning it after my shift on Tuesday."

She frowned when she heard my plan. "Have one of the staff clean the truck. I want you to look at the projections for next year. I'd like to finalize them by the end of the month."

"Aunt Jackie, it's only May. We typically do that in October." Which I thought was too early. May would be just a guessing game.

"It's just a preliminary discussion in case we're not able to do all the background work in October." She lowered her voice, glancing over to see if Harrold was listening. "It's not binding."

"Why wouldn't we be able to do it in October?" Sometimes you had to be direct with my aunt.

And sometimes, it didn't work anyway.

"Sorry, I've got to go get Harrold's lunch ready. We can talk later."

Emma and I were almost home when I remembered that my aunt's doctor appointment was today. Had they been and were already back? I'd call her Tuesday when I was reviewing the budget she'd made. And if I didn't get an answer, I'd come knocking on her door.

Chapter 14

My phone rang while I was finishing my lunch.

"Jill? Have you gone to Bakerstown yet?" Darla asked.

I glanced at the clock. Ten minutes after twelve. "Good morning, I mean, good afternoon to you as well. No, I haven't gone shopping yet. Do you need me to pick up something?"

"Actually, yes. Can you go to the record company and get the packet there for Atlantis Survivors? Keith called them this morning, and they want someone from the festival committee to pick up the packet so Mayor Baylor can officially present it to the band. I've got the mayor booked for tomorrow at noon for the actual handoff, but I can't get over there to get the paperwork today."

Well, that wasn't what I'd been expecting to be asked to pick up. Cleaning supplies, paper products, groceries, yes. But not the band's new contract. After finding what I had this morning, I figured Keith was a little anxious to get the new contract signed and in force before he lost any more band members.

"I can do that. What time do they close? Is the address on the way or past Bakerstown? I need to get groceries." I put my dishes in the sink and looked around for my shopping list. It had been here yesterday. Greg was going to add some things. I opened the drawer where we kept the notebooks and pens. Bingo, the list was in there. Sometimes Greg's neat freak habits drove me crazy. I was a "leave it out so I'd remember" kind of girl.

"I'll text you the information. Thanks for doing this. The winery is crazy this afternoon. Mondays are usually dead, but I guess a lot of people stayed over from the festival," Darla said, and then she terminated the call.

I met Emma's gaze. "Sorry, girl, I've got to do grocery shopping, and it's too hot out there today for you to stay in the Jeep."

She went over to her bed and lay down, her back to me. A signal that I was not her favorite human right now. I tucked the list into my tote, grabbed my phone and keys, and locked up the house. Three minutes later, I was turning onto the Pacific Coast Highway with my music blaring. The parking lot for the beach was almost empty, and the bandstand had been taken down and the pieces removed. Festivals went up quickly and came down just as fast. Mostly it was because Darla did a great job planning, but there was a lot of manpower there to make it look as effortless as it did.

As I drove, I thought about Axel's death and who would want to kill him. It didn't make any sense that anyone in the band would do it, unless they'd found out that he blew their first contract. But since he was working on getting another one to make up for his mistake, that didn't track. Wouldn't they just take a "sorry, my bad" from the guy? Matt loved being part of a band, even one as dysfunctional as this one. Darla just wanted Matt to be happy. Maybe Jules would be angry enough to kill over a lost contract, but did she have the strength to strangle him?

I thought about the tox screen. Maybe you didn't need strength when someone was that close to being passed out. Could I ask Jules a pointed question that would lead to her slipping up and confessing? The only problem with that was she had to be so dumb that she didn't realize she'd confessed. Otherwise, I'd be the one dead on the coroner's exam table.

And if it was Keith, I'd definitely be dead, just for asking the question. The man was cruel. You could see it in his eyes. And Emma didn't like him. That was enough for me.

I was coming up on the turnoff to Bakerstown, and the recording company's offices were right off the highway. I bet they had a good view of the ocean, like my house did. I turned into the parking lot and turned off the engine. Checking the address again in Darla's text, I realized she'd also sent me a name. Ivan Betters. I finger-combed my hair after the windy ride and headed inside.

There was no one at the reception desk. I called out, "Hello."

No answer. Great. Darla was counting on those papers. I craned my neck to look down the hall. There were three doorways. "Hello?" I called again.

Waited. Still no answer.

I moved down the hallway and knocked on the first door. When there was no response to my knock, I cracked the door a bit. Supply closet. I did the same with the second door. Empty office.

When I reached the last door, I heard sounds. Not voices, but at least it sounded human. Maybe they were listening to a record and hadn't heard me come in.

I knocked. No answer. I leaned closer, trying to hear something. There was definitely music playing. I knocked again. I didn't want to go back to South Cove empty-handed. Darla would never let me live it down. Finally, I cracked the door open and saw an arm. There was someone in the office. I opened the door wider and said, "Sorry, I'm Jill Gardner..."

I didn't get the rest of the words out before I realized the arm I'd seen was attached to a man, wrapped around a pretty blonde. They were in the middle of an intense make-out session, and as my jaw dropped, I stepped back away from the door. I didn't want to see more, just in case they were further into the act than just making out. "Sorry."

"I'll be right out," a woman's voice called out to me, and I turned and hurried back to the waiting room.

When she came out, she looked exceptionally put together for someone who had just been playing footsie with her entire body. She kept her gaze down. "Can I help you?"

"I'm Jill Gardner. Sorry, I said that already. I'm here to see Ivan Betters. I'm from South Cove. I need to pick up some papers." I didn't know why I was embarrassed. I wasn't the one who hadn't been manning the reception desk.

"I'll let him know you're here." She picked up the phone and used the intercom. "Ivan, the rep from South Cove is here to pick up the contract."

She listened and then hung up. She looked at me. Her lipstick was bleeding onto her cheek. "He'll be right out."

"Great." I stood there, waiting. I couldn't look at her. I wanted to tell her about her lipstick, but then it would bring up that embarrassing incident. I just wanted to pick up the packet and get out of there.

A noise sounded, and I turned to find a man standing there, holding an envelope. "Here you go. Darla said you'd be here this afternoon. We've signed. Your mayor or city council chair needs to sign as a formality on the contest, and then the band's rep signs the rest. Keith can drop the contract off any weekday between nine and four."

"I'll let him know." I took the envelope and put it in my tote. "Thanks for supporting South Cove's Moonstone Beach Battle of the Bands. We appreciate it."

"No problem. I'd do anything for Matt. I worked for the first record company that signed him. It was too bad he, well, couldn't keep it together. Darla's good for him. He's a changed man."

I watched as he walked back down the hall. The receptionist had reapplied her lipstick, so now she didn't look like her mouth was too large. When I didn't leave, she looked up from her computer.

"Anything else I can help you with?"

I shook my head. "Sorry. I'll get out of your hair."

When I reached the Jeep, I opened the packet and saw a note on the front. I read it to myself.

Matty, so glad you won. I would have hated to work with anyone else. Sorry about Axel, but we all know he was a tool. Someone must have gotten tired of his crap. See you in the studio soon. Call me to set up a recording time. Ivan.

I tucked the paperwork back into the package. How close was the music industry? This guy had worked with Matt before. I didn't want to think it, but had there been some way for Darla to ensure that Matt's band won?

Now I had too many questions in my head and no way to figure out the answers besides alienating one of my best friends by asking her directly. And if she had, Tina would find out, and Darla's head would be on a platter.

Turning the car back toward the highway, I continued my trip to Bakerstown. I needed to clear my thoughts before I saw anyone I knew. Especially Darla, or worse, Greg. I wasn't good at hiding what I was thinking.

The lines at the grocery store were long, and I had to stop at the house to put away the groceries before I went to the winery to drop off the contract. I decided to take Emma on the walk into town, giving me a good excuse not to sit and chat. I'd hate to upset Darla again, especially now that I had even more questions about Matt's involvement in Axel's death. But it couldn't be true. Matt was a sweet man. He'd come to South Cove out of a work-study type program where the state had covered his paycheck for two months. He'd worked hard for Darla during that time, so when it came time for his state-sponsored program to end, he and several others who'd worked at different places in South Cove, including the bookstore, got real jobs at their internship program.

I'd tried to sign the town up for a second round of interns, but the regulations had said we'd have to wait a year before applying again. By that time, the program had been shut down. Even with the success stories that came out of giving people an opportunity to get work experience without having to find a job to hire them. Now my issue was not so much finding part-time employees but having enough hours to move as many as possible from part-time to full-time without giving up my shift.

Emma paused at some of our usual stops. First, the Train Station, but I pulled on her leash. The shop was already closed for the afternoon. Maybe Aunt Jackie and Harrold were at her doctor appointment. I'd call her in the morning. The next stop Emma made was at the sidewalk leading to Diamond Lille's. Which reminded me I hadn't eaten since breakfast. But I also hadn't made a to-go order, and Emma wasn't allowed inside. I glanced at my watch. Almost three. I'd make a sandwich when I got back to the house. And maybe some soup.

When we reached city hall, Emma paused again. Apparently, I had several places I frequently visited, and I was totally confusing my dog. Greg's truck wasn't in the parking lot, but Tina's Escalade was. I didn't need to visit Amy bad enough to risk a run-in with Tina. "Come on, girl, let's keep walking. We're going to visit Darla."

She started walking and only looked back twice at the police station entrance. It seemed that my dog was missing Greg as much as I was.

We passed Coffee, Books, and More, but we were on the other side of the street. Emma didn't pause, but she kept looking at me and then at the shop. I wondered if I would send her with notes attached to her collar if she'd be able to deliver messages to several places in town. I could just sit back in the swing on the porch and read while I waited for her return with their answer.

Or I could just call or text.

That would probably be safer for my dog. We walked up the hill to the winery. From Darla's outdoor decks on each side of the building, you could see the ocean. I loved where I lived. Even with its traffic and overcrowding and expensive houses. Not to mention the possibility of an earthquake, and my house would slide into the ocean. But before that happened, I was going to enjoy every day I was given here in this paradise.

The hostess at the outdoor stand greeted me. "I've got the perfect spot for you and your dog. Corner next to the railing, so she can stretch out."

"Actually, I'm here to see Darla. I need to drop something off." I tapped my tote.

"Oh, are you Jill? She's been expecting you." The hostess looked behind me and greeted a couple who'd walked up after me. "I'll be right with you. Jill, go ahead and go around the path. She's on the back patio with Matt and some friends celebrating."

"Okay, thanks." I tugged on Emma's leash, and we stepped back around to the path. Darla couldn't pick up the package because she was celebrating? Okay, now I felt used. I took a deep breath and decided to hold my emotions until I heard Darla's explanation. Maybe she had been stuck at the winery until just now, and if she'd gone later, the place would have been closed. The people there didn't seem too busy with business, just romance.

I climbed the stairs and saw the table where Darla and Matt were sitting. With all the bandmates: Jules, Eddie, Mick, and Keith. My favorite person, not. I tried to wave to get Darla's attention, but when that didn't work, I walked Emma through the crowd of people and pulled out the contract from my tote to hand to Darla. Jules was the first to see it on the table, and she squealed.

"Is that what I think it is?" She ripped it out of my hand and pulled out the papers. Emma growled by my side, but she sat and watched for my reaction. My dog didn't like it when I was upset.

"Darla, I got your contract since you were too busy to pick it up." I stared at my friend.

To her credit, she blushed. But Matt was the one who came to her defense.

"Sorry, Jill, I know this looks bad, but Darla just sat down. Our day manager needed the day off, and she just showed up to do the evening shift. Darla's been running since six this morning." Matt stood and met my gaze. "Thank you so much for helping out. We all appreciate it."

Okay, now I felt like a witch. "No problem, I was going into Bakerstown anyway. Your new record company is pretty small. There were only two people there when I stopped by." I petted Emma's head to calm her down since she didn't understand the apology. I tried to keep the snark out of my voice when I added, "They were busy."

"Uh-oh. Ivan and Alicia were probably making out in the back." Matt snuck a look at Darla. "Maybe I should have gone. I'm sure those two weren't the most discreet. Of course, since she's married to a biker, I suppose it's the only place they can be certain their affair isn't found out."

I blew out a frustrated breath. "Everyone knows about it? Why doesn't she just get a divorce and go on with her life? And not embarrass random people who have to see it."

Everyone looked at me. Great, now I was being judgmental. I really needed to go home and have some Jill time where I wasn't opening my mouth.

Matt laughed. "You're right. They should just go on with their lives. I guess we're all just so jaded, it doesn't seem like a big deal. Now I really feel bad that you went to pick up the contract. Can I buy you a beer for your trouble? Or a glass of wine? You must be beat after the long hours this weekend."

"I'm fine. I've got to get Emma home. She's been cooped up all weekend, so I'm trying to make it up to her before I have to go back to work tomorrow."

I turned to go but then stopped. "Congratulations on the new contract. It must be especially nice to have one again since Axel tanked your last one."

I stepped away from the table but not before I heard Jules ask, "What is she talking about? The four-song contract was terminated? When were you going to tell us, Keith?"

Uh-oh. Maybe not everyone knew that piece of information. I hurried off the deck and out to the road. I pulled out my phone and called Greg. When he answered, I said, "I think I messed up."

"Jill, are you all right? Where are you?"

"I'm fine. I just said something that I probably shouldn't have. But I found out something. Jules didn't know about the terminated contract." I went on to tell him where I'd been and what I'd said.

"Well, yeah, that was something I was trying to use in my interviews, but it was bound to come out anyway. Did you say how you knew?"

"No. I was congratulating them on the new contract and should have shut my mouth then. But I blurted that Axel had tanked the first one. Jules asked Keith what I was talking about as Emma and I left the winery. I didn't stay around to hear his answer."

"I'm glad you have Emma with you. Go home. I'll be late, so don't worry about making a big dinner. Maybe Amy can meet you at Lille's."

I brightened at the thought. "I'm starving. That's a great idea. I wonder when she can get off."

We said our goodbyes, and I felt better about the screwup at the winery. Besides, they should have already known. The contract had been terminated almost a month ago. Sometimes, I needed to think before I spoke though.

When I went past the police station, Toby was standing outside. He met me on the sidewalk and took Emma's leash.

"What are you doing?" I thought I knew the answer, but I'd let him tell me.

"Greg asked me to walk home with you. Just in case." He glanced back toward where I'd come from. "No one followed you from the winery?"

"Not a one. Although I might have ruined their party." I fell into step with Toby. "I didn't mean to spill the beans. Shouldn't they have all known by now?"

"You'd think." He fake slugged me on the arm. "Now, you've been properly punished for the slipup. Feel better?"

I rubbed my shoulder. Even a faked pop from Toby hurt a little. The man didn't know his own strength at times. "A little. I was ticked off that Darla sent me on this errand because she was so busy; then I catch her drinking with the band. And I had to see these people making out in the office because she's still married."

Toby paused and looked at me. "I think you need to tell me that story."

As we headed home, I told him about the record company and Matt's explanation. It felt good to share the story with someone else. Someone I knew didn't have a vested interest in the situation. Just my feelings about it.

Chapter 15

Amy had been busy for dinner, so I'd made myself an egg dish I loved and turned on the television to find a rom-com. Now, the next morning, I was still starving. I poured a bowl of cereal and opened my new planner to check out the week. I should write in it the days that I didn't think I'd see Greg so I could figure out dinner plans. Except I never knew when he'd be free. Amy and Justin were painting their new house this week, so she wouldn't be available all week.

Darla was busy with Matt and the band things as well as running her own business that typically kept her busy at night.

And Esmeralda was in New Orleans. Evie worked nights at the coffee shop.

I was running out of friends to call to have a quick dinner with. I looked at Emma, who was watching me eat. "I guess it's you and me this week then, girl."

I could go running. Then either spend the evening watching television, or reading, or working on a review for Deek's newsletter. Or maybe I'd head into the city and see if any of my old friends wanted to get together for dinner or a coffee. I scrolled through my contacts. I hadn't reached out to many of these people for months. Maybe even longer.

I was a horrible friend. If you weren't in my daily radius, I forgot you even existed.

I glanced at the clock. I needed to open the shop. Aunt Jackie wanted me to review next year's financial goals. Then I'd call her and see if she'd meet me at Lille's for lunch. I knew she liked to eat dinner with her newish husband, but I was related to her. She could make time to have lunch with me.

With at least one of my meals for the week planned, I finished my breakfast and texted my aunt to meet me at Lille's at one. That way, I'd have the accounting review done and would use that as an excuse to have some face-to-face time. And I'd ask her about the doctor appointment.

There. I felt better about at least covering my family duties all in one swipe. I'd work on my extended friends later in the week. I wrote a note in my planner to call and make plans tomorrow with one person who I knew was still in town. And, I realized, Greg had made a date with me for tomorrow. This planner Greg bought me was making me a better person.

Who knew planning my life could be so fun?

My good mood vanished when I got to the shop. Darla sat at one of the café tables outside, waiting for me. She tucked her phone into her purse and stood as soon as she saw me walking up the street.

"Look, I wanted to explain about yesterday. What Matt said was true. Sandy wasn't supposed to show up until five to take over, but she got her running around done early. I really thought I wouldn't have time to get to the record company before it closed. And I didn't know about Ivan and his receptionist. Seriously, you know I would have told you if I had any clue. I guess it's been going on for years now."

I opened the door and waved her in. "I sounded judgmental and awful yesterday. I didn't mean either of them. I was happy to run your errand for you. It was a business-to-business event and not just your responsibility. I was just tired after a long weekend."

"So we're good? You don't hate me?" Darla climbed onto a stool.

"We're fine. And no, this doesn't affect our relationship. I was just in a bad mood yesterday. You got the brunt of it." I started the coffeepots and turned on more lights. "What can I get for you? Or did you stop by just to see me?"

"I'd love a skinny mocha." Darla pulled out a to-do list. "I've got to gird my loins before I head over to city hall to have Mayor Baylor sign the contract. I'm sure Tina's going to have a few choice words for me."

"If Matt's band won fair and square, there's nothing she can say." I made her coffee.

Darla squirmed on the stool.

I narrowed my eyes. "It was all fair, right?"

"Mostly. I mean, I knew the bands they were going against. None of them were as strong as Matt's. I didn't cull people out because they were good. I think the good bands felt our festival wasn't 'prestigious' enough for them to even submit. So the band did have an edge over the other ones." She took the coffee and took a sip. "Matt helped, and we sent flyers to all the local bars where bands play, the music stores, even the other record companies. These were the bands we got."

"Hansel had an up because he was Tina's nephew. Everyone had the same chance. Did the fact that he lost his singer to Matt's band hurt him?"

Darla shrugged. "Tina will say so, but this new guy he has, he's great too. And Mick was already looking to join Atlantis Survivors. He'd asked Axel several times, but Axel didn't want to step into the background."

"Maybe Matt's band just got all the luck cards thrown at them." I handed Darla a cookie and took one for myself. "You can't control that. You're not related to Matt, although I think you're getting close. And even if you were, you weren't judging the competition."

"True. I picked judges that I thought would be totally impartial." She glanced over her shoulder at the door. "So if Tina tries to boot me from the events coordinator position?"

"Are you paid for the position?"

Darla laughed as she broke the cookie in two. "Not a dime."

"Then Tina has no power over you. I'm the business-to-business coordinator. She can get the mayor to ask the council to fire me, but I'm not sure anyone else will take the job." I waved away the credit card that Darla held out to me. "This is on the house. We had some chatting to do."

"Oh, I wanted to ask, how did you know about Axel and the other contract? Keith said he'd just found out last week that Axel had missed his deadlines." She slipped off the stool, adjusting her tote strap over her shoulder.

"I thought I heard someone talking about it. You know how crazy it was this weekend. I'm pretty sure that must have been it. The festival was a blur." I tried to dodge the question since Greg wasn't happy about me dropping that piece of information into his suspect pool.

"It *was* crazy. Shoot me if I ever come to the council with an idea like this again. Of course, all the bands want to know is how do they sign up for next year." Darla turned toward the door to leave.

"Are you going to be able to offer such a great prize?" I called after her.

She turned and shrugged. "Probably. There are a lot of record companies around desperate to find the next big thing. This way, we do all the vetting for them, and they just have to deal with one band. And if the band doesn't fulfill the contract in six months, they don't have to put out the record. At least that's how Ivan set up the first contract. I think I'll use the verbiage as the basis for the next one. That way I don't have to get South Cove's lawyer involved again. You wouldn't believe what he charged to review the contract."

As a prior attorney, I had a clue. Especially since the city's lawyer was a friend of the mayor. He probably charged at the high end of the scale, and the mayor probably got a kickback for using him. Mayor Baylor never did anything that didn't first line his own pocketbook. Watching Darla leave the shop, I realized, except for the slipup on the contract termination, Darla hadn't asked me anything about the murder and who Greg was looking at as a possible suspect. Either she finally realized that Greg didn't tell me things about active investigations, or she was too distracted about the just-completed festival.

There was a third alternative that I didn't want to even consider. But it flashed into my head anyway. Darla didn't ask about the murder because she already knew who had killed Axel and why. My commuters started coming into the shop and distracted me from that third answer. But it still haunted me.

When Toby and Tilly showed up within a few minutes of each other, I asked Toby to take the floor while I went through the training.

As we were sitting down in the back to go over the paperwork, she met my gaze. "So that's the guy who claims to know me?"

I nodded. The first meeting had been quick, and I'd seen the confusion on Toby's face when she introduced herself. "That's Toby Killian. Are you sure you don't recognize him?"

She shook her head. "Not at all. And believe me, if I'd dated someone who looked like him, I'd remember. He's a fox."

I put the question aside and started going through her hiring packet. When I was done, I handed her a W-4. "So if you're still interested in the job, this is the last form I need. Sign it, and you'll be official."

"I'm really excited to be part of your team. I was hoping, but I didn't think you'd hire until you lost someone. And from what I've been seeing, people don't leave here unless they move or get a better job. Even then, like the guy out there, they still stay on part-time." She signed the form and handed it back to me.

"Actually, Toby was a police officer first. He was my first official employee, not counting my aunt and me." I smiled as I remembered how mad I'd been when I found out that my aunt had hired someone when she was just supposed to be minding the store. She took over a lot of the day-to-day tasks that I didn't even realize I needed to do. "So let's start with the book inventory process and software. I upgraded it last year."

By the time my shift was over, I had gone through most of the training she'd missed by being here only as a temporary staff position. I put her on the coffee bar and pulled Toby aside, and we went to the back office. "Just wanted to check in with you. Are you okay?"

"She really doesn't remember me." He sank on the edge of the desk. "It was one of the most intense relationships of my life, and she's totally forgotten."

"You were young." I felt bad for the guy. "I mean this in a good way, but maybe you imagined it?"

He laughed and nodded to the door leading to the shop. "Not hardly. We went to prom together. I have my yearbooks in a box in the shed. I'm getting them out this evening just to check my memory. Especially since you pointed out my possible brain tumor."

"I didn't say you had a brain tumor." I handed him a cookie. Cookies always soothed away pain. "Is it going to be weird between you two?"

He took the cookie, eating it in three bites. Toby had all the markings of a professional stress eater, just like me. No wonder we were friends. "I'll be fine. My pride is a little bruised, but I hear from Deek she has a boyfriend, so I'll be totally professional. She looks good though. Kind of like I'd imagined she'd look when she got older. I mean, when I thought about her."

"You're such a softie. I'm here if you need to talk. I need to go over my aunt's next year's projections, so I'll be back here for an hour or two. And if it gets slow, can you clean out the food truck?" I pointed to the rack by the door. "The keys are there."

"Sure. It will get me out of the shop so I don't have to make stupid small talk with Tilly." He glanced at the schedule. "This is the last day I'm working until Friday when Deek does his author thing. I've warned Greg about the increased amount of traffic that night."

"Deek's borrowed the community center van, and we'll be shuttling people up from the beach parking lot once the city hall parking and street parking are full. Or if people just want to park at the beach." I turned on the desktop and went to find the file. My aunt had sent me a link, so it shouldn't be hard to find. As I waited for the spreadsheet to load, I watched Toby as he got out more cheesecakes for the front. "You're sure you're okay with this? I'd hate to fire her after a week because you can't deal with it."

He smiled one of his patented Toby smiles. The one that all the customers loved. At least the female ones. "Jill, I'm a rock. Don't worry about me. This is fine."

As he walked out of the office and back to the front, tossing the keys to the food truck in his hand, I wondered if he was trying to fool me or just himself. Either way, his heart was going to take a beating before this was over. Darkest before dawn, as the saying went.

I opened a notebook and went through the projections. When I finished, I called my aunt. "Hey, I'm about ready to leave so we can meet for lunch and talk about these projections."

My aunt countered quickly. "I can come down there. No need for a lunch."

"No, I want to have lunch with you. We haven't had time to chat in ages. And I need to ask you some questions."

I heard a pause, and it went on just a few seconds too long. Finally, she sighed. Long and loud. "I'll meet you at Lille's in ten minutes. Unless you need more time to get here."

"Ten minutes will be perfect." I sent the attachment to my email, then opened my laptop to download it. I didn't know if we'd need to look at the actual numbers, but I had a half a page of questions. Which was great. Last year I would have had two pages. Had I told my aunt I was going back to school in the fall?

I turned off the computer and tucked my laptop into my tote along with a couple of ARCs I'd snagged off the table. Deck put all the ARCs out on a back table for staff to pick and choose. I think he must take the ones that weren't picked by other staff members, because by the end of the week, the table was empty. Every book deserved at least the chance to make a good impression.

I said goodbye to Tilly and then went out back to say goodbye to Toby. He was in the food truck, cleaning the coffee bar. Music played in the background, and I knocked on the door before entering. "Hey, Toby? I'm out of here."

He wiped his cheeks with the back of his hand. "I'll see you Friday then."

"You don't have to always be the strong one, you know." I walked over and gave him a hug. "Girls like the strong, sensitive type."

He snorted. "Sure, women go ape over crying men. We're in high demand. I'll be fine. It was just seeing her and knowing she didn't know me from Adam."

"Sensitive men are few and far between." I wanted to sit and talk, but I was already late for lunch with my aunt. "I'll probably be home tonight with Emma if you want to talk."

"Greg's got me on nights this week." He smiled. This time, it looked more real. "I'll be fine. I've gotten along without her for years. I'm not sure why I'm feeling like we just broke up. Again."

"The heart is a funny thing." I squeezed his shoulder. "Seriously, if it's slow, call me. You don't have to be alone in dealing with this."

"You're sweet, but I'm already over it." He took a deep breath. "Or at least I will be when I finish cleaning this truck. What did you do this weekend, hold a frat party in here? It's filthy."

"You know I use this for my personal two a.m. after-party truck. That way Greg will never be the wiser." I paused at the door. "Be good to yourself."

"I always am." He winked at me as I left the trailer and headed toward Diamond Lille's. Toby's love life was always interesting, but this twist had stuck a knife in the guy's ribs. I just hoped he would figure out a way to get over it as fast as he thought he could. I found love to be a tricky problem without an easy solution when it was unrequited.

Chapter 16

Aunt Jackie was already in a booth and talking to Lille when I walked in the door. She waved me over, and Lille turned and glared at me. Then she left the booth and went back to the front, going around the opposite side of the restaurant. Like I said before, she hated me. I wasn't sure what I'd done to her except open the coffee shop, but the truth was the truth.

I leaned down and gave my aunt a kiss on the cheek. "Glad you could get away for lunch. We're both so busy anymore I hardly see you. How's Lille?"

Aunt Jackie smirked. "I don't know what's going on with you two girls, but you really should bury the hatchet. You're a lot alike. I'm sure you'd be good friends if you just tried."

"Honestly, I'm just trying to not get banned from the diner. Friendship is a lofty goal." I glanced over the menu. With the weekend being so crazy, I wanted fish and chips. However, since I'd mainlined them during the festival, I decided to go with the California Cobb salad instead. With iced tea. If I had an ice cream craving at home, I had some tucked away from yesterday's shopping trip. I set the menu aside. "So how did your doctor appointment go? Did you get back results of your tests?"

Her eyes widened. Maybe I'd been a little too direct, but I wanted to know. Actually, I needed to know. My aunt was my only family. Not counting Greg. And Emma. And Amy and Darla and Esmeralda. Okay, so the last three were friends, one was a dog, and Greg wasn't family, quite yet. But he would be.

She set down her menu and patted it with her hand. "I guess I better just say it. They did a biopsy on a lump in my breast. I'm waiting for the results."

I blinked. Once, twice, three times. Finally, my words worked. "You have cancer?"

"I might have cancer, dear. The biopsy results will show that. Harrold's been worried since I lost a few pounds last month, but my appetite wasn't really good. Now that the biopsy is done, once we get the results, we can deal with what happens." She tapped the menu again with her soft red nail. "As of right now, I'm fine. And don't you be freaking out. I'll tell you as soon as the results are in."

"You didn't even tell me you found a lump." I choked back tears. This was not what I'd been expecting. I wasn't sure what I'd been expecting, but not this. Definitely not this.

"This is why I didn't want you to know until after the biopsy results were in. I told Harrold that, but he disagreed. Now you get to worry with me." She smiled up at Carrie. "I'm going to have the fish and chips. Jill says they're very good."

Carrie laughed. "Jill should know. She eats more fish and chips than anyone who comes into the diner. Maybe there are others somewhere else who eat more, but not here. She's the reigning queen."

She turned to me and asked, "So milkshake or iced tea to go with yours?"

"Maybe I was going to eat healthy today?"

Carrie and Aunt Jackie both stared at me.

Finally, Carrie broke the ice. "So are you eating healthy today?"

"I was." I stared at Aunt Jackie. "But I've decided to live today and worry about the calories tomorrow. I'll have the same with an unsweetened iced tea."

"Sounds great. You scared me for a minute there. I thought maybe you were sick." Carrie tucked her pen behind her ear and put the order pad in her pocket. "I'll be right back with your drinks. I know it's a normal Tuesday, but it seems so slow after this weekend. It's like the 'house that was too little' story."

As she walked away, I looked at my aunt. "Do you know what she's talking about?"

"It's an Aesop fable. At least I think it is. It's old, anyway."

She took the tea from Carrie when she came back, and took a sip. After Carrie left to attend to the next table, Aunt Jackie started telling the story.

"Anyway, there was this older couple who was sharing their hut with the son, his wife, and new baby. The hut was small and crowded. So the wife sent her husband to the wise man of the village."

"Why is it always a wise man? Weren't there wise women back then?" I sipped my tea, watching her.

"Just listen. Anyway, he went for a solution. The wise man said, 'Bring in your goats. That will make the house bigger.' The man didn't see how this was possible, but his wife convinced him to follow the wise man's words.

Then they added the cows. Then the chickens. And finally, the wise man told him to add in the pigs." My aunt took another sip.

"So the entire barn is in this house with the five people. Or four with a baby."

"Now the baby was getting almost stepped on. The goats and the cows were always getting into the cupboards. It was chaotic. The man went back and explained how awful the conditions were to the wise man. He nodded and told them to take all the animals and send them back to the barn."

"Which gave them their house back." I ended the story.

My aunt shrugged. "Almost. They cleaned and scrubbed and then made dinner. After dinner, the baby was playing on the floor, the son was reading, the wife knitting, and as she washed and put away the dishes, the old lady looked over at the husband and said, the house has grown. The wise man knew exactly what he was saying."

"And the moral of the story? I'm trying to figure it out, but I'm lost with the cows being in the house." I leaned back as a server set two orders of fish and chips with tartar and cocktail sauce on the table.

"The moral of the story is to be happy with what you have. It can always be worse." Aunt Jackie sprinkled malt vinegar over her food and handed the bottle to me.

We'd had a matching bottle in the cupboard all the years I'd lived with her. And somehow, I never noticed she loved fish and chips as much as I did. I took the bottle and sprinkled it over my fish and fries. Then I took the salt from her and did the same. "Okay, I'll be happy for today. Do you want to chat about the report you did or about your next vacation?"

"Did you have questions or changes?" She took a bite of the flaky fish and sighed. "Tiny is a South Cove treasure. I was telling Lille that just now."

"I'll agree with that. On the report, I think you're underestimating the revenue from the author signings that Deek's bringing in. Our profits from that part of our total sales have increased year over year since Deek has been involved with the planning." I grabbed some fries and realized she was staring at me. "What? Do I have ketchup on my face?"

"No, I just didn't realize I'd missed that." She didn't look up from her food when she said, "Good catch."

"Thanks. There's a few other tweaks I'd like to suggest." I took out my notebook and went down the list of things I'd noticed and my solutions.

"Is that all written down?" Aunt Jackie nodded at my notebook.

I handed it to her. "Of course. I took notes as I reviewed the document."

She ripped out the page and handed me the notebook back. "I'll make the revisions, and then we'll file this until October. We might have some new ideas then."

I didn't mention that I had already said we were working on it too soon. She'd taken my suggestions seriously. I guessed I should quit while I was ahead. "Oh, I'm going back to school this fall to finish up, so I'll be in class twice a week during fall and spring and one class during the summer, if I need it."

"Greg's okay with you being gone so much?"

Now I was going to get the "take care of your man" lecture. "He's busy too. So I'm either alone at home and reading at night or at school and reading class material at night."

"True. You both live such busy lives. I'm surprised you ever get away for a week or weekend. I'm guessing he's busy with this investigation now."

I was surprised she'd dropped the argument that fast. She was mellowing. "Yeah, he's always busy when there's an investigation going on. Which is another reason I want to get this degree done and finished. That way when we do have time to take a trip, I'm not holding us back due to an upcoming test or homework."

"Sounds reasonable." She ate one last fry, then pushed the basket away. "Was there anything else you needed my advice on? How's Toby doing knowing he's not the center of the universe?"

"That's not funny. He's fine. She really doesn't remember him, but he's certain it's the same woman. Can you forget a part of your life that completely?"

"We're sure she's not just messing with him?"

I shrugged. "Maybe. But she genuinely looked like she had no clue who he was when they met this morning. I guess she could be an amazing actress, but her resume doesn't show anything like that."

"Just keep an eye on it. Did you check the high schools they put on the applications? Maybe that's your first clue in seeing who's telling the truth." My aunt glanced at her watch. "Sorry, I told Harrold we could run to town this afternoon. He needs to pick up some train parts for the store."

"Go ahead. I'll get this. I asked you to meet me for lunch." I pulled out my purse.

She touched my hand. "Use the business credit card, dear. We spent most of the meal talking about the shop and its future. You need to keep the receipt for taxes though."

I nodded, and she stood, leaning over to give me a kiss on the cheek. "Tell Harrold I said hello."

"This was lovely. Thanks for suggesting it. And I'll call you as soon as I hear. They said Friday." My aunt wiped a spot of lipstick off my cheek like I was a child.

"I'll be thinking good thoughts." I watched as she made her way out of the diner.

She stopped and greeted people here and there, but when she got outside, I saw her pause for a second. She took a breath, then lifted her shoulders and walked away. She was more worried than she let on. But I hadn't been lying when I said I'd be thinking positive thoughts. I was going to bathe her in a golden meditation light every day for a few hours a day until I heard the news. It might not do anything, but it was all I could do while we waited.

Carrie came over with the bill and a vanilla milkshake to go. "Everything okay with your aunt? She seemed nicer today."

I put a straw into the cup. "I'd argue, but you're right. She was nicer today."

Carrie took the credit card I handed her and put it with the bill. "Just remember, you're both part of the South Cove community. So if there is anything you need, we're here for you."

"Thanks, Carrie. I appreciate that, and I'm sure Jackie would too." I put on my imitation of Toby's winning smile and continued. "Right now, everything's fine. But if we need something, I'll let you know."

I waited for my card and receipt. I'd throw it in the box I used for possible tax deductions that was in the office. It would stay there until tax time, when I'd try to remember what it was for. Maybe this time I'd take a half second and write on the back. It would save me hours of research later.

As I wrote on the back of the receipt who was at our meeting and what we talked about, I stayed in my booth. When I looked up, a man in an upscale suit stood at the doorway, talking to Lille. She laughed at something he'd said, and then she pointed to a booth by the windows where Keith sat, watching the exchange. He didn't look happy to see this guy in South Cove at all.

I tried to map out an exit route that would take me past these guys, but short of me going into the kitchen to chat up Tiny, there wasn't a valid reason for me to be walking next to their table since I was between them and the door. I could, however, get a snapshot for Greg. If he ever came home.

I fluffed my hair like I was taking a selfie, aimed the camera toward the men, and got out of the frame. I snapped several, just in case they didn't turn out.

Carrie paused at the table. "I can take a picture if you need it."

"No, I'm good, but thanks." I glanced at my phone like I was checking the photo. Which I was, but for an entirely different reason.

I got my tote and put away my phone and the notebook I'd gotten out earlier. My aunt had approved my suggestions for next year's plan. Or pretended to. Sometimes I felt like she just let me think I got my way and did what she wanted anyway. Now, with an MBA under my belt in about a year, at least I'd know when she was snowing me.

Or at least I hoped so. I headed home. I'd read for a couple of hours and let my food settle, then take Emma for a run. Greg hadn't banned me from the beach, yet. I had a feeling it might be coming. When he was working on a case, he didn't like me on an open, lonely beach with just Emma for protection. My dog was good, but she couldn't dial 911 if something happened to me.

Besides, I had some things to work out, and I thought better when I was running. As I waited, I threw in a load of laundry. Now, I just had to remember to move it to the dryer. I couldn't count the number of times I threw in laundry, then forgot about it until I decided to wash something else. So then I had to rewash the load I'd forgotten.

I opened the planner and put a note on today's list. Load in washer. Maybe that would help. Having accomplished one thing, I decided to work on the review I owed Deek for the newsletter. I opened my laptop and checked my email. Then I remembered the photo. Maybe I could do a reverse search to find out who Keith had been having lunch with. It was probably no one, but it didn't hurt to look.

I had to find the right site to do a search without giving them my credit card or being charged for the service. Then I uploaded the picture. In less than a minute, I had my results. From left to right, this was Keith Jackson and Dakota Miles.

Okay, that didn't tell me much. Who was Dakota Miles? I put his name into the search engine and found out he was a record producer for Salt Water Productions. Was that the contract that Axel had blown?

I found the pictures of the letters. Nope, it wasn't the same record company. Why would Keith be lunching with a record company that wasn't the one that the band had a contract with? Did Keith manage a second band? Did people do that? Like agents?

There were a lot more questions than answers running through my head, so I wrote them all down on my notebook. Emma nudged my foot. I'd been down the internet search rabbit hole for over two hours. I closed the laptop and went to change out the laundry to the dryer. As I grabbed her leash, I crossed off the to-do item on the wash and went to change my shoes so I could run.

When I got back, I'd cross off one more thing, my run with Emma. I was getting the hang of this planner life.

* * * *

The run was just what I needed. I stretched out at the stairs while Emma barked at the few seagulls who dared to return to their walks along the shore after she'd chased them away. We all had our habits and distractions. For the gulls, it was people and dogs like Emma. For Emma, it was her owner, who decided to do other things than just hanging out or running. For me, it was the shop, my aunt, my friends, Greg, and now, this investigation on who killed Axel. I knew I shouldn't be digging into the players' lives, but I was worried about my friend.

Darla was vulnerable. Before Matt, I hadn't seen her with anyone for more than a few dates. Now, he worked with her, and they were living together. He was a charmer. He was really good-looking. And now, he had a band that would be putting out a record. Would he be able to be Darla's Matt when the chips were down? He'd been touring with the band for the last six months, and they hadn't had problems. But what if the band exploded, and they became famous? Would he still be sweet Matt who helped Darla run the winery? Would he take their relationship to the next level?

I leaned into my hamstring stretch. And honestly, was it any of my business? I was already pushing my opinions and nose into Sadie's relationship with Pastor Bill. Now, I was questioning Matt's love for Darla?

I glanced at the ring on my left hand. Greg and I were good. We were moving to the next step in our own relationship. Was that what was getting me involved in my friends' lives?

I decided to stop thinking about Darla and Matt, Sadie and Pastor Bill, and most of all, about Axel's murder. I had my own life and problems to deal with. And as Greg told me many times, I wasn't an investigator. Nor was I a relationship coach.

I called Emma to my side, and we headed home to either make dinner or pull out a quart of ice cream. I was leaning toward the ice cream. When we got home, someone was sitting on the porch stairs waiting for me.

I opened the gate, and Matt stood up to greet Emma. He knew well enough that if he didn't stand, Emma would knock him over with her enthusiasm to see him.

"Matt, what are you doing here?"

He had one hand on Emma's head and the other tucked into his shorts. "Jill, I need your help. I think Greg's going to arrest me for killing Axel."

Chapter 17

We went inside, and I poured iced tea for both of us. I had a towel wrapped around my neck since I was still sweating from my run. He sat as far away from me as possible. "Sorry if I'm a little ripe. It was hot out there."

"Oh, no. You smell fine. I mean, it's not offensive. I just like to put a little bit of space between me and any female I'm chatting with. It makes Darla feel a little better, especially since I'm on the road so much. It's stupid, I know. If I were going to cheat, it would happen. But she's a little insecure due to some past relationships, so I try to be conscious of my physical presence." He blushed a bit and reached down where Emma sat by his knee.

"I think it's sweet. I'm sure your new occupation has a lot of relationship minefields." I'd never dated a rock star, but I'd had a few boyfriends who liked having attention from other women. And it had made me a little unsure about where we stood. "So, why do you think Greg is going to arrest you? Did you kill Axel?"

"No. I threatened to kill him several times. The last concert we played, at the after-party, I got a Coke, and he slipped vodka into it. Like I wouldn't notice. I've been clean and sober for five years now. I still remember what alcohol tastes like. Anyway, I confronted him about it, and he told me I needed to loosen up, that it was affecting my playing, my being sober." He leaned his head into his hands. "I've never wanted to punch someone so hard and so many times. He just knew how to get under my skin, you know?"

"A fight isn't going to point the finger at you without any other evidence." I sipped my iced tea. "And from what I'm hearing, you're not the only one who wanted to punch Axel."

"True, he had a very punchable face and a lot of enemies." Matt relaxed back in his chair. His hand hadn't left Emma's head. "So you really think Greg isn't going to arrest me?"

"If you killed Axel, then yes. But I don't think you killed him. Even accidentally, or you wouldn't be in my house. And Emma agrees." I smiled at my dog. "How's Darla handling all this? I talked to her this morning, but I wasn't sure how she was doing."

"She's trying to keep busy with other things. Like finalizing our contract with the city and the record company. I can't believe how much energy she's put into this project. She convinced Ivan to put up the contract, then all of you guys to hold the festival. I swear I'm taking her on a week vacation in the mountains to decompress as soon as this is all tied up. She's amazing." This time, his smile reached his eyes, and I could tell there were real feelings there.

Esmerelda was always telling me I had a gift. Maybe my talent was reading emotions like Deek read auras. At least the universe had sent an answer to one of the many questions I'd had this morning. It was obvious that Matt loved Darla. I just hoped that love was enough to get them through bad times. But that wasn't my worry.

If I kept telling myself that, I might just believe it. I decided to see what other questions I could get answered. "If you had to guess, who do you think killed Axel?"

"I guess I'm not breaking a confidence now, right, since he's dead?" He nodded and apparently answered his own question. "Axel had a bit of an addiction problem."

"Drugs?"

"Yes and no. He was addicted to a lot of things. I think he was just one of those personalities that went hard in all areas of his life. I know he owed some dealers for a few parties a couple of months back. He tried to get money back from me from our signing bonus, but I'd already turned that over to Darla." Matt blushed. "We're saving up to buy her folks out of the winery. At least this distribution center. We can't afford to buy the vineyard, but the South Cove outlet? That's doable. So all my money from this band thing is going into that pot. Then when we have enough, I'll stop touring, and we'll become partners. It's kind of an early retirement plan where we keep working, but just at the winery. I can play on weekends there and have the best of both worlds."

"So you don't want the fame and fortune that Jules is looking for?" Okay, so maybe I didn't want to just let go of the murder and the investigation. I couldn't help it if Matt had shown up on my doorstep.

He laughed and finished his iced tea. "No. I've been on that track before. You stop enjoying the music and the journey. It's all about the next step. Like we're working in a corporate environment or something. Jules is looking for something or someone to tell her that she's enough. I've got that." He stood and stepped toward the living room. "Besides, if we were famous, I'd never see Darla. You don't know how crazy it gets on tour. We go night after night, and after a while, you're not even sure what town you're in. I want a better quality of life than that. Even if I don't have the money the guys who hit it big have. I've got to be going. I'm working the early afternoon shift at the winery."

"Thanks for coming by." That was stupid to say. Words were just falling out of my mouth lately.

"No, thank you for talking me off the ledge. I let Keith wind me up. I should have realized that's just Keith's way." He moved toward the door.

"Hey, Matt? Does Keith manage any other bands?" I thought about seeing him with that record producer earlier.

"No. He's only got us. I think he wants another band, but he doesn't have any staff to promote his services. Why?" Matt paused at the door.

I pulled out my phone and showed him the picture I'd taken at the diner earlier. "I guess I was just wondering why he'd be meeting with this guy."

He held the phone for a few long seconds. "That's Dakota Miles from Salt Water Productions. When was this taken?"

"Today at lunch. I saw them at the diner."

Matt looked like he was going to punch someone else now.

"What's wrong?"

He handed me back the phone. "Nothing. I just think Keith's trying to play our offer against a bigger one. The problem is, I want this offer. I can't say the band wouldn't love a better contract, but I know what Darla did to get us this one. We need to start showing some loyalty."

I watched as he turned and jogged down my steps and out to the sidewalk.

I texted the photo and name to Greg, adding when it was taken. Then I waited. The phone rang a few minutes later. "Hi, honey."

"Jill, why did you send this picture to me?" Greg was direct. Not cold, but definitely not warm and cuddly right now.

I was wondering the same thing, actually. "I thought it was weird that Keith was taking a business meeting when things were all still up in the air. Then I showed it to Matt. He was over, by the way. He thinks you're going to arrest him. But he didn't do it."

"Jill, the picture?" Greg gently brought me back on track.

"Oh, so anyway, he was here, and I'd already looked up Dakota using a reverse image search. I asked him about it, and he thinks Keith is trying to parlay his win into more money."

"Sounds logical," he admitted. "Let me know if you find anything. I suspect you're going to keep pulling on this string?"

I sighed. "Probably. I'd made a pact with myself that I wouldn't get involved, but Matt's truly worried about what's going to happen next. I think Keith wants more than one offer for their contract so he can raise the advance amount."

"And you can change that how?"

I thought about what he said. He was right. What happened in or to the band wasn't my responsibility. "I can't. You're right."

"Wait, what? I think we have a bad connection."

I laughed as I checked the fridge for possible leftovers for dinner. "I said you were right. So are you coming home for dinner?"

"Sorry, I've got a meeting first thing in the morning with the DA, and I've got to get this stuff in order. Why don't you call Amy and go to Lille's?"

"I went to Lille's today with Aunt Jackie for lunch. Amy's busy painting the new house." I spied leftover salad. "I've got food here. I'll grill some meat and eat this salad."

"Okay, but don't forget to turn off the grill." He paused for a minute. "And it needs cleaned. And the grill might be out of propane."

"You sure are making driving down the highway until I find an open restaurant sound more appealing. I can cook food on the stove, too, you know."

He chuckled. "Sorry. I'm just tired. Can we talk later? I've got to get back to this. Just don't forget to eat."

"Same atcha." Although, he knew it was more likely for him to forget to eat than me. I might eat a meal comprised totally of junk food, but I'd eat.

I took out a piece of chicken breast from the freezer and put it in the microwave to defrost. Then I went out to check the grill. Greg was right, the propane tank was empty. I glanced at my watch. The closest exchange point was Bakerstown, which would get me home later than I wanted to eat. I decided to put it on Monday's to-do list and use the stove to cook tonight.

Once the chicken was defrosted, I put it in a baggie with herbs, olive oil, and a little wine to marinate. Then I took my iced tea and a book out to the porch. I might as well enjoy my night. Tomorrow we'd be talking finance. I couldn't see how that would be a fun discussion. Although I did have plans with Greg for dinner at Lille's before the class. So that would be fun. If he turned his phone off.

Tomorrow's worry. I snuggled on the swing and started reading.

* * * *

Wednesday morning, I had a note from Greg saying he'd meet me at five at Lille's. And a reminder to bring two notebooks and my planner to the meeting. Apparently, the class was going to really be a class. I wondered if we'd have tests and everything. At least it was a warmup for next semester's schedule.

I set out two new notebooks and two nice pens on the table. I'd be home before I had to meet Greg. With Toby cleaning the food truck yesterday and Tilly's training almost done, I didn't have much on my plate today.

Tilly was working with Deek this afternoon; then she'd work the first part of the evening shift with Evie. Judith would come in at ten, and then Deek would join her at one, and I'd be off the clock. I decided to take the planner with me to work and write down this week's schedule. That way I didn't have to remember who was working what days; it would be right there.

I glanced through today's list. I needed to take Emma running as soon as I got home. Then I'd eat a light lunch and have the rest of the afternoon free to read or write the review I still had hanging over my head. It was on this week's to-do list as well, so I wouldn't forget it if life got hectic. I could do it just before I closed the book on this week and opened a new page for next week.

I wrote down Matt's name and went back to my list of questions in a different notebook. I scanned through them, crossing off the ones I'd gotten answers to and writing down the answer below the question. Either Matt loved Darla and they were planning a life together that was being funded by the music, or he was a really good actor as well as being a strong musician. I guessed it could be possible, but I thought he was being truthful.

Which led me to the next question. If not Matt, who? I was vacillating between Jules in a fit of rage—in the study with a candlestick. I took a breath and tried to focus. Or Keith. I wanted it to be Keith. Mostly because I didn't like him. But if Greg had taught me one thing about investigations, you couldn't let your personal feelings get in the way of the truth.

I didn't have time to play this game. I closed the notebook and pushed it to the side where I wouldn't confuse it with the finance class notebooks. Then I grabbed my tote and filled my travel mug with coffee. I said goodbye to Emma and gave her a treat. Then I walked into town.

The morning was glorious, and the walk was just what I needed to clear my head. When I got to the shop, I already had a customer waiting for me. And the rest of the shift went by quickly, with a lot of people asking about the author event on Friday.

Evie must have put up a display last night with a picture of the author and his books on the edge of the coffee counter. When I got coffee for a walk-in customer, she picked up the book. "Put this on my tab too. I won't be here Friday, but I've been meaning to read this."

And another book sold because Deek thought ahead on his marketing. I really admired that guy. And my aunt, who did the books, loved him even more. As I was thinking about the different book marketing techniques he'd implemented or taken over and improved, he walked in. I checked the time. "I thought Judith was coming at ten and you were coming at noon."

"She is, and I am. I just can't write at Esmeralda's. I get into a groove, and all of a sudden, I realize I must have fallen asleep, and I've been just writing gibberish. It's words and all, but not my story. I've had to throw away more words than I've kept." He set his tote with his laptop on a table. "So I decided to write here. That way, if I fall asleep, maybe you or Judith will notice and wake me."

"Do you think it's the ghosts?"

"Not ghosts, spirits." He rubbed his chin. "And since I'm not sleeping well at night, it's got to be her house. Maybe the spirits aren't appreciating me hanging out there."

"You can bring the cat to the apartment." I studied him. He did look worn out.

"Thanks, I might just do that. I thought it would be cool staying in Esmeralda's house. I mean, Mom has a studio in her house, and I never felt any bad energy from that. Esmeralda's just feels more intense. Mom said Esmeralda always took on the hard cases. I guess she was right." He pointed to the coffee bar. "Mind if I get some java? I need the pick-me-up."

"Not a problem. And I'm serious about bringing the cat to the apartment," I called after him.

Judith had arrived during our discussion, and she looked at me. "Did I get my time wrong? I thought I was in at ten."

"You are. Deek's here to write." I headed back to the coffee bar. "Can you handle customers while I do a book order?"

"Sure." She followed me into the back office, where she put her tote on a hook on the wall. "Make sure you check the travel and music books. I think we sold most of them this weekend."

"I know we did." I held up a report I'd run the day before. "It was a really good festival, even for books. Thanks for the idea of selling books at the truck. We should have brought out kids' books for Saturday morning."

"There was just so much going on this weekend. I felt scattered. And then I heard about that guy dying. It's really sad to be following your dream and not live to see it pay off. The band he was in won the competition. I bet his spirit was smiling down from heaven." She glanced out the window in the door. "Oops, we have a customer that just came in. I'll stop jawing and get to work."

As I ordered books, I wondered if Axel would have been happy that the band won or really, really mad that they did it without him. And why on earth would he torpedo their first contract? I was certain if I knew that, I might just figure out who'd killed him at the same time.

When I was done, I went out and worked with Judith for a while. She was taking off on Saturday to attend a family wedding in Montana. "You could leave earlier, you know. You don't have to stay for the author event."

She pointed at Deek. "Tell him that. Anyway, it makes me look cool that I couldn't be there early because I've got an important job. For years, I was just a housewife, at least in their eyes. Now, I'm doing things."

"You were never just a housewife." I thought about all the jobs and travel Judith had done before she'd even retired. "You've traveled to more countries than I have. You've held more different jobs than me. And you're still volunteering and doing stuff I have on my bucket list."

She patted my arm. "That's sweet, dear, but did you ever wonder why I've been living life so hard the last few years?"

I shook my head, but before she could tell me, Deek interrupted. "Time for you to head home. According to the police dude, you two have a date tonight."

"You're talking to Greg? When did that happen?"

He shook his head. "Actually, Toby. Greg called him; Toby called me. And now I'm telling you to get your fanny out of here and go home and get ready. Police Dude's orders."

Chapter 18

Greg and I had already ordered, and we were talking about the day's events. I straightened my silverware. "Oh, I have a bone to pick with you."

"What did I do now? Leave my socks wadded up in the laundry bin?" He sipped his milkshake. We'd both decided we could use a treat.

"No. You told my employee to make sure I got out of the office on time. I don't need someone reminding me about our plans." I shook a finger at him.

"The last time I didn't remind you, I found you in sweats, reading a book and bawling your eyes out because the fictional couple had just hit the black moment. I had to take you to that police officer dinner with your eyes looking like a raccoon's."

"It was a really good romance. I don't think anyone telling me that I needed to stop was going to work. Besides, you still got that award," I reminded him. "You have it in your office at work."

"They gave it to me out of pity for having a raccoon for a girlfriend." He returned to his milkshake.

"Take it back. I'm the best girlfriend you've ever had. Admit it." I sipped my shake and got brain freeze.

"Actually, you're not."

"What? You can't mean Sherry. I mean, yeah, she would have been dressed to the nines, and it would have cost you a fortune. Okay, so I can see how going from that to me would be a bit of a letdown." We really didn't want to go into this class fighting. Not in public.

"You're silly. I said that because you're not my girlfriend any longer. You're my fiancée. And you're better than any of the others ever were. So don't get all crazy on me. I was teasing."

I sat back as a server dropped off our food. Greg was having the cube steak dinner, and I had ordered a Cobb salad tonight. I'd had it on my mind since lunch with my aunt yesterday. "Sorry, it's been a busy week. And with the murder, it just has me questioning everything about my life and what I think I know."

"What do I need to remind you of? We're in love? We've set a date for next June. And we have a shared dog who loves to go running almost as much as she loves her mommy."

"Just remember all these good things when we're arguing about our money values in a couple of hours." I took a bite of my salad. It didn't disappoint.

He shook his head. "You're wrong. We won't be arguing about values because we share the same ones. You just haven't realized that yet."

We spent the rest of the time at dinner talking about vacations we wanted to take and ways to save the money. It felt good to have some downtime after how busy the weekend had been. I knew Greg's plate was still full.

As we walked out of the diner and headed to the church for our class, I took his arm. "I know you're busy with the investigation, so I appreciate you taking the time for this class. For us."

"I figured if you were willing to go, I needed to make time in my day for this. You've been a little hesitant to talk about money with me." He squeezed my hand. "This will give us a framework for the conversations."

"You sound like my psychology professor back in school." I thought about what he'd said. "We talk about money. We just talked about how to pay for the upcoming trip."

"We talk around money. I have no idea what you make from the shop. I don't think you've ever asked me what I get paid. We make sure we have food and the lights stay on, but we've never done a deep dive. Did you know I have a retirement fund? Do you? Maybe you have a student loan that's in the thousands of dollars. You were a lawyer. These are the things I don't know about you, and you don't know about me."

My eyes widened. He was right. We hadn't ever talked about the long future. I paid my bills; he paid his. We talked about the household bills and grocery costs. Even gas prices. But not a full picture of who we were financially. "I guess since we're getting married, we should talk about these things. Or at least know about them."

"And that's why we're taking this class. Pastor Bill says when we finish, we'll have not only a full financial picture of where we are now, but we'll have a couple of goals for the future. I'm looking forward to spending the rest of our lives together. Aren't you?" He leaned into me as we passed by city hall.

"I am. Hey, not to change the subject or ruin the mood, but did you know that Darla and Matt are saving up to buy the winery, or the bar part, I guess, from her parents? He's planning on leaving the band once they save enough and just being here in South Cove." I watched as a couple passed us with a baby in the stroller. "I think that's sweet."

"The baby?" Greg nodded to the man and woman.

"No, the fact that Darla and Matt are planning a life together." I thought about what they must have done to get this far. "I guess they talk finances a lot."

"He's part of her business plan. It's probably something that came up a long time ago. We've got other things to talk about than work all the time." He glanced behind him. "Like how cute that baby was. Do you think it was a boy or a girl?"

"How would I know?" I turned and watched the couple mosey down the sidewalk. "It's a baby."

"There are clues. Like the blue clothes and the stuffed train in his stroller." He turned us down the street that would lead us to the church.

"So I can't dress in blue or like trains because I'm a girl?" I stopped walking and stared at him.

"That's not what I'm saying. Don't get upset. When a baby is little, parents put their ideas on the kid. Like dressing him in blue, because that's probably what they got at the baby shower. And Dad probably loves trains. Besides, it's just a guess. We could go back and ask, if you think the baby's a girl." He took my hand. "Ready to go to class?"

"Sorry. I am touchy tonight. This class has me tied in knots. I don't know what to expect." I squeezed his hand and continued watching. "I don't think I was this nervous the first day of law school."

"Like you said, you knew what to expect. No matter what, I'll be there with you. Maybe this is our first hurdle as a couple. Or as an engaged couple." He paused at the door to the church. "Ready to slay the lions?"

"Sure. Where you go, I go." I entered the church first as Greg held the door for me. If Amy could do this marriage thing, I could. I'd done it before, although badly. Maybe if we'd talked about more things in my first marriage, I wouldn't be divorced. I glanced at Greg as he looked for the room where the class would be held. No, I probably would still be divorced, because I knew in my heart, I was meant to be with this man.

We went down the hall together.

When Pastor Bill stood up and greeted the group of five couples, I realized I hadn't seen Sadie yet. She'd said she was attending the class too. Of course, her boyfriend was also leading it.

Greg leaned over. "What's wrong?"

"Sadie's not here." I glanced at my phone, and it was seven. Time to get started. My friend was never late. Never. I texted her. *Where are you? Class is starting.*

I saw the bubbles and kept watching the phone while Pastor Bill went over the reasons we needed the class and what we'd get out of it. I finally saw the answer pop up.

I'm not coming. I'll talk to you tomorrow when I drop off treats. I'm going to bed. Early day tomorrow.

I put my phone in my tote and focused on the class.

"First up? What and who do you owe? I hope you had time to do the pre-work package I sent you last week." Pastor Bill held up some papers. "Does anyone need a second copy?"

Greg looked at me, and I shook my head. If he'd sent it, I hadn't seen it in my inbox. Of course, we'd had the festival going, so I hadn't checked my email since last Monday. I pulled out my planner and wrote a note for tomorrow. *Check email.*

Greg held up his hand. "Can we get two? I guess we didn't do the pre-work."

"Sorry," I whispered as the other couples looked at us. We were the troublemakers.

"No problem. I know you two were probably busy with the festival and, well, other things." Pastor Bill came over and handed us each a packet. "We're focusing on section one tonight, so if you two will fill that out, the rest of the class will switch packets and discuss each item. No judging. If one of you has a few thousand in credit card debt, it's not the end of the world."

"How about ten thousand?" A man in the back held up his girlfriend's packet.

"Still not the end of the world. Maybe an opportunity to work together on a goal." Pastor Bill was still standing in front of us. "Everyone good? You have fifteen minutes; then we'll talk some more."

I pulled out a pen and went to the first question. *List your debts. Who, why, and how much do you owe?*

"Um, Jill?" Pastor Bill squatted down so he was at my level.

I looked up from the worksheet. "Look, I'm sorry I didn't get this done before. I'll be better, I promise. Life this week was just a little crazy."

"No, it's fine. A lot of couples don't do the pre-work. You're just in a class with some high achievers. I wanted to ask you something else."

I glanced at Greg, who was writing on his paperwork and not paying attention to our conversation. At least on the outside. I knew he was listening. "Go ahead."

"I was wondering, well, have you talked to Sadie? I couldn't reach her today, and she's not here." He looked around the room nervously. "Is she okay?"

"I just texted her, and she said she had an early day tomorrow." I saw relief in his eyes. "So when did you last talk?"

"This weekend. She was upset about the deacons. I told her they just needed more time to get used to the idea." He sighed. "I thought she'd accepted it when she said they could have all the time in the world. But since that conversation, she hasn't returned any of my calls. I think I misunderstood what she was telling me."

I bit my lip. He'd definitely misunderstood. "I don't think we should talk about this now. Maybe after class?"

He nodded and stood. "I'm sorry, you're right. I'm bothering you with my personal problems when I should be more professional. I'm just glad to hear she's okay. I was worried."

After he walked away to check on the other students, Greg leaned toward me. "I take it Sadie's mad?"

"I believe so. We're talking in the morning." I looked at his list. "Are you done already?"

He nodded. "I don't like owing money. After I paid off the credit cards Sherry left me, I limited the amount and type of debt I have. What about you? You only have one thing written down."

I could have lied and said, *Yep, I'm done*. But that wasn't the point of the class, right? I shook my head. "I need a few minutes to think about it. Can you get me a cup of coffee from the back? And a cookie."

He grinned. "Sure."

Thinking about my bills, I wrote down the ones that came to me. We had a business credit card, but we paid it off monthly, so I wrote it down with a zero amount. Then I had the one I used for most of my personal spending. I got points on it, and I used it for our travel costs. So I put all of our travel costs like plane tickets and hotels on it. But again, I paid it off monthly. I'd paid off my furniture when I bought it. I didn't carry any debt on my personal credit card if I could help it. I still had student loan debt. I should pay that off out of the Miss Emily fund, but I hadn't since the interest rate was so low. I called the inheritance that I'd received from my friend the Miss Emily fund. It was the slush fund I used for the business if it needed money or for a charity I wanted to support. Or in some cases, just a helping hand to a friend in need. We weren't talking resources yet, so I brushed by that and wrote down the amount left on my school loans. I'd bought my last car with cash, so no loan payment there. And the house had come free and clear from Miss Emily. I'd put some money into renovations, but I'd taken that out of the cash she'd left me. Maybe I was better off than I'd thought.

I handed my paper over to Greg. "I'm done."

"This is all? I'm impressed. Sherry had four different store cards when we got married. And they were all charged to the hilt."

"Give that back to me." I took the paper and wrote down the department store card I paid off when I used it. I wasn't sure why I just didn't use the other card, but I got rewards in coupons to use this one, and they sent me a $10 gift every anniversary and every birthday. They made me feel like a most valuable customer. I handed the paper back. "I'm pretty sure that's it. I pay my car insurance every six months, and I buy my phones when I need one."

We spent a few minutes talking about the few debts we had, and I explained how much we were earning in points for our future travel.

Pastor Bill came over. "Any issues you need help with?"

Greg shook his head. "I believe we're both on the same side of the coin with debt. We don't like it or have much of it."

He nodded to the papers. "Mind if I glance over these? A lot of people don't include things they don't think of as debt."

We turned our worksheets around.

Pastor Bill nodded. "See, you're missing a few things. Debt isn't just credit cards. What about your house?"

"Paid for," I said.

"Your Jeep? I see Greg has a truck payment, but you don't have your Jeep listed." He pointed to the two items.

"Paid for," I repeated.

Pastor Bill glanced again at the list. "Oh, you didn't add in cell phones or insurance you pay for monthly."

"Because we don't," I said. "Insurance for the house comes once a year, and the Jeep every six months. I have them set on autopay for those times, and I just have it in my budget."

He turned the papers around. "I don't think I'm going to need to teach you anything about debt."

"So we can leave?" I started to stand.

Greg pulled me back into my chair. "We'll stick around. Maybe we can be a good influence on the others."

I sipped my coffee and didn't respond.

After class, we held back as others hurried out of the room. Pastor Bill came by and sat on the table in front of us. "I'm sorry I was so unprofessional earlier. I shouldn't have used your personal connection to get information about Sadie."

"Maybe you need to be a little more unprofessional. What if the deacons told you that you couldn't see her at all anymore? Would you stand for that? Sadie needs to know you're there for her. Her first. Not your job."

"Jill," Greg warned. He really didn't want me to get involved in this.

"No, she's right. I'm not being fair to Sadie." He glanced around the now-empty room. "It looks like I'm going to have to make a choice. One love for another."

"Bill, maybe..." Greg started, but Pastor Bill held up his hand.

"I can't really talk about this right now. Again, I'm sorry I brought you into my personal problems." He walked out of the room, and Greg and I followed.

"You were hard on him," Greg said as we left the church.

I took his arm. "Probably. But Sadie's a good person. She deserves more. Especially after losing her husband. She's had bad luck."

We walked home in silence, each of us lost in our own thoughts.

Chapter 19

Thursday morning, Greg was gone before I could apologize for yelling at Pastor Bill. I probably needed to apologize to him rather than Greg, but I'd start with Greg. I decided to pack up a box of cookies and take it over to the station after work. Cookies might not solve everything, but they were great icebreakers.

My morning went by fast as I dealt with the commuters and pre-weekend shoppers. A lot of the locals stopped in before taking off for the weekend to grab a book or two for beach reading. When Deek came in, he focused on the upcoming author event details. Just before my shift was to end, he came back out front to take over the coffee bar.

"How's it looking?" I asked as I bagged up two cookies for a customer.

He rang the charge, then grinned at me. "Great. I've got a reporter coming in from the city to do a piece on the author's talk. We might just be busy next week too."

"I hope we at least sell the books we ordered." I'd checked the back, and we had over a hundred books in boxes waiting to be signed and sold.

"Clive Aarons is coming in early to sign a bunch of stock. We'll hold those back just in case he needs them for tomorrow night. He's very popular. I checked the book levels, and we've already sold ten of the books since they came in. And that's unsigned." Deek was beaming. If I could read his aura, I'd say it was joyful. Maybe that was a light blue color.

The bells went off at the front door, and Darla burst into the shop, holding up a tablet. "I need to clear out some of the festival shots so I have room for the author event tomorrow. Come look at the pictures I got for the food truck and see if you want any of them."

I smiled at Deek. "I guess you're in charge for a bit."

"I'm always in charge; you just don't know it." He went to the coffee bar. "Darla, do you want some coffee? You seem a little mellow."

"Please. I have a busy day ahead. I need all this energy and more. Matt's getting ready for a gig in the city this weekend, so he needs to get packed. I've got the winery all weekend, or at least from the time the author signing is over to Sunday night." She followed me over to the couch. "Let me set up the first picture, and you can just scroll through. Mark down the ones you want, and I'll email them to you. If I don't sort them now, I'll never get back to them."

I watched as she set up her tablet. Deek brought over Darla's coffee, black with two pumps of vanilla, and a refill for me. Finally, Darla turned the tablet my way.

"That's Thursday night just before the festival. I think there's some cute pics of your guys over at my winery if you wanted them for staff pictures." She picked up her coffee. "Just push that button to go forward and the one next to it to go back. The program numbers and dates them. So make a list based on date first, then the number."

I held up my pen and pad. "I'm ready."

"Good because I need to use your little girls' room. This is my fourth cup of coffee." She set everything down and hurried over to the restrooms.

Deek looked around the empty shop. "Okay if I glance through with you?"

"Sit down. Maybe you'll see something you want too." I moved over so Deek had room on the couch. "Were you at the winery Thursday?"

"Actually, Judith and I stopped in for a drink after our writing group. We usually either hit Lille's or the winery after the group disbands. We meet here until Evie kicks us out at nine." He grinned. "I always drink too much coffee, so I'm wired and need some time and a drink to slow down so I can at least try to get some sleep. Or I write until I'm beat. You'd be surprised how much talking about writing and critiquing other people's stuff can wind you up." He focused on the first picture. "This must have been earlier in the evening."

"How do you know that?" I studied the picture of a couple sitting at a table, wineglasses in hand. I wasn't sure I'd have the same feeling sitting and talking about writing as Deek did, but maybe if the conversation turned to books, then I could understand.

"The bandstand is empty. Matt had a trio playing Thursday night. They were pretty good. All siblings, and boy could they harmonize." He hit the button to see the next picture. "More customers. Stop me if you see someone you know that I don't."

We scrolled through picture after picture of happy customers in a bar that was more and more crowded as we went through. I leaned into a photo. Was that the band? "Wait, hold there a second. Isn't that Matt's band?"

Deek leaned closer and used his pen to point out the people. "That's Matt and Jules. Man, is she hot."

I shot him a look, and he shrugged.

"What? She is."

"That's Axel and Eddie too. I wonder where Keith was?" I looked deeper into the picture. "Hey, that's Mick. The new singer. He was there Thursday night too."

Darla spoke up behind us. "Hansel's band was sitting across the winery. Mick knows most of the band members, so he was on his way over to say hi just after this picture."

"I bet Hansel thought he was consorting with the enemy." Deek chuckled.

Darla sighed. "You're right there. Hansel yelled at Mick after he came back from the other table. Mick paid for his drink and left. I thought maybe he was going over to the bandstand to check out the setup. That's where Keith was. And just after that happened, Axel left to meet up with Keith."

"Axel was supposed to meet Keith the day he was killed?" I turned in my chair to look at Darla, but she was already walking around the couch to sit down.

"Don't read anything into that. I think everyone went down to the bandstand sometime that day. They'd just finished setting it up, and everyone was curious about how it would sound. Matt and Eddie went that afternoon right after it had been completed. Matt said it was perfect. Like you were singing on an open boat." Darla sat down and sipped her coffee. "But you're thinking Greg needs to see these pictures."

"Did you tell him you had them?" I wrote down the date and number. "How many more are there?"

Darla blushed. "A few. I wanted to see if Keith would use any of them in his marketing plan. I'd like to sell a few pictures someday."

"You're an excellent photographer." I wrote down the first band picture, then went through all the ones until the subject changed and wrote down the last one. I wrote Greg's name on top of that and started a new column for the ones I wanted.

It took about thirty minutes to go through all the pictures, but by the time I did, I had several on both lists. Pictures I wanted and pictures I thought she should send to Greg. I handed her the list. "Can you send these today?"

Darla taps back to the tablet's home screen and stands. "Sure. And I'll tell him what I told you. I really hope he finds out who killed Axel soon.

I'm tired of feeling like I'm ratting on my friends every time I remember something else."

"You may be clearing people too. If Matt was at the winery when Axel was killed, and your photo proves that, he couldn't have killed him."

Darla brightened. "True. And there is a picture of Matt and Eddie doing shots right at the time of death. Or at least the time I've heard Axel was killed. And Matt didn't leave the winery that night. After the band left, he stayed and helped me stock for the next day since the festival was keeping us busy."

"Of course, he could have hired someone," Deek said. "If I were going to off someone, I'd hire a hit man to do the wet work, and I'd have an ironclad alibi." He stood when Darla sent him a death glare. "Oops, I think there's a customer out front. Here's my list."

He dropped the paper near Darla and almost ran to the front, where there was no customer. He busied himself with setting up the coffee bar.

"Stop scaring my employees." I handed her Deek's list.

She tucked the lists into her tote with the tablet. "I just think I've got Matt cleared of everything so he couldn't have killed Axel; then someone blows a hole in my theory."

"You're not really worried about that, right?" I'd assumed that Matt had dropped off Darla's list of suspects just about as fast as he'd arrived.

"Most days, no. Then I hear something or see something that might implicate him. I know he hated the guy enough to kill him. We just needed to get the money put away for the winery buy. Then he'd stop gigging with them. Two, three years at most, even without them hitting it big, if we put everything away."

"So you two are serious. Planning a life together." I smiled as we walked toward the door. "That's nice."

"I'm hopeful. Let's just say it that way. We're good together. We're so different, but together, it seems to work. For both of us." Darla squeezed my hand. "I'll get these sent sometime today. And I'll see you at the author event."

"With bells on." I watched as she left the shop and headed down the street to Lille's. Everyone was hooking up. I turned back and glanced at the dessert case. I'd fill that up before I left. And then I realized Sadie hadn't made her delivery today. I went to the back and took out a couple of cheesecakes. We'd be good at least through today if we didn't get a bus tour in town. I started refilling the case as Deek filled a coffee order for a customer. "I hope you have enough. I'll call Sadie and see when she's coming. She should have been here already."

"Sadie called while you were talking to Darla. She said she'd be here about two and apologized for the late delivery." Deek looked at how I'd filled the case. "I should be fine with that. And I'll have Tilly help Sadie with the unloading and checking in. She hasn't done that yet, mostly because Sadie usually delivers in the morning."

I thought about my plans to take cookies to Greg. "There's a dozen chocolate chip in the back. Do you think you'd miss it if I took them to the police station?"

He nodded at the display. "It's after twelve now. And you've got the display packed. I think we'll be fine. I'll focus on selling the flower sugar cookies."

"Thanks." I went to the back and packed twelve chocolate chip cookies. There were more thawing, so I thought the shop should be fine. I grabbed my tote and headed out the door. "Have a good shift, Deek."

"You have a good night. We'll see you tomorrow." He turned back to a customer who was chatting him up about his hair. Deek was good-looking, but he was also smart and kind. And he was the perfect draw for female customers of a certain age. Although, unlike Toby, I'd never heard of Deek dating anyone he'd met at the coffee shop during work hours.

I left the shop without worrying about tomorrow's event. Deek had things in hand. In the past, my aunt and I had handled the events. I'd hated it. Especially my aunt's need for micromanaging them. Now, with Deek in charge of the events, she seemed to let him do his thing. Especially after the first quarter. Deek had doubled our previous quarter's earnings just in the event category alone. My aunt respected results. And Deek brought them. She brought any issues to me to deal with.

I crossed the street toward the police station. The weather today was amazing. I'd definitely be taking Emma for a run as soon as I got home. The air felt soft on my skin, and I was in a great mood. Then I pushed open the door to the station.

Chaos was raining down on the room. The phones were going off the hook, but no one was at the reception desk. I glanced around, but there were no officers in the lobby area. It was filled with a line of people standing at the reception desk and grumbling. I hurried around the desk, and people started yelling at me.

"I've been here for twenty minutes, and no one's even asked what's going on. If I was shot, I'd be dead by now," a man screamed at me from the other side of the desk.

I held up a hand. "Hold on a second."

I picked up a phone call. "South Cove Police Department. Can you hold?" I didn't wait for an answer. I hoped no one had been shot. I worked my way through the calls; then once I got everyone on hold, I started with the first call and took a message for Greg from the crime lab to call Horace back. Then I looked at the first guy in the lobby. "Can you tell me what you need, fast?"

"I need to file my building permit for my deck. The sign on the city hall door directed everyone over here." He held up his paperwork. "All I need to do is get this filed and pay the fee."

"The sign sent you here?" I glanced at the paperwork. "If you don't need a receipt right now, I can take this and have Amy send you a receipt to this address."

He handed me his business card. "That will work. I need to get back to the office. Tell Amy to call me if she has questions."

I looked at the others. Most of them looked like the last guy. "How many people are here to drop off city planning paperwork?"

Most of them raised their hands.

"If you have your packet and check ready, put it here with your business card." I set a folder and paper clips on the counter. "I'll give these to Amy, and you can leave. If you need something else, please line up on the right side here. I'll be right with you."

I picked up the next call. They'd hung up. I went to the next one. It was a call for a vandalism issue. I took the caller's name and address and told them that someone would get back to them.

I'd almost cleared out the lobby, and I'd answered all the calls when Greg, Toby, and Tim walked into the office from the back.

"What on earth is going on here?" Greg came over to the reception desk. "Jill, what are you doing here?"

"I brought you cookies, but when I walked into the lobby, there were all these people, and the phones were ringing, and no one was here." I handed him his messages. Then I handed Toby the other stack. "Toby, Tim, these people need a callback or a visit."

"Thanks, Jill." Toby took the messages, and he and Tim walked over to the side of the room.

"I don't understand. Where's Amy?" Greg looked around the lobby.

"I don't know. But there's a sign saying everyone should come here for help." I answered a question for the last person in line, then took his paperwork and put the applications in a file. "I'll go over to city hall and drop these off. Then I'll see what's going on. If you can handle the phones and walk-ins while I'm gone."

"I'll stay out here until you find Amy. She's supposed to be here in the afternoons this week." Greg took my seat and then logged into the computer. "I'll work on clearing up some emails. Thanks for saving the day, Jill."

"Glad to help." I tapped the box. "Don't forget to share the cookies."

He laughed, and then the bell rang over the door, and someone came in. "I can help you over here."

The woman blinked but then moved over to the counter. "I needed to drop off an application to open my business. Am I in the right place?"

"Today you are." Greg noticed I was still standing next to the desk. "Jill, go find Amy. I'm sure I'm going to quickly get out of my depth here."

I laughed and hurried through the hallways to where Amy's office was in front of the mayor's. The lights were off, and like the man had said, there was a sign directing people to the police station. Where was Amy?

I dialed my phone, and she picked up. Before I could say anything, she groaned. "I know, I'm ten minutes late getting back from lunch. Tell Greg I'll be there in just a few minutes. I'm turning onto Main Street from the highway now."

"Amy, you were supposed to take over an hour ago. I've been handling the front desk for the last thirty minutes."

I heard the sharp intake of breath. "No. Tina told me that Greg wanted me there at two, so I took my lunch from one to two. Well, two ten by the time I get there. But she said it wouldn't be a problem. I told Tina I needed to run to Bakerstown to pick up paint for the house at lunch. She said she'd tell Greg."

"She didn't. And Greg didn't change the time you were supposed to be at the station's front desk. Tina must be playing games with both of you." I glanced around the empty office, suddenly feeling very exposed. "The lights are off, and no one's here in your office."

"Tina and Marvin must have left right after I did. I wonder if she did this herself or if Marvin knew. It's not right. She shouldn't mess with people this way." Amy was breaking up. I wasn't sure if it was the call or if she was crying. I would bet it was from crying. You wouldn't know it, but when Amy got really mad, she cried.

"Don't worry about it. I'll hold down the fort until you get here." I ended the call and went to tell Greg that it hadn't been Amy's fault. We were paying for Hansel's band not making the finals. Greg was going to flip.

Chapter 20

Sitting on the couch and watching a movie, I heard Greg's truck pull into the drive. I checked my watch, not quite nine thirty. He was earlier than I'd expected. I paused the movie and watched as Emma went to greet her dad. She'd gone to the door even before I'd heard the truck in the driveway. When Toby pulled into the driveway, she went to the back door so she could greet him at the gate. Greg, she met at the front door. I guessed she could tell the difference between Fords and Rams.

After he greeted Emma, Greg came over and gave me a kiss. "Hey, you're still up."

"I don't turn into a pumpkin at nine. Why are you home so early?" I rubbed his arm as he leaned against the sofa.

"I figured explaining to Marvin what Tina did and why it wasn't 'just a mistake' was my last official duty of the day. He knew she crossed the line, but he tried to make it seem like she just got confused. I told him if that was just confusion, she needed to see a doctor to make sure she didn't have a brain tumor or something." Greg squinted at the television. "Isn't this that movie where she's talking to the guy who's putting her out of business, but she doesn't know?"

"Yep." I patted the sofa. "Come watch it with me. Or tell me how your day went after I left. Where were you guys when city hall was blowing up?"

"Our monthly meeting. Tina had been in my office talking about security for the festivals, and then she told me Amy would be right there to cover. So I went to the meeting along with all of the guys. She's lucky you came along and picked up the slack." He held up his hand. "Give me a second, and I'll get out of this uniform and be right back. Is there anything to eat?"

"You didn't eat?" Now I stood and hurried into the kitchen. I got a potpie out of the freezer and popped it into the oven. I grabbed a soda and a beer and took them back into the living room. When he came back downstairs sans uniform and gun, I held up the beverages. "Soda, beer, or iced tea?"

He grabbed the beer. "I already told Toby I'm off the clock tonight. So if something happens, he'll have to come get me, but I can have one."

I opened the soda and sat down. "I put a potpie in the oven, and I'll make you a salad to go with it, but it's going to take about an hour."

"That's fine. I need to wind down a little." He sank onto the couch. "Seriously, thank you for your help today. Jumping in like that, it really wasn't your job."

"I know a disaster in the making when I see one. I'm just thankful no one had a real problem. I would have hated for someone to have been really hurt or in danger." I curled on the sofa, watching him. "She gets why what she did was dangerous, right?"

"I don't know if Tina does, but Marvin's very aware of it. And of the possible criminal and civil suits we could have been slapped with. I'm thinking that couple is having a very serious conversation tonight." He closed his eyes and leaned back. "Speaking of serious conversations, what did Sadie say? Pastor Bill called this morning and apologized again for asking you about Sadie. The man's a wreck. I hope Sadie's not playing games with this."

I squeezed my hands together so I wouldn't say something mean in retaliation. "Sadie doesn't play games. If she's not talking to him, there's a reason. We need to take her side on this."

Greg shook his head and started the show using the remote. "I'm not taking anyone's side in this. Getting involved in a couple's spat never works out well for the third party. I'm not getting them both mad at me. You need to stay out of it too. So what did Sadie say?"

"You just want the gossip." I threw a pillow at him. "I'm not telling you. Of course, there's nothing to tell since she hadn't come into the shop by the time I left."

"All that lead-up with no payout. You're mean." He cuddled close to me. "Did you bring home any cookies?"

"No, I left the extra cookies at the station. Like I said, we were still waiting for Sadie's delivery when I left. Tomorrow's going to be a madhouse. You're probably going to be on your own for dinner."

"I can heat up a potpie or grill a steak if I get home in time to eat. Or I can stop by Lille's. What are you doing for dinner?" He turned down the volume on the television.

"I'm picking up a taco bar for the staff at five. That way we can eat in shifts and still be ready for the influx of readers at seven. I guess this guy's a big deal in the finance community." I picked up the guy's book I'd brought home from the store. "I thought maybe we'd like to read this together after we finish our class."

Greg took the book and read the back. "Sometimes you surprise me, Jill Gardner. After class on Wednesday, I didn't think I'd be able to get you to go back. Now you're picking up more material for us to work through?"

I took the book back from him. "Don't tease me. I just thought if we wanted this marriage thing to work, we should be on the same page for most things. Like finances. And raising kids."

He froze and stared at me. "You're not..."

"I'm not what?" I tried to decipher the look he was giving me. Then his eyes dropped to my stomach. "Pregnant? No. I'm not pregnant. And I hope I don't get that way for a while. Especially until after the wedding."

He sank back into the couch. "You gave me a heart attack there."

"You gave yourself a heart attack." I punched him in the arm. "So what if I was? What would you say then?"

He leaned up and pulled me toward him. "I'd say you just made me the happiest man on earth, and we need to move up the wedding."

"Oh, no. I've already put hours into this wedding. I have the venue, the catering, and I'm close to having a dress. Getting pregnant would change the dress I want to a dress that might hide the evidence." I glanced at my watch. "We've got ten minutes before your potpie is ready. Do you want a salad?"

"Please. I feel like I need to eat something light. I've had a lot of pizza and chicken lately. I'm having flashbacks to my bachelor days." He stood and followed me into the kitchen. "I'll help. What did you eat for dinner?"

"I had a piece of fish and some salad." I got the salad makings out of the fridge. "Then Emma talked me into having ice cream for dessert."

He laughed as he took the lettuce from me and pulled out the cutting board. "That's our girl, always getting you in trouble."

Speaking of trouble, I might as well ask him about the photos Darla had sent him. "Did Darla's pictures help the investigation?"

He nodded. "I got the go-ahead from the DA to pull someone back in for questioning since the pictures and Darla's testimony put that person in town that day. Their first statement didn't."

"You're using *they* so I don't know if it's Jules or Keith, right?" I took the lettuce from him and put it away after he'd cut off enough for his salad.

"Give the girl a gold star." He handed me the shaved carrots too. "Look, I don't want you involved in this. These people, they're a little bit intense about making sure Axel's murder isn't solved. It's like the fact that he's dead just corrected a problem so now we should just move on. And I get it. The guy was a tool. But he's still dead, and someone needs to pay for killing him. Unless it was the entire band. Then I'll have to charge all of them."

"You really think that's an option?"

He finished his salad before he answered. "If it is the band, then I'm afraid Darla's knee-deep in at least the cover-up if not the deed. One other reason you need to stay out of the investigation. I don't want you to find out your friend isn't who you thought she is."

I shook my head as the oven timer went off. "That's not possible. Darla is the most giving person I know. She volunteers to do all the festivals for South Cove. She doesn't need to do that."

Greg took the potholders and took his potpie out of the oven, slipping it into a soup bowl. "Jill, sometimes people do extreme things for love."

* * * *

The next morning, I tried to keep myself from thinking about Darla and Matt and the band and who killed Axel. I'd say *poor Axel,* but everyone he knew wanted him dead or at least out of their lives. Or at least all the people I knew that had known Axel. He made a perfect victim, but everyone else made perfect suspects. Even in Greg's eyes, Axel's entire band was a possibility. After my commuters had come and gone, I checked the treat levels. Sadie had delivered yesterday, including enough for our order for today's event. If I didn't know better, I'd think she was avoiding me. Actually, I knew she was avoiding me. She didn't want to talk about Pastor Bill and the breakup. I didn't blame her. I'd check in with her on Monday if I didn't see her before that.

I picked up Deek's author event list and checked off "Food." We'd make some coffee and have lemonade and ice water available to go with the cookies, but that was it. I ran my finger down the list. Most of these items we couldn't do until closer to event time. We basically closed up the dining room and filled it with chairs, moving all the tables to the side to showcase books that were either backlist titles from the author or from other authors in the same wheelhouse. I always kept a table with local travel books and another with kids' books about the subject just in case parents brought kids along with them.

Satisfied that I was done with what I could do, I opened my laptop and found Darla's email with the pictures. I'd forward this to Deek so he could put some in the next newsletter. I wanted to update our website with a few more festival pictures. Deek was making a "hire the food truck" page for the website, so we needed some good ones for that as well.

I slowly went through the pictures and frowned. I checked the file Darla had sent them in. These were taken on Thursday night before the event. Darla must have gone down to the beach near sunset, because the pictures were moody and dark with the setting sun behind the food truck and the waves lapping at the shore in the distance. The gravel parking lot was clean and empty of most cars, except a truck. One that I recognized. Jules had been at the beach when Axel was killed. The earlier shots of the band at the winery had been taken in the late afternoon. Before the winery got busy. This was later.

I downloaded the pictures of the food truck and the parking lot and then emailed them to Greg. Jules had killed Axel, then lied about being at the beach that night. She must have found the letters and confronted him. Had the production company sent her copies, or had she found the originals?

Several customers came in the front door, and I shut the laptop. Jules must be the one Greg was reinterviewing. Hopefully, these pictures would help him arrest her, and this nightmare would be over. For Darla's sake, I hoped so.

I was alone at the shop until three, when Deek and Tilly arrived. Then the shift change started. Deek glanced at the list. "We're good here. You go home and check on Emma. I'll see you at five with the taco bar, right?"

"So you're kicking me out?" I went to the back and grabbed my tote and a few cookies for Greg at home.

"You haven't eaten since breakfast. Go home and have a sandwich before you turn into a raging hunger monster." He grabbed a box of books and carried it out to the front, following me out of the back office.

"I might have brought a sandwich with me since it was so busy today." I countered his evaluation.

"Cool. Did you?"

I shook my head. It would have been smart, but I hadn't thought of it until now. "No."

"Either way, Emma needs to be let out," he reminded me. "Tilly and I are good. We can get this set up, and when Evie gets back from school, we'll finish up. It's going to be fine."

"I trust you." I put my tote over my head and moved toward the door. "Don't forget the kids' table."

"Yes, mom," Deek called out after me.

I never got any respect from my team. And I kind of liked it that way. I smiled as I headed down the sidewalk toward home. When I went past the police station, I saw Jules going inside with Toby. I guessed I'd been right. Greg had enough to charge her. The investigation was over. And starting tomorrow, I'd have Greg back, and South Cove would go back to its sleepy tourist self. Without an active murder investigation.

Boring was not a bad thing. Especially when you were involved with a police detective.

Tina and Marvin Baylor were getting out of their car when I went past Diamond Lille's parking lot. I nodded but kept going. Tina held a grudge longer than anyone I knew.

"You're not out of the woods yet, missy," Tina called after me. "You haven't even started to feel my wrath."

"Tina, be nice. You know Jill wasn't in control of what happened at the festival." Mayor Baylor took his wife's arm. "I'm sorry for the disturbance. Tina's just upset at the results of the music festival."

"Upset? I'll show you upset." Tina started after me, but as I watched, her husband blocked her way.

"Tina. Stop making a scene," he whispered, loud enough for me to hear.

I was pretty sure anyone in the parking lot heard too. I should have kept walking, but it was like watching a car wreck. I couldn't help stopping and staring.

She glared at him, but then I saw her face change, and she calmed down. How I'd become the focus of her rage wasn't clear except for the time I told her I didn't control Greg. Maybe she hadn't believed me. "Fine. I'm sorry for the harsh words."

"That's fine," I called over to the couple, who were now walking toward the diner's front door.

Tina glared at me, but the mayor smiled. "Thanks for understanding, Jill. We're having a late lunch. Do you want to join us?"

Not if Lille's had the only food in the world and I was going to die of starvation if I didn't eat. I smiled and shook my head. "Big event at the store tonight. I've got to go take care of Emma for a bit."

He nodded, and they disappeared into the diner. I figured the offer was just him trying to be nice. They didn't want to eat lunch with me. Especially not Tina. I wasn't sure she wouldn't have stabbed me with a fork while we ate.

Then instead of Greg being done with an investigation, he'd have another one. Hopefully, Carrie would be witness to my demise.

I hurried home, hoping to not run into anyone else who didn't want to talk with me.

Just before I left for the shop again, Greg pulled into the drive. When he came inside, I had my dress in a bag along with the heels I was going to wear. I had my makeup bag tucked inside. Evie had offered to do my makeup for me just before the event started so I'd look great for any pictures. But I had my hair already swept up into a clip with several curls framing my face.

Greg opened the door and whistled. "You look amazing."

"And you're home early. I take it Jules is in custody?"

He shook his head. "I don't know how you figured that one out from a picture, but yes. She's claiming she didn't kill Axel. She now admits to being there and confronting him about the old contract. The letters from the record company were copies she'd gotten when they'd told her why they weren't recording her song. I guess she reached out because she'd had an offer from another band to record it. She hadn't seen the paperwork or the money, so she went directly to the source."

"She told you all that?"

He came over and held up the dress. "Maybe I should go tonight to keep the men away from my fiancée."

I held up my ring finger. "That's what this piece of rock is for. Besides, I know where I belong. So why did Jules tell you all that?"

"I guess she thought it made her look less guilty. I asked her about the wrapper for the guitar string. She claims she bought those for Axel the last time she was in town, and he hadn't gotten them from her yet. She thought they were still in her truck." He went to the office and locked up his gun. "Either way, the DA thinks he can make a case, so my job is done."

"Do you want to come with me to the shop?"

He laughed. "You're kidding, right? My first night off in over a week, and you want me to go to an author event?" He held up a bag I hadn't noticed. "I brought home Tiny's meatloaf for dinner. You go and have fun. If you want a ride home, call, and I'll come get you. Otherwise, I need to catch up on my baseball team. I haven't even checked stats in forever."

"You don't know what you're missing." I kissed him and grabbed my bag. I was taking the Jeep since I needed to pick up the taco bar.

"Emma says she thinks I made the better choice," he said as he plopped on the sofa, and Emma joined him.

The problem was, I agreed with both of them.

Chapter 21

By the time I got the taco bar set up, the front had been completely transformed. Jackie and Harrold had arrived, and we were all in the back eating, except for Tilly. Toby looked a little worn out but kept a smile on his face. Which told me he was still hurting from Tilly not remembering him. But as Greg would say, not my circus, not my monkeys.

Except this was my circus, and Toby was one of my monkeys. I was starting to regret hiring Tilly. I'd known about the past relationship, but I'd thought both of them had put it behind them. This somehow was worse for Toby. Her moving on was one thing. Her not remembering him at all was quite another. And probably a blow to his manhood.

That was a discussion for another time. We were all here, including Judith, who was leaving the next day. After the wedding, she was heading down to see the Mayan temples in Belize. I was jealous and wanted to go along.

"You really should take a trip down there, Jill," Judith said before she took a bite from her taco. "It's magical."

"One of these days." I pointed to my aunt and Harrold. "You two should go. Then you can bring me back pictures."

"We've been talking about it." Harrold beamed at my aunt. "And now that we've got more time, it's going on the travel list."

I met my aunt's gaze. "The tests came back okay?"

She nodded, tears in her eyes. "I'm fine."

Deek looked between the two of us. "I missed something here."

"Just girl talk. Anyway, thanks for putting this together, Deek. He's a big name for such a little town." My aunt squeezed Deek's arm.

"You're welcome. Although I have to admit, he was coming to see his aunt anyway, so we're just a pit stop that makes the trip more economical."

"Where does his aunt live?" I asked, filling up a second taco shell. I was starving.

"Bakerstown. Can you believe it? He's already said he'll give us either the first or last slot for his next book tour. I'm thinking first slot would be more prestigious."

"Of course. That way we have claim to the first signed copies available." My aunt sniffed. "I would have thought you'd know that, Deek."

He smiled at her. "I just wanted your input, Ms. Jackie. You know I appreciate the support and help on these events."

I thought he was laying it on a little thick, but he went on to ask her advice on the next two events.

Harrold winked at me as he came by to get another taco. "That boy knows how to woo the ladies. He'll be setting himself up with a writer's residency here without paying rent next, and your aunt will believe it was all her idea."

I laughed. "It's a good thing he's on the side of good and not evil."

"You're telling me. I might not have a bride if he wasn't." Harrold winked at me and walked off with several tacos on his plate. Either he liked trying different varieties, or he was trying to tempt my aunt into eating and forgetting about the upcoming events.

Harrold was good for Aunt Jackie. Whether she knew it or not. I knew it, and I guessed that was all that mattered. I glanced around the room. Everyone was happy and chatty, even though we were going to have an extremely busy night.

Evie came up to me and nodded at my plate. "Once you're done, we should get you ready. You want to look like a successful bookstore owner when the media gets here."

"As long as it gets people to buy books, I'll dress up in a Batgirl costume." I went over to grab my dress.

"I'd pay to see that."

I turned around to see Greg, dressed in a suit and tie. I hurried over and gave him a hug. "I didn't think you were coming."

"I decided you needed some support. And tacos sounded better than meatloaf." He kissed me, then held me out to look me over. "You go get ready. I'm going to grab a taco, then go chat with Harrold. It's time for the official husband support group meeting to start."

"You're crazy." I kissed him again, then hurried off with Evie to get ready.

When I came back, the back office was all but cleared out. Tilly was eating with a man I hadn't met. She blushed when she saw me.

"Hi, Jill. This is my boyfriend, Andy Feedler. Deek said it would be okay if he came and had dinner with me." She set the taco down and stood to greet me. "Andy, this is my boss, Jill Gardner."

"Pleased to meet you, Miss Gardner." Andy stood, and I realized how tall he was. They made a cute couple, but my first thought was how Toby would take this. "Tilly's told me all about the job and how much she loves working here. I'm in construction, so I work where they send me. Mostly in the city doing remodels lately."

"Sounds like you're busy. Thank you for coming tonight. We're family here at the bookstore, so you're more than welcome." I nodded to the table still filled with food. "Please help us get rid of some of this."

"Tilly? Can you come out for a second? You too, Jill. The author wants to meet everyone and get a group photo." Deek stuck his head in the back room. "Oh, hi, Andy. Glad you could make it."

"I'll be right there." Tilly set her plate down and hurried to the door. "Jill, are you coming?"

"I wonder if I could have a quick word with Jill. I won't keep her long, I promise." Andy smiled at me, and I wondered what exactly this stranger could have to talk to me about.

"Tell Deek I'll be right there." I nodded. Tilly looked worried but nodded and left the room.

"Look, I know you know something's up with Tilly," Andy started and then sighed. "I hate telling people this, but she mentioned that there's this guy here, Toby, who says he knows her."

"He says they went to high school together. And dated," I corrected. "But Tilly says it's not true."

"It's probably true," Andy admitted. He must have seen the confusion on my face, because he continued. "Look, she's not lying, so don't look at this as bad. She just doesn't remember that part of her life. She was in a car accident freshman year of college. We met at University of Idaho. She was going to be a doctor. Then she was in this car accident and had to drop out of school. She lost a part of her memory. It's not anything that affects her now, and she has a great neurologist, but her high school memories are gone. She didn't even remember meeting me after the accident. We've had a long haul."

"So Toby was right about her being his high school sweetheart." I glanced at the wall that separated the back office from the front, where everyone was gathered.

"According to Tilly's mom, she thought they would get married someday. Then they had some fight just before Tilly left for college. We started dating and then, well, the accident. She doesn't know Toby." He ran a hand over his hair. "If I'd known Toby worked here, I would have told her to take another job, but she loves this. It's the first time I've seen her really happy in a job."

"She's good at it too." I tapped Andy's hand. "Don't worry about it. I'll tell Toby what happened, and he'll get over it. Right now, his heart's broken."

Andy nodded. "Losing Tilly would be a nightmare. I get what he's going through. She's amazing. Even if she's not a doctor."

"Thanks for telling me. It's been strange having the two versions of reality going on." I headed to the door. "I need to get out there. Welcome to the family, Andy. I hope to see more of you around here."

"Now that I'm not worried about Toby coming unglued on me, I think I'll be around more. Tell him I'm sorry." Andy dropped his head and pushed around a taco on his plate.

"I'll get these pictures done and then send Tilly back in to finish eating dinner." I headed out to the front. The group was lined up, and Greg was about to take a picture. I called out as I hurried over, "Wait for me."

* * * *

After the author event, I sent Tilly and Andy home along with Aunt Jackie and Harrold. There was just a little to clean up and to get ready for Saturday's opening. Toby and Deek were in the front, folding chairs and resetting the tables. I walked over and nodded to the chairs outside. "Can we chat for a minute?"

He frowned but handed a folded chair to Deek. "I'll be right back if I'm not being fired."

I laughed and looked at Deek. "He wishes. He'll be right back."

We sat down at one of the café tables I had lining the front of the shop's windows. "What's up, boss?"

"I talked to Andy, Tilly's boyfriend, tonight."

"The jerk who looks like he can bench press a motorcycle? Yeah, I saw him." Toby leaned back in his chair. "Tilly didn't used to like guys like that. She was always giving me crap about being on the football team."

"Well, they met in college." I decided to just tell him the whole story. After I did, I reached out and touched his hand. "Are you okay?"

"So she really doesn't remember me or even high school? Tilly was super smart. She was always taking the hard classes and then needing to study, so I studied too." He rubbed his chin. "Wow, I've been all up in my feelings, and she wasn't doing this on purpose to hurt me. I just never existed for her."

"Yeah, that's the story. Toby, I'm sorry. Andy said if he'd known you worked here, he would have led her to take a different job. Are you going to be okay with working with her? I can keep you off the same schedule." I didn't want to lose Toby.

"I'm fine. I might call her mom, though, and talk to her. I should have kept in touch, but you know how it is when you're a kid and you break up. You want to erase all memories of your life with the other person. I should have known something was up, but I just thought she was getting on with her life." Toby closed his eyes. "I'm such a jerk."

"You're not a jerk. You were a kid. And so was she. Now, you just have the chance to get to know her again, as a *friend*." I emphasized that word.

"Oh, believe me, I'm not planning on inserting myself into that relationship. She and Andy look happy. And he's good at taking care of her. I saw that tonight." Toby stood and paused at the open doorway. "Is that all you needed? Deek's arms are going to be sore if he has to lift all those chairs by himself."

"I can hear you, funny man," Deek called out.

I stood and followed him into the shop. "We're done. Let's get this place in shape so I can read tomorrow once my commuters are gone."

"You realize there's something very wrong with that statement," Greg said as he brought me a cookie.

"I don't think so." I took the cookie and pretended to think about his words. "Nope, I'm getting nothing."

"You're a brat." He glanced around the room.

The dining room was almost set up, and Toby was wheeling the extra chairs into the closet we'd made on the side of the bookstore. All of the author event stuff, like a lectern, projectors, microphones, etcetera, went in there after every event. That way, we didn't lose them or have stuff come up missing. A place for everything, and everything in its place. One of Aunt Jackie's favorite mottos. And I was feeling like my life was calming down as well. Now that the event was over and the investigation was complete, we might just have a little calm before the next storm.

"What do you think about getting away next weekend? Esmeralda will be back, and we could ask Toby to watch Emma. Maybe Colorado? Or do you want to find a new beach?" I went over to move books back to where they belonged. Deek had set up a display of signed books by the register, but it could use a few more. I had a feeling they'd sell quickly.

"Sounds like a plan. I'll tell Marvin on Monday." He held up his book. "I'll sit here and read while you finish up. Then I'll walk you home."

"You'll walk me home? What are we, courting? Besides, you live there too. I think it's just walking next to me as we go home." I set up a second stack of books. "And one more hiccup in your plan—I brought the Jeep."

"Whatever you want to call it. I'll be over there relaxing until you're ready to go." Greg kissed me on the cheek, then went to sit on the couch.

Evie was running the cash register report. Her eyes popped when it spit out the final numbers. "Jill, we did a lot of book sales. This says we sold two hundred books tonight."

"Are you kidding?" I came around the counter and scanned the small receipt that printed out each night. We'd put it with the bank deposit, and another copy was emailed to us for use with accounting and inventory information. I looked at the numbers and the fifteen books I had stacked on the counter. "I thought we only brought in a hundred."

Deek heard our conversation. "We brought in a hundred and fifty of his books. This is all that's left. He wanted to buy some from us, but I couldn't see letting go of these last few. I've asked him to let me know the next time he's in town, and he'll sign more if we totally sell out."

"I wonder what the other books were. Just impulse purchases?" I rubbed my arms. I could look at the report tomorrow. "I'm beat. Can you guys finish up?"

"I think someone should take the deposit to the bank. We ran a lot of cash tonight." Evie patted the bag she'd just put the money and checks into.

"I'll do it." Toby held up his hand.

"You're going the wrong way, dude," Deek pointed out. "Of course, since I'm staying at Esmeralda's, I would be too."

"I've got to get home and let Homer out, or I'd drop it off," Evie said as she finished the deposit bag that we kept in the safe for the charge slips.

"I said I'd do it," Toby repeated. "I need a little time to myself."

"I can go with you," Deek offered. "Maybe buy you a drink at the winery before we head home?"

Toby slapped Deek on the back. "I've got this. Thanks. You can buy the next time I'm off."

We watched Toby leave through the front door. Evie looked at Deek and me. "I think I missed something important."

I grabbed my tote. "I don't think you did. I'm heading home. Be sure to lock up when you leave. Deek, do you want a ride?"

He shook his head. "Nah. I'm going to go get a beer before I head to Esmeralda's. You and Greg are welcome to join me."

"I think we're heading home, but I'll let him know you offered. Thanks for organizing such a great event." I said my goodbyes, and by the time I had, Greg was standing by my side.

"I'll drive," he said as he held out his hand for my keys. "You look like you could fall asleep any minute."

"Deek asked if we wanted to go to the winery," I said as I dug in my tote for my keys. I had to stop at the desk in the office and pull my extra clothes out before I found them. I handed them over. "Did you want to go? I said no, but if you want to go, I'll go."

"I want to go home and sit on the couch with you and Emma. Although the way you look, it might just be Emma and me." He closed the door leading to the back alley where I parked and double-checked the lock. "Let's just go home."

Chapter 22

The smell of maple syrup and pancakes woke me the next morning. I loved it when Greg decided to make breakfast before we went to work. I hurried and got ready for the day. As I was coming downstairs, I heard him talking on the phone.

"What do you mean we had this information all along? When did anyone talk to this guy?"

There was an edge to his voice. I slowed down, torn between not wanting to listen in but also not wanting to miss anything. Okay, so I totally wanted to listen in. He had his back to me in the kitchen.

"Tim, just for future reference, Esmeralda typically leaves those files on my desk so I can review them. If they're in the file cabinet, it means I've already read the file." He turned and saw me. Shaking his head, he pointed to a chair. "I'll be at the station in about twenty minutes. I'm eating pancakes with Jill."

He ended the call and tossed his phone on the table.

"You'll break it if you keep doing that." I came around and got a cup of coffee. "I take it something's wrong with the investigation."

"Exactly. Jules's lawyer called the DA this morning with an alibi witness. One that Tim has actually talked to and taken his story." He stacked pancakes on my plate, then put almost a half cube of butter on top and doused them with a cup of warm maple syrup. Just like I like them. And there was crisp, almost burned, bacon on the side. "Now we have to find another suspect. One whose lawyer will be able to cite our focus on Jules as reasonable doubt that their client is guilty."

"Thanks for breakfast." I didn't really know what to say. I had thought Jules was the most likely suspect too. Either her or Keith. I cut into the stack and took a huge bite. As I chewed, I asked, "Whaaaa aboooo Keeee?"

"What about Keith? Is that what you're trying to ask through that mouthful of pancake?" He actually smiled, which had been my plan. "You know I can't talk about open investigations."

"Yep. That's what I was asking." I bit into a slice of salty, crunchy bacon. I loved Saturday breakfasts. "And technically, isn't it closed at this moment?"

"You're good at walking that fine line, missy. Honestly, I'll have to look at everything again, but he was the next on my list. If you see the creep hanging around, let me know, okay?" He stood and kissed me. "I've got to get dressed and head into work. I probably won't see you until late."

"At least we got breakfast together," I said, but then I noticed he hadn't eaten. "Aren't you going to eat? You told Tim you would."

"I was mad. I should go in." He looked at the pile of pancakes still on the counter. "Never mind, you're right. I'll eat; then I'll go in and, with a fresh attitude, figure this out."

He was sounding a little rah-rah to me, so I studied him as he stacked his plate and took the rest of the bacon. "Are you okay?"

He poured hot syrup on the cakes and then set the container down. "Not really. I really thought it was Jules. I don't think I've ever been this close to charging someone who actually didn't do it. I was going to do the paperwork yesterday, but the DA was busy, so we put it off until Monday. Jules must have gone directly to the band's attorney after we talked to her."

"Well, you didn't charge her, so no harm. Now you just need to build a case against Keith."

"Innocent until proven guilty, Jill. What if Keith didn't do it?" He took a bite of his pancakes, but it didn't look like he was enjoying them as much as I was.

I reached out and grabbed his hand. "You'll find the person. You always do."

After Greg left for the station, I cleaned up the kitchen and got ready to go into work. We opened an hour later on Saturday, just because I didn't have quite as many commuters on the weekend. Now that we had another staff member, I needed to talk to Aunt Jackie about opening up on Sunday for at least a half day. Evie said she'd take the shift and even train Tilly for it if I wanted her to. There was a lot of walk-around traffic on Sundays, so I guessed we'd have to test it out for a few weekends.

I'd need more pastries if we were going to do it, and I wanted to give Sadie at least a week's heads-up, so if we were going to open next Sunday, I needed to talk to my aunt and Sadie today. I was going through my mental to-do list when I heard a horn beep. Esmeralda pulled into her drive in her little MINI Cooper. She waved as she got out.

I crossed the street to greet her and called out, "I thought you were coming home tomorrow?"

"Change of plans. I wasn't needed for an event tonight, and I felt like Greg needed me back. Is everything okay? How's the investigation going? How was the festival?" She peppered me with questions.

"Actually, I think he'll be glad to see you. Can you stop in today?" I glanced at my watch. "I'd fill you in, but I need to open the shop. Come by and get some coffee before you head to the station, and we'll chat."

She studied me. "I knew I needed to be here. I get what you're saying. I'll get dressed and go over to help out this morning. You look well, Jill."

"Thanks. Just typical Saturday uniform." I waved my hands over my Bermuda shorts and tank top.

Esmeralda laughed. "Apparently your mind is elsewhere. I'll come by later for some coffee."

I was almost to Diamond Lille's when I realized what she'd said. That I looked well. Not how I was dressed. Sometimes I needed to listen better. In my defense, I had been thinking about Greg's murder investigation gone wrong, not so much about what she'd been saying.

I dealt with my few Saturday commuters and was just about to pull out a book to read when Darla came into the shop. She was on the phone and covered the microphone when she ordered a coffee and a box of cookies to go.

I boxed up the cookies, poured her vanilla-flavored black coffee, and then took her card. She was still talking to whoever was on the phone. I suspected it was Matt from what they were talking about. Finally, she hung up. I handed her a receipt. "Here you go."

"Thanks. Sorry about that. Matt's having a meeting with the band at the winery this morning. I guess they're making coffee there, but I thought some cookies might ease some of the bad feelings. Jules is hot."

"I heard that her lawyer already proved she couldn't have killed Axel. Greg's fit to be tied. I guess the interview got put away in a folder rather than put on his desk. He really missed Esmeralda last week." I sipped my coffee.

"She is the glue that holds that station together. Tell Greg not to worry about it. There was so much damning evidence against her that I thought she was guilty too. The band needs to be deciding what songs to work on for the record and get this Axel thing behind them." She took a sip of her coffee. "I needed this. Matt and I were up late last night talking. He's so tired of all the diva personalities. I guess since Axel's gone, Jules is being a pain in the butt. And, of course, there's Keith."

"He seems to be a handful." I didn't like talking bad about people I didn't know, but in the few times I'd talked to Keith, I'd taken an instant dislike to him. Too bad that wasn't enough to charge him for the murder. "So you're hosting a morning meeting. I figured musicians didn't get up this early."

Darla laughed. "Most of them don't, but Matt told them if they wanted to use the winery and for him to be there, the meeting had to start at eleven. They would have done it yesterday, but Jules has PT on her shoulder on Tuesdays and Fridays."

"Oh, did she hurt it?"

Darla scooted off the stool. "From what Matt's told me, she had surgery a few months ago for a tear. She's still building her strength back. The shortened set they did for the festival set her back again. I bet the axe throwing didn't help either. I better get going. I'm going to work on books while Matt does the meeting. Then he and I are going to Bakerstown to pick up some supplies and grab lunch before we have to be back at the winery for the evening shift. Got to love owning your own business, right?"

I smiled and waved the next customer up. They'd been holding back, waiting for Darla to leave. "Have a great day, Darla."

The woman came up and laid one of the signed books on the counter. "I missed last night's event. My daughter wasn't feeling well, so we stayed home. I was hoping you still had a few of the books available."

"We do, and it's signed." I opened the book to the title page and showed her. "Can I get you some coffee and a treat to go with the book?"

"Of course!" She gave me her coffee order and picked out several cookies. "Put those in a bag. I'll look like a cool mom since I brought her home cookies. She's feeling better today, just still a little under the weather."

Customers kept me busy until end of my shift when Deek showed up. He glanced around at the almost full dining area. "Lots of people today."

I nodded. "I think people came back to browse the store since the event was so crowded yesterday. I've sold another five of his books this morning."

"Well, that's unexpected. I'm glad I hung on to those last books and didn't let him buy them off us. That way, you get the profit." He started moving around the cups to the way he liked them stacked. "You might as well head home. Tilly's scheduled to be here in an hour. I can handle the shop until then."

"Okay, I'll take you up on that." I thought if Lille's wasn't busy, I'd stop there for lunch. I started to move to the back to get my things.

"Don't forget your phone," Deek called after me.

I patted my capris. My phone was in my back pocket. "Not mine. Let me look at it."

He turned it over, and I immediately saw the South Cove Winery branding logo on the back. "Darla must have left this. I'm surprised she hasn't noticed yet. If she calls, let her know I'm walking over to the winery to get it to her."

"You're a good friend." He handed the phone to me.

I took it and put it in my other pocket. "I'm planning on getting a milkshake with my lunch, so I need some steps to burn some of the calories."

Deek was busy with a customer after I'd grabbed my tote from the office, so I just waved. He knew how to reach me if he needed something, but I didn't think he would. I set my watch to count my exercise time and headed up the hill to the winery.

By the time I got there, my heart rate was up, and I paused the counter while I went inside. Darla had a small smoking area near the parking lot and away from the front door.

"Jules, you should have just let them charge you. Then they'd look like idiots when you told them about your shoulder. You couldn't physically have killed Axel. Everyone who knows you knows that." A male voice I recognized as Keith's was talking.

"You wanted me in jail? I didn't kill him, and I'm not going to take the blame for anyone, not even you." I could see through the lattice and vines into the smoking area where they sat. Jules lit a cigarette.

"What does that mean?" Keith was pacing the small area.

"You knew I had Axel's guitar strings in my truck. You drove the truck to Bakerstown the week before and got an oil change. You could have had my key copied." I heard the quaver in Jules's voice. "You were just as upset as I was about Axel ruining the original contract."

"He didn't tank the contract. I did. This new one is a stepping-stone to something big. I have a new contract lined up for the band. You just have to be on my side when I bring it up today. We back out of this no-name festival contract and sign the new one I have for you. It's easy to get another contract when you have one in hand." He sat down at the table, focusing on Jules. "Just side with me on this, and you'll be a star in no time."

I wanted to throw up. That was what all the villains said to the innocent girl when tempting them.

"I don't believe what I'm hearing. You cancel the contract where they wanted two songs I'd written. They were going to pay me for the songs and let the band record them. Now, I have to sell them to someone else or hope that Matt's friend wants us to record them as well." She stabbed out her cigarette. "Look, just leave this contract alone. We need a win here. And a bird in hand."

He laughed at her. "I didn't go to all this work to have you record with some loser record company. You're going to support me in this discussion, or I'll find that guy Axel wanted to replace you with, and you'll be out of the band completely."

"You can't do that. The band decides who leaves and who stays." Jules stood and started to walk out of the area.

"How did that mindset work for Axel?"

I didn't hear her response since I needed to get out of there before either one of them saw me. Keith hadn't come out and said he'd killed Axel, but he might as well have. Greg needed to know what was going on. At best, Keith was a bully, and the band needed to get rid of him.

I paused at the hostess desk when I entered the winery. "Hey, is Darla here?"

"Actually, she just headed to Bakerstown for a supply run. Matt's here though. Do you want me to get him?"

I handed the girl Darla's phone. "Just give him this. Darla left it at the coffee shop this morning."

"Thanks. I bet she hasn't noticed it's gone yet." She studied my face. "You own the bookstore, don't you? I'm friends with Tilly. She loves working for you."

"We love having her on our team." I patted the counter. "Tell Darla I was sorry to miss her."

"I'll tell Matt. I won't be working by the time she gets back. I'm days only." She glanced up as the door opened behind me. "Welcome to... Sorry, I thought you were customers."

I turned around, and Jules and Keith were coming in the door. I smiled like I hadn't heard them talking earlier. At least that was the plan. "Hi, guys! I bet you're here to discuss your new contract. That's so exciting. I'm so glad South Cove and the festival could help you all out with your music career. I heard your sets last weekend, and you totally deserved to win."

Keith glared at me and kept walking into the dining room. He called back to Jules, "I'll be in the banquet room. Don't be long."

The hostess and I exchanged a look. She shook her head. "He's always such a gloomy Gus. My mom told me even if I wasn't excited about something but everyone else was, I was to be gracious and act like I was excited. Fake it till you make it, right?"

I nodded. "That's my motto. How about you, Jules?"

Jules watched Keith storm through the dining room. "He's just tired. It's been a long week. I better go rejoin the meeting before they put me in charge of cleaning the bathrooms or something gross."

She hurried to catch up with Keith, and she said something to make them look back at me. I waved at them, hoping I still looked like a big fan of the band. I needed to talk to Greg. There had to be a way to prove that Keith killed Axel. Because if not, I was watching a murderer walk free.

Chapter 23

Greg was in his office going through files on his desk. He looked up and ran his hand through his hair. "Jill, this isn't a good time."

"I think I know why Keith killed Axel. Jules found out about the first contract being canceled and confronted Axel. But he didn't do it. Keith had a meeting with Axel Thursday night. Darla told me about it when she went through the festival pictures. I didn't think about it until I heard them talking this morning." I sat down in his visitor chair.

"When you heard who talking? And where were you? I thought you were going to work?" Greg leaned back in his chair, watching me.

I leaned forward. I wasn't explaining this right. "I was at work. Darla came in and said the band was meeting at the winery and bought a dozen cookies for the meeting. Then she left her phone at the shop. Deek found it, and I took it back to her."

"Where you heard Jules and Keith talking. Please tell me they didn't see you."

"No. I mean, yes, they saw me later, but not when I was eavesdropping. They were out at the smokers' den, that little area in the parking lot? Anyway, I heard them talking; then I dropped off the phone with the receptionist. Darla wasn't there. And Jules and Keith walked in as I was leaving. So they saw me then. Just not before."

Greg opened his drawer and pulled out a bottle of aspirin. "I'm not even going to remind you again that you're not an investigator. So tell me again why you think Keith killed Axel?"

I went through my logic. I'd been preparing for the discussion all the way here, but I guessed I got excited and ahead of myself. After I finished, Greg hit his intercom. "Esmeralda, can you come in and bring me all the files that mention Keith? And let's clear the desk of anything that isn't about Axel or Keith."

"I was going to go to Lille's for lunch. Do you want me to bring you something, and we can eat here while we go through the files?" I was pushing the boundary, but I was offering food as an incentive.

"No, I do not want you coming back with food and going through my files. Again, you don't work for me." He looked up as Esmeralda came into the room, a stack of folders in her arms. "Thanks, Esmeralda. I'm not sure what I'd do without you."

"Lose evidence, that's what." She set the files down and started gathering up everything on his desk. "I'll sort these out and bring you what you need once I go through them. You guys left this case in a horrible mess. No wonder I heard you call to me when I was in New Orleans. You needed some organization."

He smiled and then waved me out of the room. "Go away, little bird. I've got work to do."

"You're welcome?" I stood and met Esmeralda's gaze. "You didn't stop by for coffee."

She laughed as she followed me out to the reception desk, where more papers and files were stacked. She pointed to the mess. "I was being called back to work. Seriously, I leave for a week, and things go crazy here. Tina called me just before I got on the plane and asked what steps she needed to take to fire Amy."

"Are you kidding? Did you tell her she doesn't work here?" I repeated Greg's statement.

Esmeralda laughed, the sound deep and comforting. "I should have. Instead, I tried to calm her down and figure out why she wanted to can your friend. From what I heard, Tina's not been getting her way this week. I guess she's not used to that. Don't worry about anything. I'll have things straightened out by next Friday. Maybe you and Greg can still take that long weekend you were planning."

"How did you know?" I started to ask, then shook my head. "Don't tell me. I'm late for an appointment with Tiny's fish and chips and a milkshake."

"Have a good day, Jill. And if you see Deek, thank him for watching my cat. She told me he did a great job, even though the spirits were messing with him." Esmeralda hurried to the desk, where the phone started ringing as soon as she sat down. "See you around. South Cove Police Department. May I help you?"

I left Esmeralda to sort out the evidence and the mess that everyone had left. I headed to Diamond Lille's to eat. I had a book in my tote I'd been wanting to start, so there was that. I needed to stop thinking about if what I'd heard from Darla and Jules was enough to at least start looking at Keith as Axel's killer. I guessed Greg was right; it wasn't my job. All I could do was tell him what I knew and let him set up the case for the district attorney.

Instead of reading while I ate, I took out a notebook and my planner and pulled up the class schedule for the fall from the school's website. I'd planned exactly when I'd take each class since some of them were offered every other year. I would be going to class Tuesday and Thursday nights, and our couples' finance class would end in late July. Classes would start late August. So if we wanted to take a week or longer vacation, we had a short window.

I'd talk to Greg about it once this investigation was over. I bet he'd say to hold off on vacation until next summer when we'd have our honeymoon. He usually advocated for short trips one year and a longer one every other year. I wanted both. So maybe we did have some discussions we needed to have around that part of our lives.

Carrie came by with a glass of water when my milkshake was gone. She held it up. "Unless you want iced tea or a soda?"

"I'll be in a sugar coma if I get a soda. But an iced tea wouldn't be bad." I took the water and took a sip. "How do you and Doc handle vacations?"

She leaned on the booth. "What do you mean? Who pays? We both pay our share."

"No, I mean, scheduling around work. Do you always do a long vacation each year?"

Carrie shrugged. "We haven't been together long enough to say *always*. I like a long staycation where I get my grandkids for a week. We hit the zoo, the beach, and several historical museums. I'm sure when they're older, they won't want to hang with their cool granny."

"I'm sure they will." Maybe I was making too much of a decision that didn't need to be made for every year. Maybe we could play it by ear. "So Greg's still working on the murder investigation. Doc may be doing some long hours again."

"I'm getting used to his work schedule. The nice thing is I have time to see my friends when he's busy working. And if I'm working, he can putter around the house. It's working out nicely." She glanced over as another couple was seated at a table nearby. "Let me get you that tea."

As I was getting ready to leave the diner, my phone rang. It was Greg. "Hey, did you change your mind on lunch?"

"Wait, are you still at the diner?"

"I'm just leaving, but I was setting up my planner for next fall's school schedule. I don't have a lot of time for a real vacation, but we can talk about it when you're done with this investigation."

"I'll be home tonight. That's what I called to tell you. We found beach camera evidence showing Keith getting into Jules's truck Thursday night and then Jules leaving. Keith leaves about thirty minutes later, and it looks like there's blood on his shirt. I've got the guys over at his apartment to see if we can find his clothes. The judge didn't even question the need for the warrant. We have a solid case without the clothes, but hopefully, it will be a slam dunk, and we'll find them."

"That's amazing. I take it Esmeralda found the missing evidence." I signed for my meal and tucked my wallet away.

"Exactly. That girl's my lucky charm." He paused for a second time. "Anyway, I'll be home soon. Take out some steaks for dinner. I'll grill."

* * * *

By the time Wednesday night's class came, Keith was sitting in jail, waiting to be transferred to the county jail to await trial. He hadn't had bail set. The judge thought he was a flight risk, especially when they found the ticket to a small Caribbean island in his desk. We'd eaten dinner at home, and we chatted as we walked into town and to the class.

"Maybe we should stop by Lille's for ice cream on the way home," Greg said, linking his fingers in mine.

"I guess it depends on how much homework we get and how far we get on the discussion in class." Tonight, we were talking about net worth, and for our homework, we'd each had to list out all our bank accounts, investment accounts, real estate, and other valuables. With our debts dealt with last week, this would give us our net worth. We were calculating it as individuals and then as a couple. I wasn't looking forward to this bit of honesty. I just didn't want Greg to look at me differently. I was still just Jill. Even if I did have more money than he did. My first marriage hadn't decimated me financially like his had.

"Jill, we're going to be fine. Even if you're broke, I'll still love you." He laughed at the look on my face. "Okay, okay, I know you're not broke, but don't get all in your head about this. We're the star students in the class."

"That's true." I leaned into him. "I am a little competitive, even if it's not a real class where the grade would always be on my permanent financial record."

"Who said it wouldn't?"

I punched Greg in the arm, and we went inside the church. We ran into Sadie and Pastor Bill and saw them kissing.

Greg shielded his eyes. "Hey now, there are young, impressionable students on their way to class. No making out in the hallway. You two are supposed to be the adults here."

Pastor Bill put his arm around Sadie. "We are adults, and the two of you are our first witnesses. Show them what just happened."

Sadie held out her left hand. A small diamond ring sat on the ring finger. "Bill asked me to marry him, and I said yes."

I hurried over and gave Sadie a hug. "Congratulations. I can't believe it. I'm so happy for you."

"Well, at least someone is." Pastor Bill held up his hand. "Don't worry, they didn't fire me, but I told them that I'd given the church many years, and if they couldn't see I was in love with this woman, they were blind."

"So you still have a job." Greg shook Pastor Bill's hand. "Good, because we're planning on you doing the honors next year when we tie the knot."

"It will be my honor."

We moved toward the classroom with Sadie and Pastor Bill in front of us. She glanced over her shoulder as we followed them. "I can't believe this is happening."

"Just have fun and roll with it." I smiled at her. "The less thinking you do with your head, the better. At least that's been my experience."

As we went into the classroom and got ready for our next financial discussion, I opened my notebook and drew a heart. Love conquered all. And music was the heart song that brought everyone together. At least it did when we let our heart do the talking and didn't try to control everything.

That was a lesson I'd probably need to remind myself of over and over. I glanced over at Greg, who was grinning. And I knew it was so worth the reminder.

Recipe

I *have* noticed that Jill's go-to food is fish and chips. It's not the healthiest of food choices, but it's what she loves. In high school, when I worked a summer job, I always got fish and chips at the drive-in for lunch. And in this book, we find it's someone else's go-to stress food as well. So I started looking for a little more health-conscious foods for Jill (and me) and came across this Neptune salad. I used whole wheat tortillas, but I bet you could use Carb Balance tortillas and still be on the side of healthy. Or just use flour tortillas.

Lynn

Jill's Neptune Salad Wrap
1 package imitation crab meat
1 green onion, minced (I've also used chopped sweet onion)
1/4 cup Miracle Whip
1/4 cup sour cream
1/2 cup celery, minced
1/2 cup shredded cheese (I like the Mexican mix)
1/2 can green chilis
1/4 teaspoon salt
1/4 teaspoon coarse ground black pepper
Flour tortillas

Mix all the ingredients together and place on the flour tortillas for a wrap. Add a cup of fresh fruit or salad for your "lighter than fish and chips" lunch.

If you love cozy mysteries, you won't want to miss Lynn Cahoon's delightful Kitchen Witch series!

Keep reading to enjoy a sample excerpt from the latest Kitchen Witch mystery—

Four Charming Spells
Available from Kensington Publishing Corp.

The Lodge in Magic Springs was the go-to place for most of the town's events. Weddings, anniversary celebrations, birthday parties, the meeting rooms in the historic lodge had seen it all. But today, Mia Malone and her crew from Mia's Morsels, the new catering, cooking school, dinner delivery, and now event planning business, were catering a more solemn event. Theresa Ann Holly's funeral had been at ten this morning graveside; now the coven was holding a wake to celebrate the life and the passing of one of their members. James, the catering director over at the Lodge, had sent the coven social committee to Mia when the Lodge had already been booked for a large celebrity wedding this weekend.

Mia appreciated the referral, but the coven's requirements for the food were a little odd, even for Magic Springs. And they'd asked for a discount because Theresa didn't have family to pitch in for the expense. As she watched another box of champagne being brought out from the kitchen, Mia hoped the discounted rate would at least cover her costs. Next time, she'd build in the extra charges for the coven's special requirements plus some extra before she took off the discount.

"You look like you're ready for this to be over." Christina Adams stood next to Mia and watched the group. "I have to say, for a coven event, it's pretty mild."

"What were you expecting? A lot of chanting and spell casting?" Mia watched as a man who'd been watching his phone for the last twenty minutes raised his hands in a cheer. "That one's too busy watching the baseball game."

"I thought I heard him mumbling about a bad ref call." Christina chuckled. "All the food's out and the last trays are being passed around. The food around the floral arrangement hasn't been touched. Is there a reason?"

Mia nodded, looking at the expensive caviar and cheeses sitting on the table. "That table is for the deceased coven members. Apparently, it's tradition for the newly departed to put on a feast not only for the ones she left behind but the ones who went before. It's bad luck to eat from that table."

Christina's eyes widened. "Like the you'll-die kind of bad luck, or the general seven years' curse?"

Mia laughed, keeping the sound low. "I believe it's the general seven years' kind. But you'd have to ask Grans. I don't know a lot of the rules, especially around the funeral traditions. I wish she would have warned me before I said yes to catering this thing."

"I would have thought that Mary Alice would be here. We didn't do the ghost table for Adele's party, or maybe I've just forgotten it? It's been a while." Adele had been a friend of Grans's who had passed on a few years earlier. She'd also been Mia's Morsels first catering client. They'd planned a birthday party for her but turned it into a wake when Adele was found dead. Christina glanced around the room and pointed out one of the guests. "That woman looks like she swallowed the canary, as my mom would say. Isn't it rude to be happy at a funeral?"

"Not quite an appropriate emotion, that's for sure." Mia smiled as she saw Abigail Majors crossing the room toward them. Abigail and her husband had started Majors Grocery in Magic Springs many years before. Now, the store was run by their son, Trent, who also happened to be Mia's boyfriend. "Abigail, so good to see a friendly face."

"Yeah, these things can be intense." Abigail gave them both a hug. Christina was dating Levi, another one of Abigail's sons. "I'm really glad I wasn't part of the planning for this event, even though I'm excited to be part of the Mia's Morsels team. Ginny Willis can be a bit of a stickler for tradition. I see she made you do an ancestors table. I thought that went out of style fifty years ago."

"I thought she was making it up when she told me it was mandatory. Of course, that was after I'd finalized the bid and we'd signed the contract. Believe me, I'll be jacking up the prices of any coven event I do in the future. This one isn't turning out to be very profitable." Mia nodded to the woman Christina had pointed out. "Do you know who our Sally Sunshine is over at that table?"

"Karen Elliot?" Abigail stifled a laugh. "I've never heard anyone call Karen happy."

"Well, she looks happy today. Did she know Theresa?" Mia was taking an instant dislike to the woman, who was now watching the other mourners with interest.

"Not that I know of. Theresa was kind of a hermit. She didn't attend coven events. Or have any family to speak of. That's the reason Ginny had to step in and do the wake. Most of the time, the family takes care of this send-off. I'm sure Ginny was doing everything by the book, just in case she's questioned about it. She's had some issues as the social chair." Abigail waved at a man over by the fireplace. "I'm being summoned. I'll see you next week, right?"

"I'm looking forward to finalizing your contract with Mia's Morsels. For a lot of reasons, not just your heavenly cakes." Mia watched as Abigail moved across the room, greeting people as she passed the tables.

"Abigail knows a lot of people in Magic Springs, at least around the coven. That should bring in more business when she joins the team. Hey, who's that?" Christina pointed out a man standing by the door to the room. "He looks like he's ready to sprint as soon as anyone notices him."

"Or he's waiting so he's not the first one to leave." Mia shook her head. "I have no clue who he is. Of course, there's lot of people here I don't know. Bethanie Miller, your bestie, is over by the bar, getting another glass of wine."

"Bethanie and I aren't quite friends anymore. Not since she pulled that last stunt with Levi. I don't know if she was jealous of me having a boyfriend or of me being with Levi, but either way, I don't need that kind of negativity in my life. I can get that at home. Not our place—I mean my mom's house." Christina looked up at Mia. "Are you ready for tomorrow?"

"Moving your stuff or talking to your mom?" Mia knew Mother Adams wasn't the friendliest person, even to her only daughter.

"Talking to Mom. And maybe an appearance from Isaac. I heard from him last night. He wanted to verify what time we'd be at the house to get my things. You'd think I was moving out of a hotel or an apartment the way they're treating me, not my childhood home." Christina blinked, and Mia realized she was on the verge of crying.

"They'll figure out how to deal with you having a brain sooner or later." Mia gave her a hug. "Let's go check out what we need to do to clean up in the kitchen. I'm tired of watching these people eat and ignore the fact this woman died. I don't think anyone is here to mourn; it feels like a mandatory meeting."

Christina nodded and headed toward the staff-only door, but Mia felt a hand on her arm and she turned to see Mahogany Medford standing next to her. "Christina, I'll be there in a moment."

"Sorry to bother you. I know you're working, but I just wanted to talk to you about Theresa's death." Mahogany took in the room as she spoke. "It's just like Mom."

"I know it must remind you of your mother's wake. It hasn't been very long since you had to do this yourself." Mia felt bad for the woman. She'd come home to bury her mom, but there were some questions on how the older Mrs. Medford had died. "Did the coven help with the wake for your mother?"

Mahogany shook her head. "Mrs. Willis, she said since I came back, I was responsible for the funeral planning. And the costs. Mom had some savings, so it wasn't a hardship, but Mrs. Willis seemed really put out that I even existed. The first time I called her, she hung up on me."

"That's weird." Mia watched as Ginny Willis stood and went over to get another glass of wine. At least the woman hadn't talked Mia into including an open bar in the contract. Besides the two cases of champagne, the alcohol costs were on the attendees. "She's been pretty involved in setting up this wake. Maybe she had a lot of the work done for your mom's event too."

"Maybe. That sounds like the woman. Once she realized I was the next of kin, she sent me a list of what needed to be included in this send-off. The way she talked about the wake, it was more like a welcoming party than a traditional funeral." Mahogany took a tissue out of her bag. "Have you learned anything about my mom's death yet?"

Mia shook her head. "My grandmother, Mary Alice Carpenter, is working on finding a spell that could have masked your mom's true age. She was planning on being here, but she came down with a cold or something. She didn't want to spread it around."

"Well, come by the house on Wednesday and we can talk some more. I know you have things to do here." Mahogany paused and pointed to the man at the door. "I wonder why Jerimiah's here."

"You know him?" It was the same man Christina had pointed out earlier, who was ready to bolt at any minute.

Mahogany nodded. "He was at my mom's wake. He said he knew her from when she lived in Twin. He leads a small coven there."

"Maybe he's just here as a courtesy, then." Mia relaxed a little about the man. "Intercoven relationships are very important to keep connections, especially because there are so few of us around Idaho."

"That's probably it." Mahogany waved at another woman across the room. "I've got to go mingle. Maybe I can find out something about Mom's death while I'm at it."

Mia watched Mahogany disappear into the crowd. People were starting to leave and the mysterious Jerimiah had now left as well. This must have been just a courtesy visit, then. She turned back to the kitchen to escape the room. It wasn't a feeling of sadness that Mia felt permeating the crowd; it was worse. It was a feeling of indifference. Like Theresa's death wasn't affecting any of them. Except for maybe Mahogany, and that was just because she'd lost her mother so recently.

Theresa Ann Holly was being sent off to another life today. And it seemed like no one in this life even cared. If Mahogany Medford hadn't come home to bury her mother, she would have been sent off with a lifeless event like this. It wasn't fair, but Mia could only control one thing today, and that was the food at the wake.

Everything else wasn't on her list.

ACKNOWLEDGMENTS

When I was a teenager, we had a local radio station that was out in what was the boonies. It was between three towns, and one night after we'd gotten our drivers licenses, my friends and I decided to drop in and request a song or two. The DJ talked to us through the glass where you could watch him work. He played our requested songs, and we drove home feeling just a little more adult as we'd influenced what music our little part of the world was hearing at that time. Being band kids, we'd always known music was going to be a part of our lives. Some people went on to try to live their dreams, but most of us just let that music dream slide. Jules is based on a friend who wanted to hit the charts so bad as a kid. I hope the real person who had that dream tried as hard as my fictional Jules.

Thanks also to my new editor, Michaela Hamilton, and my agent, Jill Marsal. It's great to have you on my team.

About the Author

New York Times and *USA Today* best-selling author **Lynn Cahoon** writes the Tourist Trap, Cat Latimer, Kitchen Witch, Farm-to-Fork, and Survivors' Book Club mystery series. No matter where the mystery is set, readers can expect a fun ride. Sign up for her newsletter at www.lynncahoon.com.

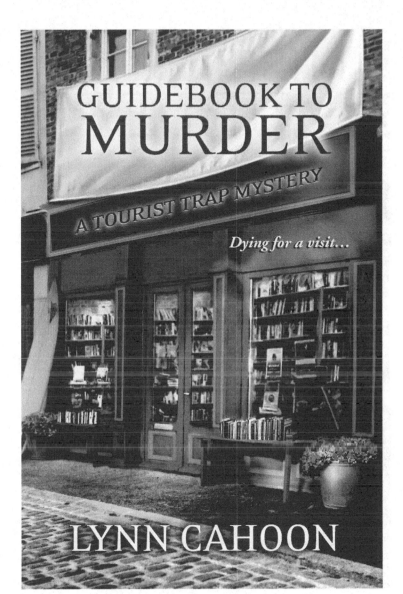

GUIDEBOOK TO
MURDER

A TOURIST TRAP MYSTERY

Dying for a visit...

LYNN CAHOON

MISSION TO
MURDER

A TOURIST TRAP MYSTERY

*Don't miss the
deadly landmark…*

ANTIQUES
by
THOMAS

CASTLE TOURS

NEW YORK TIMES BESTSELLING AUTHOR
LYNN CAHOON

IF THE SHOE
KILLS

A TOURIST TRAP MYSTERY

NEW YORK TIMES BESTSELLING AUTHOR
LYNN CAHOON

DRESSED TO KILL

A TOURIST TRAP MYSTERY

What you see
is not what
you get...

NEW YORK TIMES BESTSELLING AUTHOR

LYNN CAHOON

KILLER RUN

A TOURIST TRAP MYSTERY

She's
running
on empty...

NEW YORK TIMES BESTSELLING AUTHOR

LYNN CAHOON

MURDER
ON WHEELS

A TOURIST TRAP MYSTERY

*It's going to be a
bumpy ride...*

NEW YORK TIMES BESTSELLING AUTHOR
LYNN CAHOON

TEA CUPS
AND
CARNAGE

A TOURIST TRAP MYSTERY

The kettle's about to boil over...

NEW YORK TIMES BESTSELLING AUTHOR
LYNN CAHOON

HOSPITALITY
AND HOMICIDE

A TOURIST TRAP MYSTERY

SOUTH COVE
Bed & Breakfast

UNDERGROUND

NEW YORK TIMES BESTSELLING AUTHOR
LYNN CAHOON

KILLER PARTY

PARTY

A TOURIST TRAP MYSTERY

NEW YORK TIMES BESTSELLING AUTHOR

LYNN CAHOON

MEMORIES AND MURDER

A TOURIST TRAP MYSTERY

Coffee, Books and More

UNDERGROUND

LYNN CAHOON

MURDER
IN WAITING

A TOURIST TRAP MYSTERY

NEW YORK TIMES BESTSELLING AUTHOR

LYNN CAHOON

PICTURE
PERFECT
FRAME

A TOURIST TRAP
MYSTERY

NEW YORK TIMES BESTSELLING AUTHOR

LYNN CAHOON

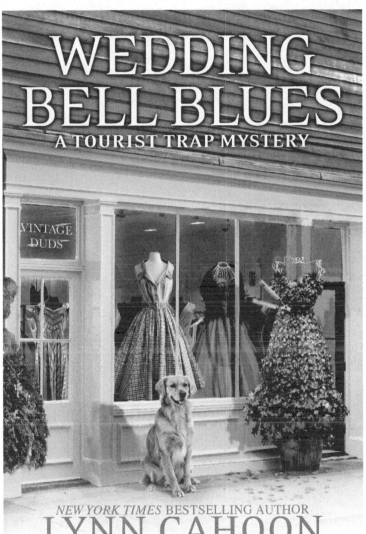

WEDDING
BELL BLUES
A TOURIST TRAP MYSTERY

LYNN CAHOON

Printed in the United States
by Baker & Taylor Publisher Services